# THE SECOND HALF OF
# THE DOUBLE FEATURE

*Also by Charles Willeford*

PROLETARIAN LAUGHTER *(poetry)*
HIGH PRIEST OF CALIFORNIA
PICK-UP
WILD WIVES
THE BLACK MASS OF BROTHER SPRINGER
LUST IS A WOMAN
THE WOMAN CHASER
DELIVER ME FROM DALLAS
UNDERSTUDY FOR LOVE
NO EXPERIENCE NECESSARY
COCKFIGHTER
THE MACHINE IN WARD ELEVEN *(coll.)*
POONTANG AND OTHER POEMS *(poetry)*
THE BURNT ORANGE HERESY
THE DIFFERENCE
A GUIDE FOR THE UNDEHEMMORRHOIDED *(autobiography)*
OFF THE WALL
MIAMI BLUES
NEW HOPE FOR THE DEAD
SOMETHING ABOUT A SOLDIER *(autobiography)*
SIDESWIPE
NEW FORMS OF UGLY *(non-fiction)*
KISS YOUR ASS GOODBYE
THE WAY WE DIE NOW
EVERYBODY'S METAMORPHOSIS *(coll.)*
I WAS LOOKING FOR A STREET *(autobiography)*
COCKFIGHTER JOURNAL *(non-fiction)*
THE SHARK-INFESTED CUSTARD
WRITING AND OTHER BLOOD SPORTS *(non-fiction)*

# THE SECOND HALF OF THE DOUBLE FEATURE

## Charles Willeford

a WitSend book

wit's end
publishing

New Albany, Indiana

to lose Willeford
we can ill afford


**First Edition**
{*August 2003*}


copyright © Betsy Willeford 2003

Set in Sabon

Published by Wit's End Publishing (www.sendwit.com)
book designed by oiva design group (www.oivas.com)

ISBN: 1-930997-29-9 (TRADE PAPERBACK)
ISBN: 1-930997-30-2 (HARDCOVER)


*All WitSend titles are edited by Juha T. Lindroos and Kathleen A. Martin.*

My work is one
long triumph
over my
limitations

—*Charles Willeford*

## Contents

## The Old Man at the Bridge

ONE DAY some years ago I drove from Miami to Palm Beach for a business appointment, and it was on the kind of day that causes a man to move to Florida in the first place. Bright, sunny, with just enough homemade divinity in the sky to break up the monotony of the flat horizon. It was a goof-off day and, because I was goofing off, I took the slower but scenic A1A route after the maze at Fort Lauderdale.

I crossed a drawbridge past Deerfield Beach and noticed the cluster of ancient fishermen on the crest of the bridge, their lines dripping over the concrete balustrade. But there was one old man down at the end of the bridge, well away from the other fishermen. The water was shallow near the bank, and I wondered why he didn't move higher up, where he could cast into deeper water. Perhaps the old man had discovered a deep pool or eddy that could not be seen from the highway. Perhaps, if the old man had not been standing all alone, I would not have noticed him.

The business transaction in Palm Beach was pleasant. The man who gave me the check was happy to do so because the money belonged to his company and not to him, and I was happy to get the check because I had already worked out a great way to spend it when I got back to Miami.

Going home, I drove even slower than on the way to Palm Beach. This time when I approached the drawbridge below Deerfield the jaws were open. I parked on the side of the road and walked over to the abutment to watch a powerboat chug through. The captain, or pilot, wore a Navy blue flannel jacket and a yellow silk scarf. The woman with him, however, was wearing an orange bikini and a heavy layer of suntan oil. I could smell the woman and the coconut in the oil as the boat passed. The boat was almost out of sight before I spoke to the old man, who was still there, fishing.

"Catching anything, Pop?"

He nodded. "Three bream. More'n I wanted to catch."

He was a clean old man, wearing stiff khaki chinos, blue canvas tennis shoes and a long-billed cap. His long-sleeved sport shirt still had starch in it, even though he had been standing out in the sun all day. His face was close-shaven and there was a scaly circle on each cheek the color of a ripe Valencia orange. Sun cancers. Benign, of course, but potentially dangerous—and sometimes they itch a little. I had one carved off my left temple by a dermatologist for $50, and it left a round white scar the size of a dime. Now that we are all wearing our hair a little longer, the scar is almost hidden. Florida fishermen get them constantly. Even if you wear a hat the reflection from the water gets to your face. But the prospect of sun cancers has had no statistical effect on the mass migration of old men to Florida.

I looked into this one's yellow plastic bucket. It held a Col. Sanders snack box, an empty Nehi bottle and a wadded Oh Henry wrapper.

"Where are the fish?"

He shrugged. "I turned 'em loose."

"But bream are supposed to be good eating."

"If you like to eat fish, they are."

"You don't eat fish?"

He shook his head. "No, and I don't like fishin', either."

I didn't laugh. I took out a cigarette, and offered the pack to the old man. His fingers reached out, and then he swiftly pulled back his hand.

"I don't smoke," he said firmly.

After lighting my cigarette I said, not unkindly, "If you don't like to fish and you don't eat fish, why have you been fishing all day? I remember seeing you in this same spot when I crossed the bridge at around nine this morning." He was silent.

"Because," he said at last, "I don't know what else to do. Before I retired I was vice-president of an insurance company in St. Louis. And this is what I always thought I wanted to do someday, retire to Florida and fish. The first day I tried it I discovered I disliked it. I had already bought a house, and my wife wouldn't let me stay home during the day.

"So I fish. Every day. In the beginning I used to take my catch home. But when I did, my wife felt that it was her duty to cook them. And I hate the taste of fish, the stink of fish and even the smell of other fishermen. That's why I stand down here by myself. Now when I go home in the evening I tell my wife that I didn't catch anything. It's simpler that way. She doesn't have to prepare the fish, and I don't have to eat any."

"Why don't you stay home and get a hobby of some kind?"

"I'd love to, but a woman can't stand to have a man around all day. I'd like to stay home and watch TV. The house is air conditioned, and"—he fingered the sun cancers—"maybe I could get these things cleared up. But my wife gets jittery when I'm around the house, and runs me out. And after talking about wanting to come to Florida for 30 years I can't tell her that I hate to fish."

"To get it straight: you hate to fish, but you're forced by circumstances to fish every day."

"That's about the size of it. I believe I will take one of those cigarettes if you don't mind."

"Sure."

He was a fine old man with fissured character lines and pale but keen eyes. The white hair that puffed out below his cap was more plentiful than mine. I thought about the check in my billfold. If this tough old man had handled the insurance deal instead of the young guy in Palm Beach, the check would have been halved. At least 67, maybe 68, the fisherman had several more unhappy years ahead on this bridge.

"I guess that you'll be fishing here tomorrow, then?" I said.

"That's right." He returned the cigarettes and lighter. "When 8:30 rolls around, I'll be standing right here with my line out."

"I—I hope you don't catch anything!"

"Thanks," he said gravely. "I appreciate that."

I returned to my car, and driving over the bridge wondered about the other old men who were there. How many fished because they had to and not because they wanted to? It was a cinch that none of them fished out of necessity, out of hunger. How many of these fishermen, like the man I had talked with, hated fishing as much as he did but didn't have the guts to admit it?

I reviewed my own fishing experiences. When I was younger and living in Los Angeles, a gang of us occasionally went out to the all-night fishing barge off Santa Monica. But we never did much fishing. We would try for half an hour or so, and someone might catch a barracuda or a sand shark, and then we would all go inside where it was warm and drink beer and play poker for the rest of the night. None of us really liked to fish. We used the overnight barge merely as an excuse to get drunk and play poker.

Once in Bimini I tried sail fishing on a charter boat, but I got seasick after an hour and, to the captain's disgust, made him take me back to the dock. The only other time I could remember going out to fish was in Georgia while I was stationed at Fort Gordon. A sergeant I knew had a musette bag full of concussion grenades. We killed half a dozen bass, a dozen frogs and a cottonmouth that day. The bass, after being roasted over a smoky fire, tasted like salted buffalo chips. By the end of the day I had a swollen face full of mosquito bites, and chiggers all over my arms and hands. By the following morning the scratches on the backs of my hands had festered, and they resembled yellow worms. All day long I had been fearful of getting caught with the bag of grenades. The sergeant claimed, falsely as I discovered later, that the laws against fishing with explosives didn't apply to professional soldiers.

After reviewing these admittedly limited experiences I knew that I hated fishing and that I would never go fishing again.

This was five years ago. Since then, on my own and without the help of a federal grant, I have talked to a lot of fishermen, more than a hundred altogether. My random sampling has included cane pole fishermen, commercial fishermen, charter boat captains and clients and even some of the men who go out on the shrimp boats at Fort Myers Beach. It is something no fisherman likes to admit, but after you work on them for a while, gain their confidence and break down their defenses (*machismo* is definitely tied up with this thing, you know), every man I have talked the matter over with has finally admitted, or confessed, that he truly hated fishing!

The only excuse for fishing, like hand-to-hand combat, is that it gives you something to do with your hands. There it is, the ugly truth about fishing for "pleasure" and for profit. I spend a good deal of time—too much—just sitting and don't get nearly enough exercise. Last night, to do something about it, I dug out my bowling shoes and ball and drove to the nearest alley. Not wanting to bowl alone, I asked a guy who was putting on his shoes if he wanted to bowl with me.

"If you want to," he replied.

"Fine. You can go first."

"No," he said, "go ahead."

"All right. You can keep the score."

"No." He shook his head. "I don't keep score."

I laughed. "You sound like a guy who doesn't like. . ." I didn't finish the sentence. In the morning my back muscles would ache, and the stiffness would bother me all day. My thumb and middle finger would be swollen and sore.

Without another word, and without keeping score, we grimly rolled about ten lines before we earned enough manhood to call it quits and get the hell out of there. ◉

# The Condemned

WE WERE in the Baguio market one morning, walking around and looking at the bare breasts of the Igorot women. Their breasts were brown and taut, and the nipples stuck straight out. This was because, D'Angelo said, none of these women had ever worn brassieres, which break down the muscles under the arms and cause breasts to sag. We ran into Tom Higdon in the market, and Higdon had a grande of gin. Higdon was an M.P. from Manila who came from Terrell, Texas, and he was already a little drunk. He offered us each a drink from his bottle, and told us that they were going to hang an Igorot in the morning. The Igorot had killed a man, and then he had eaten the man's heart after roasting it on a charcoal fire. Because of the American influence, the Philippines were sensitive to things like cannibalism, and they were making an example of this Igorot, although they had never bothered them much before, not while the Philippines were still under Spain, anyway. After all, it was a tribal custom to eat the heart of an enemy after killing him. The bolo fight, apparently, had been a fair one, so they were hanging the Igorot more to stamp out cannibalism than they were for murder.

"What I'm worried about," Higdon said, "is that this here Igorot's a pagan. What I'm going to do is go down to the jail and talk to him and show him the light. If I can convert the little fucker, he'll have a chance to go to heaven instead of purgatory."

Higdon was Southern Baptist, and even though he was a little drunk, he seemed serious about this mission.

"I don't think they'll let you talk to him, Higdon," I said. "And even if you did, he won't understand English."

"That's right," D'Angelo said. "With your Texas accent, I can hardly understand you myself."

"Look who's talking!" Higdon said, bristling. "You got a black dago Brooklyn accent that only foreigners talk."

"I'm as white as you are," D'Angelo said. I think he was probably sensitive about his dark Mediterranean skin. Texans like Higdon didn't make any distinction between Negroes, Mexicans, Portuguese, Italians, or anyone else with dark skins—they were all black to Higdon. I didn't want to see these two guys get into a fight about something stupid. I stepped between them.

"We'll go with you, Higdon. The constabulary might let three of us see the Igorot, where he might turn down just one guy."

"It's not that I want to go," Higdon said, shrugging, "but I wouldn't be much of a Christian if I didn't try."

So we walked to the jail, finishing the rest of the gin on the way.

There was an uneasy relationship between the Philippine Constabulary and the armed forces in P.I. As a national police force, they could, technically, arrest a soldier or a sailor, but they never did. They might hold on to some soldier who was tearing up a bar or something, but they turned him over to the M.P.'s as soon as possible.

The constabulary, anywhere you went, was a smart group of policemen. They were well trained and bore no resemblance to the sloppy new Philippine Army. I don't think they were paid well, but they undoubtedly had several kinds of graft working for them, and you never saw a member of the constabulary in a dirty or sloppy uniform. Higdon was an M.P., but he was on furlough and had no official capacity in Baguio.

There were three members of the constabulary at the jail, a corporal and two patrolmen. The sullen corporal didn't want us to see the Igorot.

"No." He shook his head. "I can't let you bother the Igorot. He's going to be hanged in the morning."

"That's why we have to see him today," Higdon explained. "Tomorrow will be too late. I've got to show him the light." Then Higdon pulled out his M.P. I.D. card, and that placed the corporal in a quandary. He knew that he was supposed to cooperate with American M.P.'s, so he reluctantly took us back to the cells.

The Igorot, wearing a pair of dirty white pants, was a dark little man of about four six. When we stopped outside his cell he scrambled up the tier of six bunks and peered down at us over the edge of the top bunk with the terrified dark eyes of a lemur.

"Come down here a minute," Higdon said. "I want to talk to you."

"He don't understand English," the corporal said.

"You tell him then."

"I talk Tagalog, not Igorot."

"Tell him in Tagalog."

The corporal said something in Tagalog, but there was no response. The little Igorot just backed away in that top bunk until all we could see were his nose, brown eyes, and his fingers gripping the iron rail of the top bunk.

"I guess you'll have to open the door," Higdon said. "I'll have to go in there and get him."

"No," the corporal said. "I can't let you bother that Igorot. He's going to be hanged in the morning."

Higdon was six four, and he must have weighed at least 190 pounds. He had red hair, bright blue bloodshot eyes, and long arms. He squatted down until his eyes were level with the corporal's. He lowered his voice to a whisper: "Open the door."

The way he said it, anyone would have reached for the keys, let alone a little constabulary cop in a small town like Baguio. He opened the cell.

Higdon went inside while we stayed outside and watched. After a few minutes our sides were hurting from laughter. I've never laughed so hard before in my whole life. The little Igorot didn't come as high as Higdon's chest, and he was faster than greased owl shit. Higdon would climb the tier, and then the Igorot would scramble down headfirst, as slippery as mercury. Then, as Higdon started down, up the Igorot would climb again to the top bunk. Higdon was getting angrier by the minute, calling him a pagan sonofabitch, and anything else he could think of. By the time Higdon finally caught the Igorot by the leg, he was breathing heavily through his mouth. He twisted the little man's arm behind his back, forced him to kneel, and said:

"Do you accept Jesus Christ as your Lord and Savior?"

The Igorot didn't say anything, so Higdon jerked the arm up a little higher and asked him the same question. This time the corporal said something in Tagalog, and the Igorot nodded his head vigorously. Higdon accepted the nod for a yes and released the man. He immediately scrambled up the tier again and looked down at us from the top bunk. If the Igorot was saved, he sure as hell didn't know it.

"I'm sorry if I hurt you, boy," Higdon apologized. "But you'll thank me for it someday when we meet in heaven."

D'Angelo also thanked the constabulary corporal for his cooperation, and I gave him a cigarette and lighted it for him. The cell was locked again, and Higdon seemed oddly subdued and sobered. The corporal was happy to see us leave the jail, and he shook his head solemnly as we left. "You shouldn't have bothered that Igorot. He's going to be hanged in the morning."

"Does he know it?" I asked.

"No, no. That would be too cruel, to know that you were going to be hanged. No, he doesn't know."

"He was tried, wasn't he?"

"Oh, yes, he was tried. The judge decided."

"But they didn't tell him?"

"No, that would be too cruel. We are not a cruel people, we Filipinos."

"Nobody said you were."

When we got outside again, we decided to walk back to Camp John Hay. There was plenty of time before noon chow. On the way, D'Angelo said that they didn't tell prisoners in France when they were going to be executed either. In America, of course, we always told our prisoners well in advance, down to the exact date and minute. We discussed which was the best way, whether to know or not, and concluded that the American way was best. How in the hell could a man sleep at night, knowing that any time someone could come in and put a noose around his neck?

"I'm sorry if I hurt that little fucker," Higdon said suddenly. "But I think I saved his soul. He doesn't know he's going to be hanged and he doesn't even know that what he did was wrong. They probably didn't tell him that it was against the law to eat his enemy, either. Jesus, what a fucking backward country this is! Can you imagine what this place'll be like when we pull out? As soon as they begin starving to death, they'll probably start eating each other again, and that little bastard's death will be in vain. It makes me sick to my fucking stomach."

"Don't look at it that way, Hig," D'Angelo said. "It's their country, not ours, and they're entitled to run it the way they want, just as we do ours. Besides, you did your Christian duty. So look on the bright side."

"Of course," I added, "you should've baptized him while you were at it—"

"Jesus!" Higdon said, slapping his forehead. "I should of baptized him, shouldn't I? Let's go back!"

"It's too late for that now, Hig. That corporal wouldn't let us in again."

"I guess you're right. Besides, a baptism without total immersion is a half-assed way to baptize anybody, and they don't have any tank or water trough at the jail."

When we got back to the barracks, Higdon didn't go with us to the mess hall. He wasn't hungry, he said, and he had a headache. He stretched out on his bunk and put the pillow over his face.

"You know," D'Angelo said after we sat down at the table and filled our plates, "that was the hardest I've ever laughed in my life. My stomach still hurts. But I don't think I'll ever tell anybody about it."

"Me neither," I said. "But I might write something about it someday."

"That's the best way, Will. That way, nobody'll understand why we laughed."

"Fuck you."

D'Angelo laughed, reached out, and speared another pork chop. @

# The Pop-Off Caper

MRS. WHEELER was at her picture window in her favored half-crouched position, late in the afternoon, when the cruising car tooled slowly down Fairfax Street. She was bent over crookedly, easing her back, peering out between the seventh and eighth ribs of the venetian blinds. The nasty little brown-and-white terrier that belonged to the irresponsible Crandall's up the street was due to make its daily appearance to use her lawn, and she had the broom ready by the front door. When the dog arrived, always looking about him warily before darting onto her neat lawn from the sidewalk, she would dash out the front door wildly swinging her broom. As feeble as she was she couldn't run after him, and she had never hit the filthy little beast yet. But one of these days she hoped to fetch him up such a good smack he'd never darken her lawn again.

Not many cars, except for those that belonged there, came down Fairfax, because it was a dead-end street. The cars that turned onto Fairfax accidentally, not noticing the "Dead End" sign at the corner, were easy to distinguish from those that belonged on the street. The disappointed drivers always got so angry. They would drive quickly to the circle turnaround, and on their way back to the corner they would race their engines in roaring annoyance that the street had turned out to be a dead end.

But this car was merely cruising, the driver obviously looking for an address. When he was abreast of Mrs. Wheeler's house and reading the number on her door, it seemed as if he were looking straight into her eyes. And although she knew that he couldn't possibly see her behind the drawn blinds, she stepped back from the window. The car continued to the end of the street, made the circle, and on the way back stopped at the curb in front of her house. The driver was a husky young man, more than six feet tall, and his red face was perspiring freely as he lumbered up the walk. He was wearing a blue gabardine suit that was much too heavy for this warm weather, and he carried a huge, bulging brown-paper sack under his left arm. His thick black curly hair was damp, and he didn't wear a hat.

Mrs. Wheeler had the door open before his finger could push the buzzer. A little old gray-haired lady in a green-and-purple flowered muumuu, she shaded her eyes with her hand as she stared up at the big man's sunburned face.

"Mrs. Wheeler?" He took a letter (it was one of *her* letters; she recognized her pink stationery with the white borders) out of his jacket pocket.

She nodded in reply, setting her thin lips in a determined line, wondering which company he was from. She wrote a good many letters of complaint and, as long as things continued to remain as they were, she was going to write a good many more.

"I'm Art Duncan, Mrs. Wheeler, from Regimental Can Company. The company sent me down to answer your complaint. I'm in the Public Relations Division."

"Come in." She stepped aside and closed the door behind him as he stumbled slightly in the dark living room. She turned on the overhead light at the wall switch, instead of opening the closed venetian blinds. When she pointed, Mr. Duncan backed awkwardly and sat on the couch. Mrs. Wheeler sat primly across from him in her old Morris rocker.

"We're awfully sorry that you've had trouble with our cans, Mrs. Wheeler," Duncan began earnestly. "In your letter you suggested that we include directions on the can for opening the tab-top pop-off, and that's the kind of constructive criticism Regimental Can appreciates. But the reason we don't do that is that once you get the hang of it, popping the top off is as easy as rolling off a log. I've brought some practice cans along with me to teach you how to do it. They're empty cans, of course, but the pop-off tops are exactly the same as they are on full cans of beer."

Mrs. Wheeler crossed her bony arms and glared at the man

as he took a plain, unlabeled can out of the paper sack.

"Now—watch my fingers closely," he said. In his big hairy hands the 16-ounce can looked like a small and shiny toy of some kind. "The trick is in the two distinct and separate movements, but the second follows the first so closely, you should think of them both as being only one continuous movement. With your thumb you pop up, like so, and then almost at the same time—and without a pause—with a continuing follow-through, the way you'd use a Number Five iron for a 150-yard hole, you simply jerk it open the rest of the way. See? See how simple it is?"

"No, Mr. Duncan, I do not see. Nor do I know what a Number Five iron is either."

Duncan laughed boyishly. "It's a golf club, Mrs. Wheeler. I only mentioned it because of the follow-through. That's the important thing in opening your pop-top can of beer—the old follow-through. If you stop pulling too soon, the top gets stuck midway, you see, and then you really have to pull on it hard to get it the rest of the way off."

"How much do you weigh, Mr. Duncan?"

"Weigh? Well, to tell you the truth, I'm a little overweight right now, although I'm trying to do something about it. When I played football in college I was two-ten, but I'm up around two-thirty now."

"I suspected as much. And how old are you?"

"Twenty-eight."

"Exactly!" She wet her thin lips and leaned forward painfully. "And so the Regimental Can Company sends a young man, 200 pounds of ex-football player, out to demonstrate how *simple* it is for a 70-year-old lady weighing 102 pounds to open a pop-top beer can!"

Mr. Duncan blushed beneath his sunburn and opened his mouth to speak, but Mrs. Wheeler held up a hand for silence. "No, don't say anything else, Mr. Duncan. You probably have a moral argument all prepared; but to say simply that a 70-year-old lady should not be drinking beer does not excuse your company's misrepresentation of the facts."

"I wasn't going to say anything like that—"

"I'm still talking, young man. Mind your manners. Not only that, but you actually brought along *trick* cans to teach me with, which are altogether different from full cans. What bothers me most of all, Mr. Duncan, is the absolute contempt your company has shown for the general public."

"I don't understand."

"I think you do. But I'll tell you anyway. I mean the little boy, about eight or nine, in your television commercial who pops open the cans of beer one after another, as though the tops were tissue paper, before handing the opened cans to his father. Do you actually think that we, the television audience, don't know that he has special, trick cans to open?"

"Honestly, Mrs. Wheeler—"

"Is a word your company should learn the meaning of. However, I'm willing to give you the benefit of the doubt, so I'll be honest with you, Mr. Duncan. When I wrote your company I didn't expect a reply, nor did I expect them to send a representative. I hoped they would, but I didn't think they would. But I did save—on the off chance that someone might possibly be sent to see me—the can of beer that I was unable to open. I popped the top all right, and although it stung when it jabbed its way into the meaty heel of my palm, it didn't break the skin. And that's as far as I could get it open, Mr. Duncan. Tug and pull as I might, the can would open no farther. So if you are here to demonstrate in good faith, let me see if you can get it the rest of the way off."

Mr. Duncan smiled confidently. "Gladly, Mrs. Wheeler."

The little old lady got out of her Morris rocker and went into the kitchen. She opened her refrigerator, removed a frosty can of beer, and picked out a clean glass from the drain rack beside the sink before returning to the living room. She handed the cold can of beer to Mr. Duncan. The big man, exposing his teeth in a broad smile, jerked the tab-top off the rest of the way as if it were indeed made of tissue paper.

With a shrug, Mrs. Wheeler handed him the clean glass. She lifted the corners of her lips slightly. "It's flat now, I suppose, having been partly opened for so long, but as warm as you are from your exertions, you might as well go ahead and drink it.

At least it's ice-cold."

"Thank you, ma'am." Mr. Duncan smiled happily, a victory smile, and poured the cold flat beer into the empty jelly glass.

The moment he set the partially emptied can on the cobbler's bench coffee table and tipped the bubbleless glass of beer to his lips, Mrs. Wheeler hastily snatched up the can. And not a moment too soon either. With only half of the contents emptied down his throat, Mr. Duncan's face twisted into a terrible grimace of mingled surprise and pain. A moment later his face was contorted and his pale blue eyes were bulging crazily in their sockets. He dropped the half-empty glass, clutched madly at his throat with both hands, and his heavy legs, as limp now as molten wax, buckled beneath his weight. He slid off the couch, falling sideways onto the floor with a resounding 230-pound thump, and lay still.

The sight of his distorted face, with its lolling tongue and glazed staring eyes, was distasteful to Mrs. Wheeler. She covered his face and the upper part of his body with a yellow silk Spanish shawl that she removed from her closed upright piano. She sponged up some of the spilled beer that had splashed onto her couch—fortunately, most of it had spilled on his suit—and washed the glass under hot water at the sink. She took the sack full of "trick" cans, together with the can of cold poisoned beer, out the back door and dumped all of them into her garbage can. And then, because it was Monday (Tuesdays and Fridays were garbage pick-up mornings for Fairfax Street), she carried the can out to the front curb. The galvanized iron garbage can was four years old, and the bottom had rusted places that were jagged, slit holes. She checked the lid to make certain it was on securely, reflecting as she did so, that if the garbage men had been as careful as she in replacing the lid, particularly on rainy mornings, her cans would last much longer than they did. Every eight or ten years, it seemed, she was forced to buy a new can. She had written twice to the mayor about their laxity, but instead of action, all she had received was a grateful letter of acknowledgement. If there were such a rule, as the mayor claimed, it wasn't filtering down to the garbage men.

Reentering her cottage through the kitchen door, Mrs. Wheeler paused for a moment to study the problem of the huge body on her rose rug. She had so many, many things to do, and one of the hardest of them would be the burying of Mr. Duncan in her basement. It was a pity that she hadn't managed to think of some way to lure him into the basement before he drank the poisoned beer; it would take literally hours of time and more effort than she wanted to expend to drag his heavy body down the cellar stairs.

But first, she would have to get rid of his car. As soon as it was dark she would drive it to the supermarket lot— there were some things she had to buy anyway—and she could simply leave the car on the lot and walk the three blocks home. So much for the car.

Mrs. Wheeler crossed to the window, crouched slightly, and peered through the venetian blinds to see if it was dark enough yet to drive the car away.

"Oh, dear!" she exclaimed, putting thin trembling fingers to her lips.

The nasty little Crandall dog was on her walk and sniffing about her garbage can at the curb. He shook his ugly brown-and-white head violently, staggered comically across the side-walk, and fell over dead on her lawn. It served him right, she thought, lapping up the beer that had seeped through the rusted bottom of *her* garbage can—but now, she realized unhappily, she would have to bury the dog as well as Mr. Duncan in her crowded basement.

And where would she put the dog? She could bury Mr. Duncan between the salesman, who had sold her the kitchen linoleum that had buckled, and the man from the department store, who had sold her the television that had promptly burned out the picture tube only two days after the guarantee had run out. But it didn't seem right to bury a dog in a human cemetery.

There were so many terrible problems she had had to face of late, and she wasn't getting any younger—she often forgot things lately, important things, too. She would simply have to make a list. For one thing, as quickly as she tired of late, it would take at least three days to dig a grave for Mr. Duncan in the basement. This meant that she would be much too tired to attend her granddaughter's birthday party on Friday. She would be so tired she would want to stay in bed from Friday through Monday and not even go to church on Sunday. So she mustn't forget to telephone her granddaughter that she couldn't come to the party. Close to tears and whimpering, the little old lady sat wearily in the Morris rocker.

If only people were nicer to each other, she thought, kinder, more considerate, instead of everybody trying to cheat everybody else. Oh, how simple and beautiful life could be if only people would meet each other halfway and pull together toward a common goal! God knows she tried her best to right the evils in this harsh world, but she was getting older and older every day, and sometimes, she sobbed now with indulgent self-pity, it was almost more than a body could stand. . . ⦿

## The Deserted Village

*Sweet smiling village, loveliest of the lawn,*
*Thy sports are fled, and all thy charms withdrawn;*
*—Oliver Goldsmith*

*MONDAY; MIAMI, Fla.* This morning, Joseph ate my Sensodyne toothpaste. All he left was an empty tube with tooth marks, and there wasn't enough paste left for me to brush my teeth. Emilie, Joseph's wife, had filled the tub with her washing, and I couldn't take a shower. Pedro and Alejandro, our two middle-aged anti-Castro Cuban refugees, had argued half the night away in the kitchen, and they had finished off the coffee. So I couldn't make any coffee.

Pedro and Alejandro were snoring way out-of-sync on their mattress in the kitchen, while Emilie and Joseph, our Haitian couple, huddled together on our pile of beach towels in the living room. Emilie, several months pregnant, will soon present us with another problem. . .

Dressed, I tiptoed into the bedroom and awoke my wife, Sally, by gently shaking her shoulder. Teresa, the fourteen-year-old Vietnamese orphan, clutching Sally's battered Teddy bear, one of my wife's childhood relics, slept soundly in the space I used to occupy. I sleep on the floor beside the bed now, and Sally and I haven't made love for four weeks—not since Teresa was assigned to us and we were made her unwilling foster parents.

"After all," Sally said, "we can't make a fourteen-year-old girl sleep on the floor."

I could have, yes, I could have. Four weeks—32 days, actually—is a long time when a man has been married for only a year.

"It's five A.M.," I whispered to Sally.

"Already? Pedro and Alejandro kept me up with all their shouting—"

"I know. But Pedro made five dollars yesterday, washing windows, and I think they're going out tonight to see if they can buy some dynamite to make a bomb."

"Thank God! Maybe I can get some sleep tonight, I'm exhausted."

I kissed Sally good-bye and drove to work. I felt bad. This was the first time since our marriage that I hadn't been able to hand her a cup of hot coffee. Perhaps it would be a good idea to buy a jar of instant and hide it somewhere in the apartment where Pedro and Alejandro couldn't find it. (Ha. Ha.) Fat chance.

No, sir, as I will show—or hope to show—the Reagan Refugee Resettlement Plan of 1982 simply isn't working. That's all there is to it.

† † †

*Wednesday; Miami, Fla.* When I started this record on Monday, I meant to keep it every day, but things were so hectic around here yesterday I was simply too tired. Joseph got sick last night. He ate four cans of sardines and four boxes of Granola and the mixture didn't agree with him. The hall smells terrible. I wanted to get a doctor, but Emilie found a voodoo priest who lives in a pup tent behind McDonald's, and the priest fixed Joseph up okay by brewing some mango leaf tea in the kitchen. Unhappily, the priest is still here. Emilie wants him to stick around in case Joseph gets sick again.

Then, around midnight, Pedro came home alone, all excited. I finally made out that someone had shot Alejandro in the Publix parking lot. I drove down there with Pedro, and we found Alejandro wedged beneath a Honda Civic. He had been shot at, all right. He and Pedro had been ripped off on their dynamite deal, losing their Timex watches and five-dollar bill, but Alejandro had saved himself when Pedro ran by diving under the Honda Civic. We dragged him out, despite his protests. His nose and forehead were scraped, but otherwise he was unhurt. He was frightened out of half of the few wits he has left.

When we got back to the apartment, Teresa was missing. Sally and I went out to look for her, and we found her with Old Man Zuckerman (301-C) in the boiler room behind the emergency stairs. Mr. Zuckerman is 82, a retired furrier from Chicago, and although he hadn't done anything to Teresa he had certainly been trying. We made Teresa return the twenty-dollar bill he had given her and took her back to the apartment. She kept crying, even after Sally made her go to bed.

The voodoo priest was squatting in the living room, dribbling white sand on our beige carpet, trying to form some kind of nine-sided star. I twisted his arm behind his back and gave him the bum's rush out of the door. Joseph and Emilie stared at me with round, terror-stricken eyes, afraid that they, too, would be given the bum's rush. They are both gentle and shy, and downright humble. In fact, they are so bewildered about everything that they are "out of it." They only speak Creole, of course, and neither one of them can read or write. They will eat anything that comes in a paper bag, a tube, a package, or a box, including soap chips. In the month they have been with us, they only leave the apartment one at a time, and then only for a few minutes. They're afraid that they may not be able to get back in again. The naked terror in their eyes was so pitiful when I bum-rushed the priest that I had to let the fraud back in.

Little do they know; I couldn't get rid of them if I wanted to, and I do, I *do* want to. . .

"Mr. Zuckerman," Sally told me, as she came into the living room, "wants to marry Teresa."

"That's wonderful."

"But she's only fourteen, and in Florida—"

"She's wise beyond her years. Let's get her married off tonight. Mr. Zuckerman can elope with her to Georgia. There's no age limit there, and no waiting period for marriages."

"The government made us her foster parents, and we could get into trouble if we let her run off with the old man. However, I do think that Mr. Zuckerman would be willing to wait three days if we can get official permission. This morning, he said, he made an appointment with his doctor to add three batteries to his pacemaker."

"He's really smitten, isn't he? I hope you didn't tell him that Teresa still wets the bed every night?"

"Of course not."

"Good. I'll check out the legal aspects tomorrow, and if we can get her married off this week, we can be back together by Sunday."

"I hope so. And by Sunday the mattress will be dry."

† † †

*Thursday; Miami, Fla.* It was no dice on marrying off Teresa. We have to wait until she is sixteen, and I doubt if Mr. Zuckerman will live two more years. If we let her run away to Georgia with the old man, we would be in violation of the Reagan Refugee Resettlement Plan, which would make us liable for a $1,000 fine and a year in jail.

Somehow, it just isn't fair. Not to us, and not to Old Man Zuckerman.

This is not the kind of life Sally and I had in mind when we saved our $50,000 for the down payment on this one-bedroom condo in Kendall and got married. Because we both are willing to work hard, we can make the $1,000-a-month mortgage payments, but some months it is a real struggle.

Sally pumps gas at the Exxon station from 6 A.M. until noon. At 1:00 P.M. she works at the Blue Carpet Real Estate Company until 6:00 P.M. She's a house scout. Her job is to find a house or an apartment for sale. If she finds one she gets a $1,000 bonus from the firm, no questions asked. She's good at her job, but she has to give kickbacks to the home owner and pay for her own gas. In some neighborhoods, as she drives around looking for sellers, she has to hire an armed, uniformed Wackenhut guard, which runs $25 an hour. So she usually ends up with only $250 or $300 left from the bonus.

I work as a mechanic at Ryder Trucks from 7 A.M. until 4

P.M. I then act as a school crossing guard from 4:30 to 7:30 P.M. at N. Kendall and 107th Avenue. It's a real madhouse when those 80,000 students at M-DCC South try to make a left on Kendall. Then, three nights a week, I'm a projectionist at the Tropicaire Drive-in on Bird Road. The Metro government gives free Spanish lessons there at night, and I show educational films and slides. It's really something to hear 5,000 voices shout in unison,

## "Arriba, Spot, Arriba!"

Both of us were almost always tired at night when we got home, even before the R.R.R. Program started. We both had to do some piecework at home, too, before going to bed. Sally made macramé neckties to sell to the customers she pumped gas for in the morning, and I tie-dyed T-shirts, which I sold on Sundays from a booth at Dadeland Tent City. We needed all the extra money for those monthly mortgage payments; and the F.P.L. fuel adjustments were killing us. We no longer use the air conditioning, so the F.P.L. bills are a little lower now. Joseph and Emilie start shivering when the temperature drops below 85 degrees, so we had to turn it off. The Cubans took the screens off the windows and sold them, claiming that no fresh air could get through the screens.

It is sweltering in the apartment right now, at 2 A.M., as I write this, and the marsh mosquitoes are settling in packs on the back of my neck. I'm going to lie down on the floor and cover myself with a sheet.

Something *has* to be done—but what?

† † †

*Friday; Miami, Fla.* Our real troubles began with the Third Mariel Boatlift, as we called it. The Second Mariel Boatlift hardly touched us out here in the Kendall area of Miami, but the Third overwhelmed the entire county and overran the Keys. Castro hired three cruise ships from the Costa Lines, and the ships, packed with about 5,000 refugees at a time, dumped them off daily at Port Everglades. Baby Doc Duvalier's successors made a deal to get the Norway Princess, and loaded in Haitian refugees like curled anchovies. When the Norway Princess docked it looked like flies on a rotten mango.

The INS was overwhelmed, so it closed its offices and went back to Washington. Then Reagan came out with his Resettlement Plan, and each Dade County resident who owned his own home or apartment was forced to take in a quota of refugees. That's how Sally and I got saddled with Joseph and Emilie, Pedro and Alejandro, and little doe-eyed, bed-wetting Teresa.

Tonight, after finishing work at the Tropicaire, I got into my car and placed my .45 pistol on the seat beside me. I hated to drive home. As I drove swiftly through the dark streets, I speeded up at the intersections, where knots of people were gathered. At night men gather around empty oil drums, which they use for gambling tables, and gamble through the night by the light of tiny oil lamps. There are lots of fights, knifings and shootings.

There was plenty of activity and lots of light at the Dadeland Tent City, however, where free bean lines have been established. The parking lot looks like downtown Tangier, what with all the noise and the milling, raggedy crowds. According to the *Miami Herald,* there was a big rally there this afternoon for more refugee rights, and Mayor Steve Clark was scheduled to sing "Your Cheating Heart" in both Spanish and Creole. Mayor Clark is largely responsible for setting up the processing tent cities and free bean lines at Dadeland, Cutler Ridge, Westland, and Omni, and he is very popular with the refugees.

As I passed under the Palmetto on Kendall, I could hear the booming of the voodoo drums from atop Dadeland's Burdine's, and they sounded ominous and threatening. No matter where you are in Miami at night, you can always hear voodoo drums and steel band music and the crackle of guns firing.

After I parked in my condo slot, I took the safety off my .45 and stuck the pistol in my belt. I picked my way through the cluttered courtyard. Many of the new Haitian residents of the condo were cooking fish over charcoal fires around the polluted swimming pool, and there were huge piles of trash and garbage scattered throughout the compound and against the new barbed wire fence. The buildings, less than two years old, resembled the tenements in the old photographs of the Tenderloin district of old New York. The elevator, out of order, was being used as a domino parlor by six Colombians. They had a flashlight, and they shouted with joyful glee as they slammed their dominoes down on the bare metal floor. The elevator rug was stolen two weeks ago.

I climbed the three flights of stairs to our apartment and unlocked the door. Emilie, Joseph and Teresa were watching the news on Channel 10, the all-Creole station. Ann Bishop is as cute as she can be when she does the news in Creole, and ordinarily I would have watched her myself for a while, but tonight I was too depressed.

I don't know why; I was just depressed.

Sally was sitting on the edge of the bed, crying.

"What's the matter, honey?"

"Pedro and Alejandro. . ."

"What have they done this time?"

"They. . ." She wiped her eyes. "They went to the Westland Mall Processing Center to get their families. Their wives and children finally arrived today from Mariel."

"That's good news, isn't it? Now they'll be reassigned to larger quarters, and we'll be rid of them. That's the rule, according to the Plan—"

She shook her head. "Eventually, yes. But they'll all be here for at least three months. That's what the man told me on the phone. He said there was no place else to put them right now—" She started to cry again.

"What about our letter to Congressman Benitez? Can't he do something?"

"It came back today. It was stamped, 'Unread. Please correspond in Spanish only.' If you want to see it, it's crumpled up over there in the wastebasket."

"I'm sorry now," I said, "that I voted for him instead of Dante Fascell. But Fascell was so damned ineffectual. . ."

"We were fools, Bob, that's all." She wiped her face with a macramé necktie.

Sally looked terrible. There were dark circles beneath her eyes, and tiny lines creasing her temples. The dark lines from the corners of her nose to the corners of her mouth had deepened almost overnight it seemed. She was only 25, but she could have passed for 35.

"You know something, Sally?"

"What?"

"We've got to do something."

† † †

*Monday. Six weeks later. Port-de-Paix, Haiti.* It wasn't as hard as I thought it would be.

Three days after the last entry in this notebook, I picked up a quit-claim deed form from a stationery store, and signed over the condo apartment to Joseph and Emilie. Now *they* can worry about the $1,000 a month mortgage payments. With the addition of three middle-aged Cuban ladies and five children to our crowded apartment, the situation became unbearable.

We packed up our clothes and utensils, and drove both cars down to the Dinner Key marina. We traded both cars for a 32-foot sailboat that had a serviceable if puttery inboard engine.

Four days later we arrived here, in beautiful, deserted Port-de-Paix, Haiti. Except for Sally and me, there isn't a living soul within miles of here. The residents who lived here have all gone to South Florida. (There may be two or three hundred people left in Port-au-Prince, the capital, but I'm not going over there to find out.)

We selected a sturdy, three-story house on the beach, and cleaned it up. We have a vegetable garden started, and we can get all of the fish and lobsters we need from the sea. This is beautiful country. The rains have come, and the nearby hills are a shimmering, emerald green. We walk the beach in the mornings, and swim in the afternoons. The silence is like the music of the spheres, golden—

—as golden as my tanned and happy Sally.

As I write this on the veranda, having finished my rum and coconut water, I watch Sally, in her white bikini, running from the beach toward the house. She is holding a lobster at arm's length in each hand, giggling with delight as she runs.

She's beautiful, and so happy she looks like a 16-year old.

We plan to stay here forever in this peaceful deserted village. We made a vow, and there is only one thing we *won't* do: And that is to start a family.

We tried that in Miami, and we didn't like it. ❧

# Give the Man a Cigar

SEÑOR ARMANDO Martinez came into my shop a little before noon, and I uncrossed my fingers. He usually came by for a cigar every weekday, but sometimes he missed a day. I had been waiting for him, and I was very glad to see him. Martinez was the big shot editor of *El Grito,* perhaps the most strident of the ten weekly Spanish newspapers published in Miami.

He was wearing a brown silk suit with tiny gold threads in it, a white silk shirt, and a lemon-yellow Countess Mara necktie.

He pointed to the box of Queen Isabellas in the glass case. I smiled, shook my head, and unlocked the drawer beneath the cash register. I took out the box of Ramón Navorones, placed it on the counter, and raised the lid.

"Jesus," he said, with a little laugh. "Navarones! I haven't seen one of them for at least three years. Where'd you get them?"

"A friend in the Isle of Pines. He ships a few boxes every year to a friend of mine in Toronto. Then, when my friend from Toronto comes down for the season, he sometimes brings me one or two boxes to sell. This year he only brought one box."

Martinez fingered a couple of the Navarones in the box with a gentle touch. The cigars were ten inches long, hand-rolled, maduro, oily, and as black as Castro's heart.

Martinez selected a cigar. I put the box away, locked the drawer, and then lit a kitchen match. Martinez held the tip of the cigar an inch above the flame, and turned the cigar slowly as he lighted it.

"Jesus, this is good," he said. "I could *eat* the damned thing."

He held the cigar between his teeth, took out his wallet, and placed three one-dollar bills on the counter.

I shook my head. "Two more."

"Five dollars?"

I shrugged. "It's a Navarone." He added two more ones to the three bills on the counter. I lighted a Winston 100 with my Bic throwaway lighter.

"Don't you smoke Navarones?"

"I can't afford them," I said.

Martinez still had his wallet out. He removed a five. "Give me another."

"No." I shook my head. "The others are spoken for."

"It's not for me," Martinez argued. "It's for my father-in-law."

"The others are spoken for."

Martinez put his wallet away. As he pulled his coat back, I noticed the handle of the .38 pistol in the shell clip-on holster on his belt. He buttoned the middle button of his jacket.

I lowered my voice. "Perez is looking for you, Señor Martinez."

"Perez?"

I nodded. "He didn't like what you said about the bombing in your editorial."

"I told the truth."

I shrugged. "Truth or no truth, don't go to the Café Toledo for lunch today."

"Is that where he is?"

I nodded. "Raul and Anibel are with him."

Martinez went to the window, and looked across the street at the Café Toledo. He had his own special table at the Toledo, and ate lunch there every day. He stood there for a long time, puffing on his cigar, wasting it. His white Mercedes was parked in front of my shop. I knew that he was afraid to leave the shop and get into his car.

"Señor Martinez," I said, "why don't you go out the back? Leave me your keys, and when my son comes home from school, I'll have him drive your car to your father-in-law's house."

He turned. "What's out back?"

"The alley. Fifty yards down the alley is the back of the Granada Supermarket. You can go through the market, and catch a cab on Seventh Street."

"I do not fear Perez," he said, throwing out his chest. Beads of sweat glistened in his moustache.

"Perez alone, no," I said, "but he has Raul and Anibel with him."

"That is true. But I have many friends and supporters in Miami."

"At least as many as Perez."

"More. Because I tell the truth in my paper."

"If you want to tell the truth in your paper tomorrow," I said, "you should go out the back today."

Martinez hesitated for a moment, and then took out his key case. He removed the key to his Mercedes, and placed it on the counter. "Does your son know my father-in-law's house?"

"I will tell him."

I unlocked the back door to let Martinez out. I pointed down the alley to a huge pile of empty cardboard boxes. "The back door to the market is on the other side of those boxes," I said. "There are always one or two cabs waiting out front."

He slipped out the door, and I locked it behind him. I picked up the phone on the wall and dialed. I let the phone ring twice, then hung up.

I waited about five minutes, and then I unlocked the back door. I stuck my head out and listened. I had not heard the shots, but I could hear the sirens of the police cars as they pulled up in front of the Granada Supermarket on Seventh Street.

I closed and locked the back door. I took the box of Ramón Navarones from the drawer, opened it, and selected one. As I rolled the cigar between my fingers I could feel the fine film of oil. There was no crackle, and the cigar was firm. I lighted the Navarone with a kitchen match.

Now I could afford to smoke Ramón Navarones; every cigar in the box. ❧

## Citizen's Arrest

IT WAS fairly late in the afternoon when I stopped at Gwynn's Department Store on my way home to look at some new fishing tackle. Gwynn's is the best store in the entire city; there are three full floors of everything imaginable. So I always took my time shopping at Gwynn's; a man who's interested in the outdoors can spend several hours in there just looking around.

My back was to the man at the counter—the thief, I should say—because I was looking at the shotguns in the rack behind the locked glass doors. He must have seen me, of course, but he didn't know, I suppose, that I could see his reflection in the glass doors as he stood at the next counter. There was no clerk in the immediate vicinity; there were just the two of us in this part of the store on the ground floor. Casually, as I watched him in the polished glass, he snatched the heavy lighter off the counter and slipped it into the deep right-hand pocket of his green gabardine raincoat.

I was pretty well shocked by this action. As a kid, I had pilfered a few things from ten-cent stores—pencils and nickel key-rings, and once a twenty-five-cent "diamond" ring—but this was the first time in my life I had ever seen anybody deliberately *steal* something. And it was an expensive table lighter: $75 not counting tax. Only a minute or two before I had examined the lighter myself, thinking how masculine it would look on the desk in my office or on the coffee table in a bachelor's apartment. Of course, as a married man, I couldn't afford to pay that much money just for a cigarette lighter, but it was a beautiful piece of work, a "conversation piece," as they say in the magazine ads. It was a chromium-plated knight in armor about six inches tall. When you flipped up the visor on the helmet a butane flame flared inside the empty head, and there was your light. There had been a display of these lighters in shining armor on the gift counter, and now, as the big man sauntered toward the elevators, there was one less.

If I'd had time to think things over I am inclined to believe now that I would have ignored the theft. As I've always said, it was none of my business, and nobody wants to get involved in a situation that is bound to be unpleasant, but at that particular moment a young clerk appeared out of nowhere and asked me if I needed any help. I shook my head, and pointed my chin in the general direction of the elevators.

"Do you see that man over there in the green raincoat? I just saw him take one of those knight table lighters off the counter and put it into his pocket."

"Do you mean he stole it?" he asked, in a kind of stage whisper.

"No." I shook my head again. "I didn't say that. All I said was that he put the lighter into his pocket and then walked over to the elevators."

The big man entered the elevator, together with a teen-aged boy who badly needed a haircut, and the operator clanged the door closed.

The clerk, who couldn't have been more than twenty-two or three, cleared his throat. "I'm afraid, sir, that this sort of thing is a little out of my province. Would you mind talking to our floor manager, Mr. Levine?"

I shrugged in reply, but there was a sinking sensation in my stomach all the same. By mentioning the theft I had committed myself, and now I knew that I had to go through with it no matter how unpleasant it turned out to be.

The clerk soon returned with Mr. Levine, a squat bald man in his early forties. He wore a plastic name tag and a red carnation on the left lapel of his black silk suit coat.

I briefly explained the theft to Mr. Levine. He pursed his lips, listened attentively, and then checked out my story by going over to the glass case of shotguns to prove to himself that the gift counter was reflected perfectly in the polished surface.

"Would you be willing, Mr.—"

"Goranovsky."

"Would you be willing, Mr. Goranovsky, to appear in court as a witness to this shoplifting? Providing, of course, that such is the case."

"What do you mean, if such is the case? I told you I saw him take it. All you have to do is search him, and if you find the lighter in his raincoat—in the right hand pocket—the case is cut and dried."

"Not exactly, sir. It isn't quite that simple." He turned to the clerk, whose eyes were bright with excitement, and lowered his voice. "Call Mr. Sileo, and ask him to join us here."

The clerk left, and Mr. Levine steepled his fingers. "Mr. Sileo is our security officer," he explained. "I don't want you to think that we don't appreciate your reporting this matter, Mr. Goranovsky, because we do, but Gwynn's can't afford to make a false accusation. As you said, there was no clerk in the vicinity at the time, and it's quite possible that the gentleman might have gone off to search for one."

I snorted in disgust. "Sure, and if he can't find one on the second floor, maybe he'll find one on the third."

"It's possible," he said seriously, ignoring my tone of voice. "Legally, you see, no theft is involved unless he actually leaves the store without paying for the item. He can still pay for the lighter, or put it back on the counter before he leaves.

"No, please. I merely wanted to explain the technical points. We'll need your cooperation, and it's Mr. Gwynn's policy to prosecute shoplifters; but you can't make charges without an airtight case and a reliable witness. If we arrest him within the store, all the man has to say is that he was looking for a clerk, and there isn't anything we can do about it. He very well may be looking for a clerk. If such is the case, we could very easily lose the good will of a valuable customer."

"I understand; I'm a businessman myself. In fact, I hope I'm wrong. But if I'm not, you can count on me to appear in court, Mr. Levine. I've gone this far."

We were joined by Mr. Sileo. He was slight, dark, and businesslike. He looked more like a bank executive than a detective, and I had a hunch that he had an important job of some kind with Gwynn's; that he merely doubled as a security officer. In a businesslike manner, he quickly and quietly took charge of the situation.

I was directed to stand by the elevators and to point out the thief when he came down. Mr. Levine was stationed in the center aisle and Mr. Sileo took up his post by the Main Street entrance. If, by chance, the shoplifter turned right after leaving the elevator—toward the side exit to 37th Street—Mr. Levine could follow him out, and Mr. Sileo could dart out the main door and circle around the corner to meet the man outside on 37th Street. Mr. Sileo explained the plan so smoothly, I supposed it was some kind of standing procedure they had used effectively before. The eager young clerk, much to his disgust, was sent back to work by Mr. Levine, but he wasn't needed.

To my surprise, when I looked at my watch, only ten minutes had passed since I reported the theft. The next ten minutes were much longer as I waited by the elevators for the man in the green raincoat to reappear. He didn't look at me as he got off, and I pointed him out by holding my arm above my head, as Mr. Sileo had directed, and then trailed the man down the wide corridor at a safe distance. I wondered if he had a gun, and at this alarming thought I dropped back a little farther, letting Mr. Levine get well ahead of me. Mr. Sileo, who had picked up my signal, went out the front door as soon as it became apparent that the man was going to use the Main Street exit. I could see Mr. Sileo through the glass door as he stood on the front sidewalk; he was pretending to fumble a cigarette out of his pack. A moment later, just about the time I reluctantly reached the Main Street doorway myself, Mr. Levine and Mr. Sileo were escorting the big man back inside the store.

I couldn't understand the man's attitude; he was smiling. He had a huge nose, crisscrossed with prominent veins, and he had a large mouth, too, which probably looked bigger than it was because of several missing teeth.

The four of us moved silently down the right side aisle a short distance to avoid blocking the doorway. For a strained moment nobody said anything.

"I'm sorry, sir," Mr. Sileo said flatly, but pleasantly, "but this gentleman claims that you took a desk lighter off the counter and put it in your pocket without paying for it."

I resented the offhand way Mr. Sileo had shifted all the responsibility onto me. The big man shrugged and, if anything, his genial smile widened, but his bluish white eyes weren't smiling as he looked at me. They were as cold and hard as glass marbles.

"Is that right?" He chuckled deep in his throat. "Is this the lighter you mean?" He took the chrome-plated knight out of his raincoat pocket.

"Yes," I said grimly, "that's the one."

He unbuttoned his raincoat and, after transferring the lighter to his left hand, dug into his pants pocket with his right.

"This," he said, handing a slip of paper to Mr. Sileo, "is my receipt for it."

Mr. Sileo examined the receipt and then passed it to Mr. Levine. The floor manager shot me a coldly furious look and returned the slip of paper to the man. The thief reached into his inside jacket pocket for his checkbook. "If you like," he said, "you can look at the check stub, as well."

Mr. Sileo shook his head, and held his hands back to avoid taking the checkbook, "No, sir, that's quite all right, sir," he said apologetically.

Mr. Levine made some effusive apologies for the store which I thought, under the circumstances, were uncalled for— but the big man cut him off in the middle of a long sentence.

"No harm done," he said good-naturedly, "none at all. In your place, I'd have checked, too. In all probability," he qualified his remark.

"It was my mistake," I said, finally. "I'm sorry you were inconvenienced." And then, when neither Mr. Levine nor Mr. Sileo said anything to me, and the big man just stood there— grinning—I turned on my heel and left the store, resolving, then and there, never to spend another dime in Gwynn's as long as I lived.

There had been no mistake. I had seen the man take the lighter, and there had been no clerks anywhere near us at the time. I stood beside my car at the curb, filled with frustration as I ran things all over again in my mind. A trick of some kind had been pulled on the three of us, but how the man had worked it was beyond my comprehension. I opened the door on the sidewalk side and slid across the seat. As I fastened my seat belt, a meaty hand opened the door and the big man in the green raincoat grinned at me. He held out the shining knight for my inspection.

"Want to buy a nice table lighter, buddy?" he said, chuckling deep in his throat. "I can let you have it without any tax."

I swallowed twice before I replied. "I knew you stole the lighter, but how did you get the receipt?"

"Will you buy the lighter if I tell you?"

"No, damn you; I wouldn't give you ten cents for it!"

"Okay, Mr. Do-Gooder," he said cheerfully, "I'll tell you anyway. This morning there were several lighters on the counter, and I bought one of them at ten A.M. After stashing the first one in a safe place, I came back late this afternoon and got this one free. Unfortunately, you happened to see me pick it up. The receipt I got this morning, however, served me very well for the second. The store stays open until nine-thirty tonight, and I had planned to come back after dinner and get another one. So long as I took them one at a time, one receipt is as good as three, if you get my meaning. So the way I figure it, you ought to buy this one from me because I can't come back tonight for my third lighter. You cost me some money, fella."

"I've a good mind to go back in and tell Mr. Sileo how you worked it."

"Really? Come on, then. I'll go in with you."

"Get the hell out of here!"

He chuckled, slammed the door, and walked away.

My fingers trembled as I lit a cigarette. There was no mistaking my reaction now—I was no longer frustrated, I was angry. If the man had been my size—or smaller—I would have chased after him and knocked out the remainder of his front teeth. I also considered, for a short moment, the idea of telling

Mr. Levine how he had been cheated. All they had to do was to inventory their remaining lighters (there couldn't be too many of them in stock, an expensive item like that) and they would soon find out that they were one short. But after the cold way they had treated me, I didn't feel like telling them anything.

A policeman's head appeared at the car window. "Is this your car, sir?"

"Of course."

"Will you get out, please, and join me on the sidewalk?" He walked around the front of the car, and I unfastened my seat belt and slid back across the seat; I was more than a little puzzled.

"Take a look," he said, pointing at the curb when I joined him on the sidewalk. "You're parked well into the red zone."

"That isn't true," I said indignantly. "Only the front bumper's in the zone; my wheels are well behind the red paint. There's supposed to be a little leeway, a limit of tolerance, and I'm not blocking the red zone in any way—"

"Don't argue with me, sir," he said wearily, taking a pad of tickets out of his hip pocket. "Ordinarily, I'd merely tell you to re-park or move on, but this time I'm giving you a ticket. A good citizen in a green raincoat reported your violation to me at the corner just now, and he was a gentleman who had every right to be sore. He said he told you that you were parked in a red zone—just as a favor—and you told him to go to hell. Now, sir, what is your name?" ◉

## Sentences

MY FIRST wife spoiled me, as new brides are wont to do, by giving me a glass of freshly squeezed orange juice every morning with breakfast.

I loved it. What is better in the morning than cold, freshly squeezed orange juice? True, there were always two or three orange seeds I had to fish out of the glass with a spoon before I could drink it, but who would complain about something so petty?

And then one afternoon, after I had been married for almost a year, I had a headache. The characters in the novel I was working on were no longer speaking to each other. There was no aspirin in the bathroom, so I rummaged around in the kitchen shelves. I found a small tin aspirin box, but when I opened it I discovered 34 dry orange seeds.

I then looked in the freezer compartment of the refrigerator and found three small cans of frozen orange juice. What she had been doing, you see, was to mix the frozen juice in the kitchen, and then serve it to me after adding two or three seeds so that I would think I was drinking freshly squeezed juice.

Why did she do it? I don't know. There was no way that I could fathom her motivation. The deception was so trivial, so minor, I didn't know how to handle it. Should I confront her with my newly gained knowledge? And if I did, what purpose would it serve? Besides, it was partly my fault. I shouldn't have gone into her kitchen, her territory, in the first place.

No, I decided, the gentlemanly thing to do would be to continue on as if nothing had changed. I would keep on fishing those seeds out with my spoon each morning, and drink my frozen orange juice (made from concentrate).

However, small seeds of suspicion had been planted. If, I thought, she would deceive me by putting dry seeds into frozen orange juice, perhaps there were other things as well. . . ? I started to check around—but that's another story. In time, my first wife became my ex-wife.

I told this little story at our regular poker game the other night. When I finished, there were appreciative, affirmative nods around the table. Another player cleared his throat and told this story:

"I went out with my present wife for almost three months before I found out that she was already married.

"Of course," he added virtuously, "if I had known that she was married, I never would have dated her in the first place."

She had fooled him neatly. She would meet him at his office when he finished work for the day. Then they would go out to dinner, movies, motels, and things like that.

But when he drove her home, she always made him drop her off a block away from her house. She lived with her mother, she explained, and her mother was dying with a terrible disease. Her mother was so ravaged with pain that she couldn't stand to have a stranger in the house. The explanation seemed reasonable, so he went along with it without concern.

Later on, he discovered that her mother had been dead for 18 years.

The deception could have continued indefinitely, but her husband found out about him. There was a messy, expensive divorce, and he had to pay her lawyer's fee. She also got the custody of her two children when he married her after the divorce was final.

"She promptly had another baby with me," he concluded, "so now I'm stuck with a deceitful wife and three ungrateful children to support."

The poker game was forgotten now, as another player told his story of a woman's deceit; and then another, and another, with each vignette more trenchant than the last.

Confession is good for the soul, but it ruined the poker game. The game, which usually runs until midnight, broke up at ten P.M. The married men in the game all quit and went home to check on their wives, to see what they were doing while they—the husbands—were out playing poker.

That left two of us, Ed Lewis, an accountant, and me, at the table: Two bachelors, twice married, twice divorced: lonely, middle-aged men. We didn't say anything for a long time after the others left. We just sat there, drinking beer and trying to make interesting circle patterns on the felt-covered poker table with our damp cans of beer.

Finally, Ed said, "Do you still drink orange juice every morning for breakfast?"

"No," I replied. "Prune." ◉

## Saturday Night Special

IT STARTED out as kind of a joke, and then it wasn't funny any more because money became involved. Deep down, nothing about money is funny.

There were four of us at the pool: Eddie Miller, Don Luchessi, Hank Norton, and me—Larry Dolman. It was just beginning to get dark, but the air was still hot and muggy and there was hardly any breeze. We were sitting around the circular, aluminum table in our wet trunks. Hank had brought down a plastic pitcher of vodka martinis, a cupful of olives, and a half-dozen Dixie cups. That is one of the few rules at Dade Towers; it's all right to eat and drink around the pool so long as only plastic or paper cups and plates are used.

Dade Towers is a singles only apartment house, and it's only one year old. What I mean by "singles only" is that only single men and women are allowed to rent here. This is a fairly recent idea in Miami, but it has caught on fast, and a lot of new singles only apartments are springing up all over Dade County. Dade Towers doesn't have any two- or three-bedroom apartments at all. If a resident gets married, or even if a man wants to bring a woman in to live with him, out he goes. They won't let two men share an apartment, either. That's a fruitless effort to keep gays out. But there are only two or three circumspect gays in the 120-apartment complex, and they don't bother anyone in the building. The rents are on the high side, and all apartments are rented unfurnished. The rules are relaxed for women, and two women are allowed to share one apartment. That rule is reasonable, because women in Miami don't earn as much money as men. And by letting two women share a pad, the male/female ratio is evened out. So some of the one-bedrooms have two stewardesses, or two secretaries, living together. Other women, who have more money, like school teachers, young divorcees, and nurses, usually make do with efficiencies. If a man wanted to, he could get all of the women he wanted simply by hanging around the pool.

Under different circumstances, I don't think Don, Hank, Eddie and I would have become such good friends. But the four of us were all charter members, so to speak, the first four tenants to move into Dade Towers when it opened. And now, after a solid year together, we were tight. We swam in the pool, went to movies together, asked each other for advice on the broads we took out, played poker one or two nights a month, and had a good time, in general, without any major fights or arguments. In other words, we truly lived the good life in Miami.

Eddie Miller is an ex-Air Force pilot. After he got out of the service, he managed to get taken on as a 727 co-pilot. Flying is just about all Eddie cares about, and eventually he'll be a captain. In the meantime (he only flies 20 hours a week), Eddie studies at the University of Miami for his state real estate exam. That's what many of the airline pilots do in their spare time; they sell real estate. And some of them make more money selling real estate than they do as pilots, even though real estate is a cutthroat racket in Dade County.

Hank Norton has an A.B. in Psychology from the University of Michigan. He has a beautiful job in Miami as a detail man, or salesman, for a national pharmaceutical firm. He only works about ten or fifteen hours a week, when he works at all, and he still has the best sales record in the U.S. for his company. As the top detail man in the field the year before, his company gave him a two-week, all-expenses paid, vacation to Acapulco. He is a good-looking guy, with carefully barbered blond hair and dark, Prussian-blue eyes. He is the best cocksman of the four, too. Hank probably gets more strange in a single month than the rest of us get in a year. He has an aura of noisy self-confidence, and white flashing teeth. His disingenuous smile works as well on the doctors he talks with as it does on women. He makes about twenty-five thousand a year, and he has the free use of a Galaxie, which is exchanged for a new model every two years. His Christmas bonus has never been less than two thousand, he claims.

Don Luchessi makes the most money. He is the Florida rep for a British silverware firm, and he could make much more money than he does if the firm in Great Britain could keep up with his orders. They are always two or three months behind in production and shipping, and Don spends a lot of time apologizing about the delays to the various department and jewelry stores he sells to. What with the fantastic increase of the Miami Cuban population, and the prosperity of the Cubans in general, Don's business has practically doubled in the last four years. Every Cuban who marries off a daughter (as well as her friends and relatives, of course) wants the girl to start off her married life with an expensive silver service. Nevertheless, even though Don makes a lot more money than the rest of us, he is paying child support for his seven-year-old daughter and giving his wife a damned generous monthly allowance besides. As a Catholic he is merely legally separated, not divorced, and although he hates his wife, we all figure that Don will take her back one of these days because he misses his daughter so much. At any rate, because of the money he gives to his wife, by the end of the year he doesn't average out with much more dough than the rest of us.

Insofar as I am concerned, what I considered to be a bad break at the time turned out to be fortuitous. I had majored in police science at the University of Florida, and I had taken a job as a policeman, all gung-ho to go, in Florence City, Florida, two weeks after I graduated. Florence City isn't too far from Orlando, and the small city has tripled in population during the last few years because of Disney World. After two years on the force I was eligible to take the sergeant's exam, which I passed, the first time out, with a 98. They were just starting to build Disney World at the time, and I knew that I was in a growth situation. The force would grow along with Florence City, and because I had a college degree I knew that I would soon be a lieutenant, and then a captain, within a damned short period of patrolman apprenticeship.

So here I was, all set for a sergeancy after only two years on the force. None of the other three men who took the exam with me was even close to my score. But what happened, I got caught with the new ethnic policy. Joe Persons, a nice enough guy, but a semiliterate near-moron, who had failed the exam for five years in a row, finally made a minimum passing score of 75. So the Board made him a sergeant instead of me because he was black. I was bitter, of course, but I was still willing to live with the decision and wait another year. Joe had been on the Florence City force for ten years, and if you took seniority into account, why not let him have it? I could afford to wait another year. But what happened was incredible. The chief, a sharp cracker from Bainbridge, Georgia, called me in and told me that I would be assigned to Sergeant Persons fulltime to do his paperwork for him. I got hot about it, and quit then and there, without taking the time In think the matter out. What the chief was doing, in a tacit way, was making it up to me. In other words, the chief hadn't liked the Board's decision to make Joe Persons a sergeant instead of me any more than I had. By giving me the opportunity to do the sergeant's actual work, which Persons was incapable of handling, he was telling me that the next vacancy was as good as mine, and laying the groundwork to get rid of Sergeant Persons for inefficiency at the same time.

I figured all this out later, but by that time it was too late. I had resigned, and I was too proud to go back and apologize to the chief after some of the angry things I had said to him.

To shorten the story, although it still makes me sore to think about the raw deal I was handed in Florence City, I came down to Miami and landed a job with National Security as a senior security officer. In fact, they could hardly hire me quickly enough. National has offices in every major city in the United States, and some day—in a much shorter period than it would have taken me to become the chief of police in Florence City—I'll be the director of one of these offices. Most of the security officers that National employs are ex-cops, retired detectives usually, but none of them can write very well. They have to dictate their reports, which are typed later by the girls in the pool. If any of these reports ever got out cold, without being edited and rewritten, we would lose the business of the department store industry receiving that report in five minutes flat. That is what I do: I put these field reports into some semblance of readability. My boss, The Colonel, likes the way I write, and often picks up phrases from my reports. Once, when I wrote to an operator in Jacksonville about a missing housewife, I told him to "exhaust all resources." For about a month after that, The Colonel was ending all of his phone conversations with, "Exhaust all resources, exhaust all resources."

So down at National Security, I am a fair-haired boy. Four years ago I started at $10,000, and now I'm making $15,000. I can also tell, now, from the meetings that they have been asking me to sit in on lately, "just to listen," The Colonel said, that they are grooming me for a much better job than I have already.

If this were a report for National Security I would consider this background information as much too sketchy, and I would bounce it back to the operator. But this isn't a report, it's a record, and a record is handy to keep in my lock-box at the bank.

Who knows? I might need it some day. In Florida, the guilty party who spills everything to the State's Attorney *first* gets immunity. . .

† † †

We were on the second round of martinis when we started to talk about picking up women. Hank, being the acknowledged authority on this subject, threw out a good question. "Where, in Miami," Hank said, "is the easiest place to pick up some strange? I'm not saying the best, I'm talking about the easiest place."

"Big Daddy's," Eddie said.

I didn't say so, but I agreed with Eddie in my mind. There are Big Daddy's lounges all over Miami. Billboards all around Dade County show a picture of a guy and a girl sitting close together at a bar, right next to the bearded photo of Big Daddy himself, with a caption beneath the picture in lower case Art type: *"Big Daddy's—where you're never alone. . ."* The message is clear enough. Any man who can't score in a Big Daddy's lounge has got a major hang-up of some kind.

"No," Hank said, pursing his lips. "I admit you can pick up a woman in Big Daddy's, but you don't always score. Right? In fact, you might pick up a loser, lay out five bucks or so in drinks, and then find her missing when you come back from taking a piss."

This was true enough; it had happened to me once, although I had never mentioned it to anyone.

"Think, now," Hank said. "Give me one surefire place to pick up a woman, where you'll score, I'll say, at least nine times out often."

"Bullshit," Don said. "Nobody scores nine times out of ten, including you, Hank."

"I never said I did," Hank said. "But I know of one place where you *can* score nine times out often. Any one of us at this table."

"Let's go," I said, leaping to my feet.

They all laughed.

"Sit down, Fuzz," Hank said. "Just because there is such a place, it doesn't mean you'll want to go. Come on, you guys—think."

"Is this a trick question?" Eddie said.

"No," Hank said, without smiling, "it's legitimate. And I'm not talking about call girls either, that is, if there're any left in Miami."

"Coconut Grove is pretty good," Eddie said.

"The Grove's always good," Hank agreed, "but it's not a single place, it's a group of different places. Well, I'm going to tell you anyway, so I'll spare you the suspense. The easiest place to pick up a fast lay in Miami is at the V.D. clinic."

We all laughed.

"You're full of it, Hank," Don said. "A girl who's just picked up the clap is going to be turned off men and sex for a long time."

"That's what I would have thought," Hank said. "But apparently it doesn't work that way. It was in the *Herald* the other day. The health official at the clinic was bitching about it. I don't remember his name, but I cut out the piece and I've got it up in my apartment. He said that most of the girls at the clinic are from sixteen to twenty-two, and the guys and girls get together in the waiting room to exchange addresses and phone numbers because they know they're safe. They've all been treated recently, so they know there's no danger of catching anything. Anyway, according to the *Herald,* they've brought in a psychologist to study the problem. The health official wants to put in separate waiting rooms to keep the men and women apart."

"Would you pick up a girl in a V.D. clinic?" Don asked Hank.

Hank laughed. "Not unless I was pretty damned hard up, I wouldn't. Okay. I'll show you guys the clipping later. Here's a tougher question. Where's the *hardest* place in Miami to pick up a woman?"

"The University of Miami Student Union," Eddie said solemnly.

We all laughed.

"Come on, Eddie," Hank said. "Play the game. This *is* a serious question."

"When a man really needs a piece of ass," I said, "any place he tries is hard."

"That's right," Eddie said. "When you've got a woman waiting for you in the sack, and you stop off for a beer, there'll be five or six broads all over you. But when you're really out there digging, desperate, there's nothing out there, man. Nothing."

"That's why I keep my small black book," Hank said.

"We aren't talking about friends, Hank," I said. "We're supposed to be talking about strange pussy."

"That's right. So where's the hardest place to pick up strange?"

"At church—on a Sunday," Eddie said.

"How long's it been since you've been to church?" Hank asked. "Hell, at church, the minister'll even introduce you to a nice girl if you point one out to him."

"But who wants a nice girl?" Eddie said.

"I do," Hank said. "In my book, a nice girl is one who guides it in."

"If that's true," I said, "every girl I've ever slept with has been a nice girl. Thanks, Hank, for making my day. Why don't we give up this stupid game, get something to eat, and go down to the White Shark and play some pool?"

"Wait a minute," Eddie said, "I'm still interested in the question. I want to know the answer so I can avoid going there and wasting my time."

"A determined man," Don said, "can pick up a woman anywhere, even at the International Airport. And you can rent rooms by the hour at the Airport Hotel."

"It isn't the airport," Hank said. "As you say, Don, the airport's not a bad place for pick-ups. A lot of women, usually in pairs, hang around the Roof Lounge watching the planes take off."

"We give up, Hank," I said. "I've had my two martinis, and if I don't eat something pretty soon, I'm liable to drink another. And on my third martini I've been known to hit my best friend—just to see him fall."

"Eighty-six the Fuzz," Eddie said. "Tell us, Hank." Eddie poured the last drink into his Dixie cup.

"Drive-in movies," Hank said.

"I don't get it," Don said. "What's so hard about picking up a woman at a drive-in, for Christ's sake? Guys take women to drive-ins all the time—"

"That's right," Hank said. "They *take* them there, and they pay their way in. So what're you going to do? Start talking to some woman while she's in her boy friend's car, while he's got one arm around her neck and his left hand on her snatch?"

Eddie laughed. "Yeah! Don't do it, Don. The guy might have a gun in his glove compartment."

"I guess I wasn't thinking," Don said.

I thought about the idea for a moment. "I've only been to a drive-in by myself two or three times in my whole life," I said. "It's a place you don't go alone, usually, unless you want to catch a flick you've missed. The last time I went alone was to see *Two-Lane Blacktop*. I read the script when it came out in

*Esquire,* and I really wanted to see the movie."

"I saw that," Eddie said. "Except for Warren Oates in the GTO, none of the other people in the movie could act."

"That isn't the point, Eddie," I said. "I didn't think the movie was so hot either, although the script was good. The point I'm trying to make is that the only reason I went to the drive-in alone was to see *Two-Lane Blacktop,* and it didn't come on until 1:05 A.M. Where're you going to find anyone to go to the drive-in with you at one in the morning? And when I didn't like the movie either, I wanted to kick myself in the ass."

"I don't think I've ever been to a drive-in alone," Don said. "Not that I remember, anyway."

"Well, I have," Hank said, "just like Larry. Some movies only play drive-ins, and if you don't catch them there you'll miss them altogether."

"I've been a few times, I guess," Eddie said, "and you'll always see a few guys sitting alone in their cars. But I've never seen a woman alone in a car at a drive-in, unless her boyfriend was getting something at the snack bar."

"Let me tick it off," Hank said. "First, if a woman's there, she's either with her parents, her husband, or her boy friend. Second, no woman ever goes to a drive-in alone. They're afraid to, for some reason, even though a drive-in movie's safer than any place I know for a woman alone. Because, third, a man would be stupid to look for a broad at a drive-in when there're a thousand better places to pick one up."

"That's the toughest place, all right," I said. "It's impossible to pick up a woman at a drive-in."

Hank laughed. "No, it isn't impossible, Larry. It's hard, but it's not impossible."

"I say it's impossible," I repeated.

"Better than that," Eddie said, "I'm willing to bet ten bucks it's impossible."

Hank, shaking his head, laughed. "Ten isn't enough."

"Add another ten from me," I said.

"I'll make it thirty," Don said.

"You guys aren't serious," Hank said.

"If you don't think thirty bucks is serious enough," Eddie said, "I'll raise my ten to twenty."

"Add another ten," I said.

"And mine," Don said.

"Sixty dollars is fairly serious money," Hank said. "That's twice as much dough as I'd win from you guys shooting pool at the White Shark."

"Bullshit," Eddie said. "We've offered to bet you sixty hard ones that you can't pick up a broad at the drive-in. And we pick the drive-in."

"You guys really love me, don't you?" Hank said, getting to his feet and rotating his meaty shoulders.

"Sure we love you, Hank," I said. "We're trying to add to your income. But you don't have to take the bet. All you have to do is agree with us that it's impossible, that's all."

"What's my time limit, Eddie?" Hank said.

"An hour, let's say," Eddie said.

"An hour? Movies last at least an hour-and-a-half," Hank said. "And I'll need some intermission time as well to talk to women at the snack bar. How about making it three hours?"

"How about two?" I said.

"Two hours is plenty," Don said. "You wouldn't hang around any other place in Miami for more'n two hours if you couldn't pick up a broad."

"Let's compromise," Hank said. "An hour-and-a-half, so long as I get at least ten minutes intermission time. If the movie happens to run long, then I get more time to take advantage of the intermission, but two hours'll be the outside limit. Okay?"

"It's okay with me," I said.

"Then let's make the bet a little more interesting," Hank said. "For every five minutes under an hour, you add five bucks to the bet, and I'll match it."

Hank's self-confidence was irritating, but I considered it as unwarranted overconfidence. We took him up on his addition to the bet, and we agreed to meet in Hank's apartment in a half-hour.

We all had identical one-bedroom apartments, but we furnished them so differently none of them looked the same. I don't have much furniture, but the stuff I've got is unique. On Saturday nights I often get the early Sunday edition of the *Miami Herald* and look for furniture bargains in the Personals. That's how I got my harpsichord. It was worth at least $850, but I paid only $150 for it. I can pluck out "Birmingham Jail," but I plan to take lessons if a harpsichord teacher ever moves to Miami. I'm not in any hurry to complete the furnishings; I'm willing to wait until I get the things I want to keep.

Eddie has a crummy place, a real mess, but his mother drives down from Ft. Lauderdale every month to spend a couple of days with him, and that's the only time it's clean.

When Don left his wife, he took all of his den furniture, and his living room is furnished as a den. He's got two large comfortable leather chairs, tall, old-fashioned, glass-door bookcases, and a half-dozen framed prints of "The Rake's Progress" on the walls. When we're watching football and drinking beer in Don's place, it's like being in some exclusive men's club.

Hank, because he doesn't have an office, has almost a third of his living room taken up with cardboard boxes full of drugs and samples of the other medical products his company manufactures. Hank serves as our "doctor." We get our pain killers, cold remedies, medicated soap, and even free toothbrushes from Hank. Before the strict accountability on drugs started, he could sometimes spare sleeping pills and a few uppers. But not any longer. His company counts them out to him now, in small quantities, and he has to account for the amphetamines he passes out free to the doctors he calls on.

Hank's apartment is overcrowded with possessions, too, in addition to the medical supplies. Once he has something, he can't bear to part with it, so his apartment is cluttered. On top of everything else, Hank has a mounted eight-foot sailfish over the couch. He caught it in Acapulco last year, had it mounted for $450 and shipped to Miami. Across the belly, in yellow chalk, he's written, "Hank's Folly." He still can't understand how the boat captain talked him into having the sailfish mounted, except that he was so excited, at the time, about catching it. He's so genuinely unhappy now, about his stupidity in mounting a sailfish, we no longer kid him about it.

When I got to my apartment, I was feeling the effects of the two martinis, so before I took my shower, I put on some coffee to perk. After I showered, I put on a T-shirt, khaki shorts, and a pair of tennis shoes. I fixed a very weak Scotch and water in a plastic glass, and carried it with me down to Hank's apartment.

The other guys were already there. Don, wearing yellow linen slacks and a green knit shirt, was checking the movie pages in the *Herald*. Eddie wore his denim jacket and jeans with his black flight boots, and winked at me when I came in. He jerked his head toward the short hallway to the bedroom. Hank, of course, was still dressing, and a nose-tingling mixture of talcum powder, Right Guard, and Brut drifted in from the bedroom.

Eddie grinned, and jerked his head toward the bedroom. "An actor prepares," he said. "Stanislavski."

"Jesus," Don said, rattling the paper. "At the Tropical Drive-in they're showing *five* John Wayne movies! Who in hell could sit through five John Wayne's for Christ sake?"

"I could," I said.

"Me, too," Eddie said, "but only one at a time."

"If you go to the first one at seven-thirty," Don said, "you don't get out 'til three A.M.!"

"I wouldn't mind," Eddie said, "if we all went and took along a couple of cases of beer. It's better than watching TV from seven-thirty 'til three, and I've done that often enough."

"Yeah," I said, "but you can watch TV in air-conditioned comfort. You aren't fighting mosquitoes all night."

"They fog those places for mosquitoes," Eddie said.

"Sure they do," Don said, "and it makes them so mad they bite the shit out of you. Here's one. Listen to this. At the Southside Dixie. *Bucket of Blood, The Blood-Letters, The Bloody Vampires,* and *Barracuda!* There's a theater manager with a sense of humor. He put the barracuda last so they could get all that blood!"

We laughed.

Eddie got up and crossed to the kitchenette table, where

Hank kept his liquor and a bucketful of ice. "What're you drinking, Fuzz-O?"

"I'm nursing this one," I said.

"Pour me a glass of wine, Eddie," Don said.

"Blood-red, or urine-yellow?"

"I don't care," Don said, "just so you put a couple of ice cubes in it."

Eddie fixed a Scotch over ice for himself, and brought Don a glass of Chianti, with ice cubes.

"The Southside's probably our best bet," I said. "There'll be fewer women at the horror program than at the John Wayne festival. And besides, there's a Burger Queen across the highway there on Dixie. We can eat something and watch for Hank when he comes out of the theater."

"Shouldn't one of us go with him?" Eddie said.

"It wouldn't be fair," Don said. "I don't think he'll be able to pick up any women there anyway, but it would be twice as hard to talk some woman into getting into a car with two guys. So we let him go in alone. As Larry says, we can watch the exit from across the Dixie Highway."

Hank came into the living room, looking and smelling like a jai-alai player on his night off. He wore white shoes with leather tassels, and a magenta slack suit with a silk blue-and-red paisley scarf tucked in around the collar. Hank had three other tailored suits like the magenta—wheat, blue and chocolate—but I hadn't seen the magenta before. The high-waisted pants, with an uncuffed flare, were double-knits, and so tight in front his equipment looked like a money bag. The short-sleeved jacket was a beltless, modified version of a bush jacket, with huge bellows side pockets.

Don was the only one of us with long hair, that is, long *enough*, the way we all wanted to wear it. Because of our jobs, we couldn't get away with hair as long as Don's. Hank had fluffed his hair with an air-comb, and it looked much fuller than it did when he slicked it down with spray to call on doctors.

"Isn't that a new outfit?" Eddie said.

"I've had it awhile," Hank said, going to the table to build a drink. "It's the first time I've worn it, is all. I ordered the suit from a small swatch of material. Then when it was made into a suit, I saw that it was a little too much." He shrugged. "But it'll do for a drive-in, I think."

"There's nothing wrong with that color, Hank," Don said. "I like it."

Hank added two more ice cubes to his Scotch and soda. "It makes my face look red, is all."

"Your face is red," I said.

"But not as red as this magenta makes it look."

"When you pay us off tonight," Eddie said, "it'll match perfectly."

Hank looked at his wristwatch. "Suppose we synchronize our watches. It is now, precisely . . . seven-twenty-one. We'll see who ends up with the reddest faces."

We checked our watches. For the first time, I wondered if I had made a bad bet. If Hank lost, I consoled myself, at least his over-confidence would preclude my giving him any sympathy.

We decided then to meet Hank at the Burger Queen across from the Southside Drive-in. He would take his Galaxie, and the rest of us would ride down in Don's Mark IV.

Because we stopped at the 7/Eleven to buy two six packs of beer, Hank beat us to the Burger Queen by about five minutes. Don gave Hank a can of beer, which he hid under the front seat, and then Hank drove across the highway. It was exactly seven-forty-one.

† † †

We ordered Double Queens apiece, with fries, and then grabbed a tile table on the side patio to the left of the building. The Burger Queen didn't serve beer, and the manager couldn't see us fish our beers out of the paper sack around to the side. We could look directly across the highway and see the drive-in exit.

Unless you're going out to dinner somewhere, eating at eight P.M. in Miami is on the late side. We were all used to eating around six, and so we were ravenous as we wolfed down the double burgers. We didn't talk until we finished, and then I gathered up the trash and dumped it into the nearest garbage can. Don ripped the tops off three more beers.

Below Kendall, at this point on the Dixie Highway, there were six lanes, and the traffic was swift and noisy both ways. Eddie began to laugh and shake his head.

"What's so funny?" I said.

"The whole thing—what else? I know there isn't a hellova lot to do on a Thursday night, but if I ever told anyone I sat around at the Burger Queen for two hours waiting for my buddy to pick up a woman at a drive-in movie—"

"You'd better hope it's at least an hour-and-a-half," Don said.

"I know, I know," Eddie said, "but you've got to admit the whole business is pretty stupid."

"Yes, and no, Eddie," I said. "It isn't really money, either. You and Don both know that we'd all like to take Hank down a notch."

Don smiled. "I think you may be right, Larry."

"I'm not jealous of Hank," Eddie said.

"Neither am I," I said. "All I'm saying is that for once I'd like to see old Hank lose one. I like Hank, for Christ's sake, but I hate to see any man so damned over-confident all the time, that's all."

"Yeah," Eddie said. "I know what you mean."

Don snorted, and looked at his watch. "You'll have to wait until another time, I think. It's now eight-twelve, and here comes our wandering over-confident boy."

Don had spotted Hank's Galaxie as it cleared the drive-in exit, and Hank, waiting to make a left turn, was hovering at the edge of the highway when I turned to look. He had to wait for some time, and we couldn't see whether there was a woman in the car with him or not. He finally made it across and parked in the Burger Queen lot. We met him about half-way as he came toward us—by himself.

"How about a beer?" Hank said.

"We drank it," Eddie said.

"Thanks for saving me one. Come on. I'll introduce you to

Hildy."

We followed Hank to the Galaxie. When he opened the passenger door and the overhead light went on, we saw the girl clearly. She was about thirteen or fourteen, barefooted, wearing a tie-dyed T-shirt, and tight raggedy-cuffed blue jeans with a dozen or more different patches sewn onto them. On her crotch, right over the pudenda, there was a patch with a comic rooster flexing muscled wings. The embroidered letters, in white, below the chicken read: *I'M A MEAN FIGHTING COCK*. Her brownish hair fell down her back, well past her shoulders, straight but slightly tangled, and her pale face was smudged with dirt. She gave us a tentative smile, and tried to take us all in at once, but she had trouble focusing her eyes. She closed her eyes, and her head hobbled on her skinny neck.

"She's only a kid," Eddie said, glaring at Hank.

Hank shrugged. "I know. She looked older over in the drive-in, without any lights, but you guys didn't set any age limit. A girl's a girl, and I had enough trouble snagging this one."

"It's a cop-out, Hank," I said, "and you know it."

"Suit yourself, Fuzz-O," Hank said. "If you guys don't want to pay off, I'll cancel the debt."

"Nobody said he wouldn't pay," Don said. "But the idea was to pick up somebody old enough to screw. You wouldn't fuck a fourteen-year-old girl—"

"That wasn't one of the conditions," Hank said, "but if that's what you guys want, I'll take Hildy home, give her a shower, and slip it to her. I sure as hell wouldn't be getting any cherry—"

The girl—Hildy—whimpered like a puppy, coughed, choked slightly, and fell over sideways in the seat.

"Nobody's going to hurt you, kid," Don said.

"She's stoned on something, Hank," I said. "You'd better get her out of there before she heaves all over the upholstery."

Hank bent down, leaned inside the car, and pushed up the girl's eyelids. He put a forefinger into her throat and then grabbed her thin right wrist to check her pulse. He slammed the passenger door, and leaned against it. His red, sunburned face was watermelon pink—about as pale as Hank was capable of getting.

"She's dead," Hank said. He took out his cigarettes, put one in his mouth, but couldn't get his lighter to work. I lighted a cigarette myself, and then held the match for Hank. His fingers trembled.

"Don't play around, Hank," Don said. "Shit like that isn't funny."

"She's dead, Don," Hank said.

"Are you sure?" Eddie said.

"Look, man—" Hank ran his fingers through his fluffy hair, and then took a long drag on his cigarette. "Dead is *dead,* man! I've seen too many . . . too fucking many—"

"Take it easy, Hank," I said.

"What do we do now, Larry?" Don said. Hank and Eddie looked at me, too, waiting. At 28, I was the youngest of the four. Hank was 31, and Don and Eddie were both 30, but because of my police background they were dumping the problem in my lap.

"We'll take her to Hank's apartment," I said. "I'll drive Hank's car, and Hank'll go with me. You guys go on ahead in the Continental and unlock the fire door to the northwest stairway. Meet us at the door, because it's closest to Hank's apartment. Then, while you three take her upstairs to the apartment, I'll park Hank's car."

"Okay," Don said. "Let's go, Eddie."

"Don't run, for Christ's sake," I said.

They slowed to a walk. Hank gave me his car keys, and I circled the car and got in behind the wheel.

On the way back to Dade Towers I drove cautiously. Hank sat in the passenger bucket seat beside me, and held the girl's shoulders. He had folded her legs, and she was in a kneeling position on the floor with her face level with the dash glove compartment. He held her steady, with both hands gripping her shoulders.

"How'd you happen to pick her up, Hank?" I said.

"Thursday's a slow night, apparently," Hank said. "There're

only about twenty-five cars in there. No one, hardly, was at the snack bar. I got a paper cup from the counter, and went outside to pour my beer into it. Sometimes, you know, there's a cop around, and you're not supposed to drink beer at the drive-in, you know."

"I know."

The girl had voided, and the smell of ammonia and feces was strong. Moving her about hadn't helped any either. I pushed the button to lower the windows, and turned off the air conditioning.

"That was a good idea," Hank said. "Anyway, I got rid of the beer can in a trash basket, and circled around the Knack bar to the women's can. I thought some women might come out, and I could start talking to one, but none did. Then I walked on around the back of the building to I he other side. Hildy, here, was standing out in the open, not too far from the men's room. She was just standing there, that's all, looking at the screen. The nearest car was about fifty feet away—I told you there were only about twenty-five cars, didn't I?"

"Yeah. A lot of people don't come until the second feature, which is usually the best flick."

"Maybe so. The point is, nobody was around us. 'Hi,' I said, 'are you waiting for me?' She just giggled and then she mumbled something.

" 'Who?' I said, and then she said, 'The man in the yellow jump suit.'

" 'Oh, sure,' I said, 'he sent me to get you. My name's Hank—what's yours?'

" 'Hildy,' she said.

" 'Right,' I said. "You're the one, all right. I hope you don't mind magenta instead of yellow.'

"Then she asked me for some of my Coke. She thought I had a Coke because of the red paper cup, you see. So I gave her a drink from the cup and she made a face. Then she took my hand, just like I was her father or something, and I led her over to my car. It was dark as hell in there, Larry, and I swear she looked older—around seventeen, anyway."

"That doesn't make any difference now," I said.

"I guess not. I wish to hell I had a drink."

"We can get one in your apartment."

The operation at Dade Towers worked as smoothly as if we had rehearsed it. I parked at the corner, ten feet from the door. Hank wrapped a beach towel around Hildy, an old towel he kept in the back seat, and Eddie opened the car door. The fire door to the stairway, which was rarely used, only opened from the inside. Don held the door partly open for Hank and Eddie, and they had carried her inside and up the stairs before I drove across the street and into the parking lot. After parking in Hank's slot and locking the car, I shoved Hildy's handbag under my T-shirt.

I knocked softly at Hank's door when I got upstairs. Don opened it a crack to check me out before he let me in. Hildy was on her back on the couch, with the beach towel beneath her. She was only about four-eight, and the mounted sailfish on the wall above her looked almost twice as long as she did. The sail's name in yellow chalk, "Hank's Folly," somehow seemed appropriate. When I joined the group, Hank handed me a straight Scotch over ice cubes.

The four of us, in a semi-circle, stared down at the girl for a few moments. Her brown eyes were opened partially, and there were yellow "sleepies" in the corners. There was a scattering of pimples on her forehead, and a few freckles on her nose and cheeks. There was a yellow hickey on the left corner of her mouth, and she didn't have any lipstick on her pale lips. Her skin, beneath the smudges of dirt, was so white it was almost transparent, and a dark blue vein beneath her right temple was clearly visible. She wasn't wearing a bra beneath her T-shirt; with her adolescent chest bumps, she didn't need one.

"She looks," Eddie said, "like a first-year Brownie."

Don began to cry.

"For God's sake, Don—" Hank said.

"Leave him alone, Hank," I said. "I feel like crying myself."

Don sat in the Danish chair across from the TV, took out his handkerchief, wiped his eyes, and then blew his nose.

I emptied the purse—a blue-and-red patchwork leather bag, with a long braided leather shoulder strap—onto the coffee table. There were two plastic vials containing pills. One of them was filled with the orange heart-shaped pills I recognized as Dexies. The other pills were round and white, but larger than aspirins, and stamped "M-T." There was a Mary Jane, a penny piece of candy wrapped in yellow paper, the kind kids buy at the 7/Eleven; a roll of bills held together by a rubber band; a used and wadded Kleenex; and a blunt, slightly bent aluminum comb.

As I started to count the money, I said to Eddie, "Search her body, Ed."

"No," he said, shaking his head.

"Let me fix you another drink, Ed." Hank took Eddie's glass, and they moved to the kitchenette table. Don, immobilized in the Danish chair, stared at the floor without blinking.

There were thirty-eight dollars in the roll; one was a five, the rest were ones. I emptied the girl's front pockets. This was hard to do because her jeans were so tight. There were two quarters and three pennies in the right pocket, and a slip of folded notebook paper in the left. It was a list of some kind, written with a blue felt pen. *"30 ludes, 50 Bs, no gold."* There was only one hip pocket, and it was a patch that had been sewn on in an amateurish manner. The patch, in red denim, with white letters, read, *KISS MY PATCH.* The pocket was empty.

"There's no I.D., Hank," I said.

"So what do we do now," Eddie said, "call the cops?"

"What's your flying schedule?" I said.

"I go to New York Saturday. Why?"

"How'd you like to be grounded, on suspension without pay for about three months? Pending an investigation into the dope fiend death of a teenaged girl?"

"We didn't do anything," Eddie said.

"That's right," I said. "But that wouldn't keep your name out of the papers, or some pretty nasty interrogations at the station. And Hank's in a more sensitive position than you are with the airline, what with his access to drug samples and all.

If—or when—he's investigated, and his company's name gets into the papers, as soon as he's cleared, the best he can hope for is a transfer to Yuma, Arizona."

Hank shuddered, and sat down at the coffee table beside me in a straight-backed cane chair. He opened the vial holding the pills that were stamped "M-T."

"Methaqualone," Hank said. "But they're not from my company. We make them all right, but our brand's called 'Meltin.' There're twenty M-T's left in the vial, so she could've taken anywhere from one to a dozen—or more maybe. Four or five could suffocate and kill her." Hank shrugged, and looked at the girl's body on the couch. "The trouble is, these heads take mixtures sometimes of any and everything. She's about seventy-five pounds, I'd say, and if she was taking a combination of Dexies and M.T.'s, it's a miracle she was still on her feet when I picked her up." He tugged on his lower lip. "If any one of us guys took even three 'ludes, we'd sleep for at least ten hours straight. But if Hildy, here, was on the stuff for some time, she could've built up a tolerance, and—"

"Save it, Hank," I said. "The girl's dead, and we don't know who she is—that's what we need to know. The best thing for us to do, I think, is find the guy in the yellow jump suit and turn her over to him."

"What guy in what yellow jump suit?" Eddie said. Hank told them what the girl had said, that she was waiting for a man in a yellow jump suit.

"Do you think it was her father, maybe?" Don said. "Hell, no," I said, "whoever he is, she's his baby, not ours."

"How're we going to find him?" Eddie said.

"Back at the drive-in," I said. "I'm going to get my pistol from my apartment, and then we'll go back and look for him."

"D'you want me to take my pistol too, Larry?" Eddie asked.

"You'd better not," I said, "I've got a license, and you haven't. You and I and Hank'll go back. You'd better stay here with the girl, Don."

"I'd just as soon go along," Don said.

"No," I said. "Somebody'd better stay here with the girl. We'll go in your car, Hank." I handed him his keys. "I'll meet you guys down in the lot."

I went to my apartment, and changed into slacks. I put my pistol, a Colt Cobra .38, with a two-inch barrel, into its clip holster, and shoved the holstered gun inside the waistband of my trousers. To conceal the handle of the weapon, I put on a sand-colored lightweight golf jacket, and zipped up the front. Hank and Eddie were both in the Galaxie, Eddie in the back seat, and Hank in the driver's, when I got to the parking lot. I slid in beside Hank.

On our way to the drive-in I told them how we would work the search party. Hank could start with the first row of cars, going from one to the next, and Eddie could start from the back row. I'd start at the snack bar, checking the men's room first, and then look into any of the cars that were parked close to the snack bar. I would also be on the lookout for any new cars coming in, and I would mark the position of new arrivals, if any, so we could check them out when we finished with those already there.

"One other thing," I said. "If you spot the guy, don't do anything. We'll all meet in the men's room, and then we'll take him together. There aren't that many cars, and we should finish the search in about five minutes."

"What if he isn't there?" Eddie said.

"Then we wait. I think he'll show up, all right. My worry is, he might not be alone, which'll make it harder to pick him up. But there aren't that many guys wearing jump suits, especially yellow ones, so we should be able to spot him easily enough."

"Not necessarily," Hank said. "He might be a hallucination, a part of the girl's trip. Hell, she came with me without any persuasion to speak of, and she would've gone with anybody. She was really out of it, Larry."

"We don't have to look for the guy, Hank," I said. "If you think it's a waste of time, let's go back and get the girl and dump her body in a canal some place."

"Jesus, Larry," Eddie said, "could you do that?"

"What else do you suggest?"

"Nothing," Eddie said. "But before we do anything drastic, I think we'd better look for her boyfriend in the jump suit."

"That's why we're going to the drive-in," Hank said.

I took a five and a one out of my wallet, and had the money ready to pass across Hank to the girl in the box-office the moment Hank stopped the car. Hank had cut his lights, but I regretted, for a moment, not taking my Vega instead of returning in his Galaxie. The Galaxie, because it was leased by Hank's company, had an "E" prefix on the license plate. But because there were three of us in the car instead of only one, it was still unlikely that the girl would make an earlier connection with Hank.

We parked in the last row. The nearest car was three rows ahead of us. As we got out of the car, Eddie laughed abruptly. "What do we say," he said, "if someone asks what we're looking in their car for? Not everybody comes to this fingerbowl to watch the movie, you know."

"Don't make a production out of it," I said. "Just glance in and move on. If somebody does say something, ask for an extra book of matches. That's as good an excuse as any. But look into each car from the side or back, and you won't get into any hassles. Remember, though, if you do spot the guy, keep on going down the line of cars as before. Don't quit right then and head for the men's room. He might suspect something."

A few minutes later we met in the men's room. I lit a cigarette, and Eddie and Hank both shook their heads. I wasn't surprised. I hadn't expected to find any man in a yellow jump suit. In fact, I suspected that Hank had made up the story. And yet, it was wise to get all three of them involved. I had realized, from the beginning, that I would have to be the one who would have to get rid of the girl's body, but it would be better, later on, for these guys to think that they had done everything possible before the inevitable dumping of the kid in a canal.

"Okay," I said. "To make sure, let's start over. Only this time, you start with the first row, Eddie, and you, Hank, start with the back. It won't hurt anything to double-check."

"If you really think it's necessary," Hank said.

"We've got to wait around anyway," I said.

They took off again. It wasn't necessary, but I wanted to keep them busy. They didn't have my patience. These guys had never sat up all night for three nights in a row at a stake-out in a liquor store. But I had. I went around to the back of the snack bar, where it was darkest, and kept my eye on the box-office entrance, some hundred yards away. Two more cars, both with their parking lights on, came in. The first car turned at the second row and squeezed into an empty slot. The second car, a convertible, drove all the way to the back, and parked about three spaces to the right of Hank's car. If you came to see the movie, it was a poor location, so far from the screen, and angled away from it. A man got out of the car, and started toward the snack bar.

I caught up with Hank, and pointed the man out as he came slowly in our direction, picking his way because his eyes weren't used to the darkness. "I think we've got him, Hank," I said. "Go straight up to him and ask for a match, and I'll circle around in back of him."

"What if he's got a gun?" Hank said.

"I've got a gun, too. Hurry up."

When Hank stopped the man, I was behind him about ten yards or so. He gave Hank a light from his cigarette lighter; then he heard me and turned around. I clicked the hammer back on my .38 as he turned.

"Let's go back to your car, friend," I said.

"A stick-up in the drive-in? You guys must be out of your fuckin' minds," he said.

"Stand away from him, Hank," I said. "If he doesn't move in about one second, I'll shoot his balls off."

"I'm moving, I'm moving," the man said. He put his arms above his head and waggled his fingers.

"Put your arms down, you bastard," I said. "Cross your arms across your chest."

When we reached his car, a dark blue Starfire, with the top down, I told him to get into the passenger side of the front seat. Eddie, breathing audibly through his mouth, joined us a moment later.

"Okay, Hank," I said, "the same as with the girl. You drive on ahead, get Don, and have the fire door open for us. Eddie'll drive this car, and I'll watch the sonofabitch from the back seat. Okay, friend, put one hand on top of the dash, and pass over your car keys with the other."

"No dice," he said. "If you guys want my dough, go ahead and take it, but I ain't leavin' the drive-in—"

He sat erect in the seat with his arms crossed, looking straight ahead. He was wearing a yellow jump suit, and from the cool way he was taking things I knew that he was the right man. I slapped the barrel of the pistol across his nose. His nose broke, and blood spurted. He squealed, and grabbed for his nose with his right hand.

"Cross your arms," I said.

He quickly recrossed his arms, but he turned his head and eyes to glare at me. "Now," I said, "slowly—with one hand, pass over your car keys to the driver." He kept his right fore-arm across his chest, and dug the keys out of his left front pocket. Eddie slid into the driver's seat, shut the door, and took the keys.

"Get going," I said to Hank, who was still standing there. "We'll be right behind you."

Hank walked over to his car. I climbed over the side of the Starfire, into the back seat, and Eddie started the engine.

"Wait till Hank clears the exit before you pull out," I said to Eddie.

"Where're you guys takin' me, anyway?" the man said. "I got friends, you know. You're gonna be sorry you broke my fuckin' nose, too. It hurts like a bastard." He touched his swollen nose with his right hand.

"Shut up," I said, "and keep your arms crossed. If you move either one of your arms again, I'm going to put a round through your shoulder."

Eddie moved out, handling the car skillfully. He drove to the extreme right of the row before turning onto the exit road, and without lights. There was a quarter-moon, the sky was cloudless, and we'd been in the drive-in so long by now that we could see easily.

When we reached the fire door at Dade Towers, Don and Hank were waiting for us. I ordered the man in the yellow jump suit to follow Don, and Hank followed me as we went up the stairs. Eddie parked the convertible in a visitor's slot across the street, and came up to Hank's apartment in the elevator.

While we were gone, Don had turned on the television, but not the sound. On the screen, Doris Day and Rock Hudson were standing beside a station wagon in a suburban neighborhood. She was waving her arms around.

The man in the yellow jump suit didn't react at all when he saw the dead girl. Instead of looking at her, he looked at the silent television screen. He was afraid, of course, and trembling visibly, but he wasn't terrified. He stood between the couch and the kitchen, with his back to the girl, and stared boldly at each of us, in turn, as though trying to memorize our faces.

He was about twenty-five or -six, with a glossy Prince Valiant helmet of dark auburn hair. His hair was lighter on top, because of the sun, probably, but it had been expensively styled. His thick auburn eyebrows met in the middle, above his swollen nose, as he scowled. His long sideburns came down at a sharp point, narrowing to a quarter-inch width, and they curved across his cheeks to meet his moustache, which had been carved into a narrow, half-inch strip. As a consequence, his moustache, linked in a curve across both cheeks to his sideburns, resembled a fancy, cursive lower case "m." His dark blue eyes watered slightly. There was blood drying on his moustache, on his chin, and there was a thin Jackson Pollock drip down the front of his lemon-yellow poplin jump suit. His nose had stopped bleeding.

Jump suits, as leisure wear, have been around for several years, but it's only been the last couple of years that men have worn them on the street, or away from home or the beach. There's a reason. They are comfortable, and great to lounge around in—until you get a good profile look at yourself in the mirror. If you have any gut at all—even two inches more than you should have—a jump suit, which is basically a pair of fancied up coveralls, makes you look like you've got a pot-gut. I've got a short-sleeved blue terrycloth jump suit I wear around the pool once in a while, but I would never wear it away from the apartment house. When I was on the force and weighed about 175, I could have worn it around town, but since I've been doing desk work at National, I've picked up more than twenty pounds. My waistline has gone from a 32 to a 36, and the jump suit makes me look like I've got a paunch. It's the way they are made.

But this guy in the yellow jump suit was slim, maybe 165, and he was close to six feet in height. The poplin jump suit was skin tight, bespoke, probably, and then cut down even more, and he wore it without the usual matching belt at the waist. It had short sleeves, and his sinewy forearms were hairy. Thick reddish chest hair curled out of the top of the suit where he had pulled the zipper down for about eight inches. He wore zippered cordovan boots, and they were highly polished.

"What's the girl's name?" I said.

"How should I know?" he said. "I never seen her before. What's the matter with her, anyway?"

"There's nothing the matter with her," Don said. "She's dead, now, and you killed her!" Don started for him, but Hank grabbed Don by the arms, at the biceps, and gently pushed him back.

"Take it easy, Don," Hank said. "Let Larry handle it." When Don nodded, Hank released him.

"Step forward a pace," I said, "and put your hands on top of your head." The man shuffled forward, and put his hands on his head. "Here, Don," I said, handing Don the pistol. "Cover me while I search him. If he tries anything, shoot him in the kneecap."

"Sure, Larry," Don said. His hand was steady as he aimed the .38 at the man's kneecap.

"I'll hold the pistol, Don," Hank said, "if you want me to."

Don shook his head, and Eddie grinned and winked at me as I went around behind the man in the jump suit to frisk him.

"Leave him alone, Hank," I said. "Why don't you fix us a drink?"

I tossed the man's ostrich skin wallet, handkerchief, and silver ballpoint pen onto the coffee table from behind. He didn't have any weapons, and he had less than two dollars worth of change in his front pockets. He had a package of Iceberg cigarettes, with three cigarettes missing from the pack, and a gold Dunhill lighter.

At his waist, beneath the jump suit, I felt a leather belt. I came around in front of him, and caught the ring of the zipper. He jerked his hands down and grabbed my wrists. Don moved forward and jammed the muzzle of the gun against the man's left knee. The man quickly let go of my wrists.

"For God's sake, don't shoot!" he said. He put his hands on top of his head again.

"It's all right, Don," I said.

Don moved back. I pulled down the zipper, well below his waist. He wasn't wearing underwear, just the belt. It was a plain brown cowhide suit belt, about an inch-and-a-half in width. I unbuckled it, jerked it loose from his body, and turned it over. It was a zippered money belt, the kind that is advertised in men's magazines every month. If he had been wearing the belt with a pair of trousers, no one would have ever suspected that it was a money belt. I unzipped the compartment. There were eight one-hundred dollar bills and two fifties tightly folded lengthwise inside the narrow space. I unfolded the bills, and counted them onto the coffee table.

"That ain't my money!" the man in the yellow jump suit said.

"That's right," Eddie said, laughing. "Not any more it isn't."

"I'm telling you, right now," the man said, "that dough don't belong to me. You take it, and you're in trouble. Big trouble!"

I sat down at the coffee table, and went through his wallet. Eddie sat beside me in another straight-backed chair. Hank set Scotches over ice in front of us. He held an empty glass up for

Don, and raised his eyebrows. Don shook his head, but didn't take his eyes off the man in the yellow jump suit. Hank, with a fresh drink in his hand, leaned against the kitchenette archway, and stared at the man.

There were three gas credit cards in the billfold: Gulf, Exxon, and Standard Oil. The Gulf card was made out to A.H. Wexley, the Exxon to A. Franciscus, and the Standard card was in the name of L. Cohen. All three cards listed Miami Beach addresses. There was no other identification in the wallet. There was another eighty dollars in bills, plus a newspaper coupon that would entitle the man to a one-dollar discount on a bucket or a barrel of Colonel Sanders' fried chicken. There was a parking stub for the Dupont Plaza Hotel garage, an ivory toothpick in a tiny leather case, and a key to a two-bit locker. Bus station? Airport? Any public place that has rental lockers. And that was all.

"I've never seen a man's wallet this skimpy," I said to Eddie.

"Me either," Eddie said. "I can hardly fold mine, I got so much junk."

"Which one is you?" I said, reading the gas credit cards again. "Cohen, Franciscus, or Wexley?"

"I don't like to use the same gas all the time, man," he said, then he giggled.

I got up and kicked him in the shin with the side of my foot. Because I was wearing tennis shoes, it didn't hurt him half as much as he let on, but because he was surprised, he lost some of his poise.

"Look, you guys," he said, "why don't you just take the money and let me go. I haven't done anything—"

"What's the girl's name?" I said.

"I don't know her name. Honest."

"What's her name? She told us she was waiting for you, so there's no point lying about it."

"Her name's Hildy." He shrugged, yawned, and looked away from me.

"Hildy what?"

"I don't know, man. She worked for me some, but I never

knew her last name."

"Doing what?" I said.

"She sold a little stuff for me now and then—at Bethune."

"Mary Bethune Junior High?"

"Yeah."

"Did you drop her off, earlier tonight, at the drive-in?"

"No. I was supposed to collect some dough from her there, that's all."

"Do you know how old she is?"

"She's in the eighth grade, she said, but I never asked how old she was. That's none of my business."

"So you turned her on to drugs without even caring how old she was?" Hank said. "You're the lowest sonofabitch I've ever met."

"I never turned her on to no drugs, man," the man said. "She was takin' shit long before I met her. What I was doing, I was doing her a favor. She lives with her mother, she said. Her mother works at night, over at the beach, she said. And her father split a couple of years back for Hawaii. So Hildy asked me if she could sell some for me. She was trying to save up enough money to go to her father in Hawaii. That's all. And the other kid, a black kid, who used to sell for me at Bethune, he took off for Jacksonville with fifty bucks he owed me. I needed someone at Bethune, and I told Hildy I'd give her a chance. She needed the bread, she said. She wanted to live with her father in Hawaii. So what I was doing, I was doing her a favor."

He ran down. We all stared at him. Beneath his heavy tan, his face was flushed, and he perspired heavily in the air-conditioned room.

"I ain't no worse'n you guys," the man in the yellow jump suit said. "What the hell, you guys picked her up to screw her, didn't you? Well, didn't you?"

"You mean you were screwing her, too?" Don said.

"No—I never touched her. She might've gone down on me a couple of times, but I never touched her."

"What do you mean, 'might have'?" Don said. "Did she or didn't she?"

"Yeah, I guess she did, a couple of times. But I never made her do it. She wanted to, she said."

Don fired the pistol. It was like a small explosion in the crowded room. Hank, standing in the kitchenette archway, dropped his glass on the floor. It didn't break. Eddie, sitting beside me, sucked in his breath. The man in the yellow jump suit clawed at his chest with both hands. He sank to his knees and his back arched as his head fell back. The back of his head hit the couch and his arms dropped loosely to his sides. He remained in that position, without toppling, his face in the air, looking up at nothing, on his knees, with his back arched and his head and neck supported by the couch. Don made a funny noise in his throat. There was a widening red circle on the man's hairy chest, as blood bubbled from a dark round hole. I stood up, took the pistol away from Don, and returned the gun to my belt holster. The man in the yellow jump suit had voided and the stench filled the room. I crossed to the TV and turned up the volume.

"I didn't—" Don said. "I didn't touch the trigger! It went off by itself!"

"Sit down, Don," Hank said. He crossed to Don, and gently pushed him down into the Danish chair. "We know it was an accident, Don."

"Eddie," I said, "open the windows, and turn the air conditioning to fan."

Eddie nodded, and started toward the bedroom where the thermostat was on the wall. I opened the door to the outside hallway. Keeping my hand on the knob, I looked up and down the corridor. A gunshot sounds exactly like a gunshot and nothing else. But most people don't know that. I was prepared, in case someone stuck his head out, to ask him if he heard a car backfire. The sound from the TV, inside Hank's apartment, was loud enough to hear in the corridor. I waited outside for a moment longer, and when no heads appeared, I ducked back inside and put the night lock on the door.

"Larry," Hank said, "d'you think I should give Don a sedative?"

"Hell, no," I said. "Let him lie down for a while on your

bed, but we don't want him dopey on us, for Christ's sake."

Don was the color of old expensive parchment, as if his olive tan had been diluted with a powerful bleach. His eyes were glazed slightly, and he leaned on Hank heavily as Hank led him into the bedroom.

Eddie grinned, and shook his head. "What a night," he said. "When I opened the damned window behind the couch, I accidentally stepped on the guy's hand. One of his damned fingers broke." Eddie looked away from me; his mouth was twitching at the corners.

"Don't worry about it, Ed," I said. "You and I are going to have to get rid of him, you know—both of them."

"That figures. Any ideas?"

Hank came back from the bedroom. "I'm treating Don for shock," he said. "I've covered him with a blanket, and now I'm going to make him some hot tea."

"Never mind the fucking tea," I said. "I'm not worried about Don. We've got to get these bodies out of here."

"I know that," Hank said. "What do you suggest?"

"We'll put them into the back seat of the convertible, and then I'll drive his car over to the Japanese Garden on the MacArthur Causeway. I'll just park the car in the lot and leave it." I turned to Eddie. "You can follow me in my Vega, and pick me up."

"Okay," Eddie said. I gave Eddie my car keys.

"I'll go with you, if you want," Hank said.

"There's no point, Hank. You can stay here after we load the bodies, and make some fucking tea for Don."

"Wait a minute," Hank said, "you don't have to—"

"I don't have to what?" I said.

"Cut it out, you guys," Eddie said. "Go ahead, Larry. Get the convertible and park it by the fire exit. I'll bring the girl down first, but it'll take all three of us to carry him down."

"All right," I said. "Except for the money, put the girl's bag and his wallet and all their other stuff into a paper Hack." I pointed to the stuff on the coffee table. "And we'll need something to cover him up."

"I've got a G.I. blanket in the closet," Hank said.

Taking the car keys to the convertible from Eddie, I left the apartment.

While Eddie and I wedged the girl between the back and front seats on the floor of the convertible, Hank held the fire door open for us. We covered her with the beach towel, and I tucked the end under her head.

"Shouldn't one of us stay down here with the car?" Eddie asked.

"No," I said. "He's too heavy. It'll take all three of us to bring him down. It won't take us long. We'll just take a chance, that's all."

On the way back to Hank's apartment, we ran into Marge Brewer in the corridor. She was in her nurse's uniform, and had just come off duty at Jackson Memorial. She was coming toward us from the elevator.

"I'm beat," she said, looking at Hank. "A twelve-hour split shift. I'm going to whomp up a big batch of martinis. D'you all want to come down in ten minutes? I'll share."

"Give us a rain check, Marge," Hank said. "We're going down to the White Shark and shoot some pool."

"Sure," she said. " 'Night."

We paused outside Hank's apartment. Hank fumbled with his keys at the door until she rounded the corner at the end of the corridor.

"Go inside," I said. "I'd better pull the emergency stop on the elevator. You can take it off after we leave, Hank."

They went inside. I hurried down the hall, opened the elevator door, and pulled out the red knob. There was an elevator on the other side of the building, and the residents who didn't want to climb the stairs could use that one.

Hank and I, being so much bigger than Eddie, supported the man in the yellow jump suit between us. We each draped an arm over our shoulders, and carried him, with his feet dragging, down the corridor. If someone saw us, it would look—at least from a distance—as if we were supporting a drunk. Eddie, a few feet in front of us, carried the folded army blanket and the sack of stuff. It was much easier going down the stairs. I went down first, carrying the feet, while Hank and

Eddie supported him from behind. After we put him on top of the girl, in the back of the car, and covered him with the G.I. blanket, I got into the driver's seat. The fire door had closed and locked while we loaded him, so Hank started down the sidewalk toward the apartment entrance.

"Look, Eddie," I said. "Drive as close behind me as you can. If I'm stopped—for any reason—I'm going to leave the car and run like a striped ass ape. And I'll need you behind me to pick me up. Okay?"

"No sweat, Larry," Eddie said, "if you want me to, I'll drive the convertible. I'm a better driver than you."

I shook my head. "That's why I want you behind me, in case we have to make a run for it in the Vega. Besides, I'm not going to drive over thirty, and when I cross the bridge, before the Goodyear landing pad, I'm going to throw my pistol over the side. It'll be a lot easier to throw it over the rail from the convertible."

"Move out, then. I'm right behind you."

I got rid of the gun, leaving it in the holster, when I passed over the bridge, and a few moments later I was parked in the Japanese Garden parking lot. There were no other cars. The Garden itself was closed at night, and fenced in to keep the hippies from sleeping in the tiny bamboo tearoom. But the parking lot was outside the fence. Sometimes lovers used the parking lot at night, but because most people knew that the Garden was closed at night, they didn't realize that the parking lot was still available. Eddie pulled in beside me and cut his lights.

I got some Kleenex out of the glove compartment of my Vega, and smudged the steering wheel and doors of the convertible. I did this for Eddie's benefit mostly; it's almost impossible to get decent prints from a car. Then I got the G.I. blanket and the beach towel and the paper sack of personal belongings. As we drove back toward Dade Towers, I folded the blanket and the towel in my lap.

Eddie said: "What do you think, Fuzz-O?"

"About what?"

"The whole thing. D'you think we'll get away with it?"

"I'm worried about Don."

"You don't have to worry about Don," Eddie said. "Don's all right."

"If I don't have to worry about Don," I said, "I don't have to worry about anything,"

"You don't have to worry about Don," Eddie said.

"Good. If you don't scratch a sore, it doesn't suppurate."

"Hey! That's poetry, Larry."

"That's a fact," I said. "When you hit Twenty-seventh, turn into the Food Fair lot. I'll throw all this stuff into the Dempsey Dumpster."

When we got back to Hank's apartment, Don and Hank were watching television. The color was back in Don's face, and he was drinking red wine with ice cubes. Hank had found an old electric fan in his closet, and some Christmas tree spray left over from Christmas. The windows were still open, but the pungent spray, diffused by the noisy fan, made the room smell like a pine forest. I turned off the TV, fixed myself a light Scotch and water, without ice, and sat in front of the coffee table. I counted the money, and gave two one-hundred-dollar bills each to Eddie, Hank, and Don, and kept two of them for myself. I folded the remaining money, and put it into my jacket pocket.

"I'll need this extra money to buy a new pistol," I said. "I got rid of mine—and the holster."

"What did you do with it, Larry?" Don said.

"If you don't know, Don, you can't tell, can you?" I looked at Don and smiled.

"What makes you think Don would ever say anything?" Hank said.

"I don't," I said. "But it's better for none of you guys to know. Okay? Now. If anybody's got anything to say, now's the time to say it. We'll talk about it now, and then we'll forget about it forever. What I mean, after tonight, none of us should ever mention this thing again. Okay?"

Hank cleared his throat. "While you and Eddie were gone, Don and I were wondering why you had us bring the girl here in the first place."

"I was waiting for that," I said. "What I wanted was a make on the girl. I figured that if I could find out her address, I could call her father, and have him come and get her. Either that, or we could take her to him after I talked to him. That way, he could've put her to bed and called his family doctor. That way, he could've covered up the fact that she died from an O.D., if that's what it was."

"That wouldn't have worked," Hank said.

"Maybe not. But that was the idea in the back of my mind. You asked me why I brought her here, and that's the reason."

"It would've worked with me," Don said. "I wouldn't've wanted it in the papers, if my daughter died from an overdose of drugs."

"Okay, Larry," Hank said. "You never explained it to us before, is all. I just wonder, now, who those people were."

"The papers will tell you." Eddie laughed. "Look in the *Miami News* tomorrow night. Section C—Lifestyle."

"Don?" I said.

"One thing," Don said, looking into his glass. "I didn't mean to pull the trigger. I'm sorry about getting you guys into this mess."

"You didn't get us into anything, Don," Eddie said. "We were all in it together anyway."

"Just the same," Don said, "I made it worse, and I'm sorry."

"We're all sorry," I said. "But what's done is done. Tomorrow, I'm going to report it at the office that my pistol was stolen out of the glove compartment of my car. They may raise a little hell with me, but these things happen in Miami. So I'm telling you guys about it now. Some dirty sonofabitch stole my thirty-eight out of my glove compartment."

No one said anything for a few moments. Don stared at the diluted wine in his glass. Eddie lit a cigarette. I finished my drink. Hank, frowning, and looking at the floor, rubbed his knees with the palms of his hands.

"Eddie," I said, "do you want to add anything?"

Eddie shrugged, and then he laughed. "Yeah. Who wants to go down to the White Shark for a little pool?"

Hank and Don both smiled.

"If we needed an alibi, it wouldn't be a bad idea," I said. "But we don't need an alibi. If there's nothing else, I think we should all hit our respective sacks."

Eddie and I stood up. "You going to be okay, Don?" Eddie asked.

"Sure," Don stood up, and we started toward the door.

"Just a minute," Hank stopped us. "I picked up the girl in the drive-in, and bets were made! You guys owe me *money!*"

We all laughed then, and the tension dissolved. We paid Hank off, of course, and then we went to bed. But as far as I was concerned, we were still well ahead of the game: four lucky young guys in Miami, sitting on top of a big pile of vanilla ice cream. ◉

# To a Nephew in College

DEAR WESLEY,

I am enclosing this letter with the book I have sent you. The book will come as a surprise, I know, not merely because it is *The Metamorphosis,* by Franz Kafka, but because it is from me, an old uncle you haven't heard from in five years.

But threads of conscience have been bothering me since your mother wrote three weeks ago and informed me that you were barely hanging on to a "D" average. That doesn't bother me too much; a "D" average means that you have a great many friends, but what does make me feel remorseful is that I have neglected you completely for so many years. Of course, I thought of you a year ago when your mother told me of your decision to attend an Ivy League school instead of coasting through one of our fine Florida universities, but to tell you the truth, I haven't thought of you since. I am trying to make up for it now with some sage, avuncular advice.

Examine the book. Observe how *slim* it is, how easy to read. It is set in ten-point type, the way all books should be printed. Although this edition was printed in 1946, and is not a first edition, it is worth two dollars more now than it was then. The only flaw is a small spot on Page 67. Because this is a very sad part of the story—where an apple has pierced Gregor's back—you may think this blemish was caused by a tear falling onto the page. Such is not the case; it is a drop of gin from an overflowing martini.

There is a purpose in my sending you *The Metamorphosis,* although you might think that it is pointless at this stage; but as Kafka said, "We must break the frozen sea within us."

You are now in your sophomore year and it is time you became an expert in something. Inasmuch as you are not an athlete, and obviously not a scholar, I am recommending to you, out of my knowledge gained by 24 years in public relations, that you become an expert on Franz Kafka.

I offer you this advice with the same sincerity I give $10,000 retainers. To get by in this world, and to have the sharpened edge on his fellow men that means the difference between mediocrity and success, a man must be expert in at least *one* thing. Kafka may not sustain you throughout your entire life, but an extensive knowledge of his works will bring your average in college up to a "C" or possibly a "B" before you graduate into the Kafkaesque world. No teacher would dare give a "D" to a Kafka scholar.

Not only is it a simple matter to become an expert on Kafka, it is inexpensive. All of Kafka's books are in English now, and all of them are available in handsome, paperback editions. Recently, *The Basic Kafka* was published. It is basic, but not enough: you also need *The Trial, The Castle, Amerika, The Diaries,* and *The Complete Stories.* There are also three volumes of letters, but I advise you to save these for graduate school, when you must begin work on an M.B.A. Today, you can obtain this entire list for less than thirty dollars. Now let me impress you: With this rack of books purchased and in plain sight in your dormitory room at college, *you do not even have to open a single one of them to obtain a "C" average by the end of the year!*

Such is the quiet power of Franz Kafka in an academic setting. The mere fact that you have these books in your room will spread to every corner of the campus. The setting, however, is still incomplete. There is a scene in *The Trial* where K., the protagonist, buys three heathscapes from Titorelli, the court painter. It isn't possible for you to go right out and buy three heathscapes for your room, but for three dollars apiece you can get one of the fine arts students at school to paint you three of them. If you know a female art student you can probably get them done for nothing. Unfortunately, none of the do-it-yourself painting kits feature heathscapes. Heathscapes are quite depressing; two gnarled trees in the foreground, a patch of dirty gray-green grass, and a sun at its nadir. Three of these paintings, exactly alike, hanging in a row in your room, will speed your reputation as a Kafka expert. They will also serve to remind you how bleak your prospects will be if you get bounced out of college.

Next you must read all of Kafka's books. This will take time, but you have three more years to go in college, and the short list will do. After reading *The Metamorphosis*, read *The Trial* and then *The Castle*. Most readers give up halfway through *The Castle,* so when you finish it you will be a front runner. Many Kafka experts specialize by reading only one book over and over again, but this is the cowardly way, and not for you.

Always carry a Kafka book with you from class to class. By reading a page at a time you will eventually get through them all.

As soon as you have read at least three books, write an article on some fragment of Kafka's works and have it published in the school magazine. At this early stage I know it sounds difficult even to think about writing an article on a man you haven't read yet, but Kafka experts *have* to write about him. In fact, after reading his books, you won't be able to prevent yourself from writing about Kafka.

To get started, choose any phrase that interests you and explain it as well as you can, giving it your own interpretation. Your interpretation will be valid, and will not brook contradiction. Kafka's "The Hunger Artist" interested me at one time and I wrote seven different interpretations for my own elucidation. Every one of them was valid.

You won't have to bribe the editor of your college magazine to publish your article; he will be delighted to get it. Everything written about Kafka is eventually published somewhere. Even if I were to send a copy of this letter to a newspaper it would be published immediately.

After the publication of your article you will be invited to join the college literary societies. Join them, by all means, but do not take an active part in their activities. This calls for some preparation, however. It will be necessary for you to memorize several quotations from Kafka's works. To avoid being elected to any office a good quotation is, "One must not cheat anyone, not even the world of its victory." Or you could refuse just as gracefully by saying, "Beyond a certain point there is no return. This point has to be reached."

It will be better for your studies if you do not join any of the fraternities. To turn down the many requests you will receive after your article appears, quote: "What is gayer than believing in a household god?" You will, of course, lose some friends this way, but you will have ample time for your studies. Kafka has quotations to fit every situation; however, they must be delivered dead-pan to obtain maximum effectiveness. When you reach your senior year it will be best to quote Kafka in German . . . but I'm getting too far ahead for you, I'm afraid.

Your work is cut out for you, Wesley, but you will never regret the effort. As Kafka stated in *In the Penal Colony,* "Up till now a few things still had to be set by hand, but from this moment it works all by itself."

> Fraternally,
> Uncle Charles

# Checking Out

THE WOMAN sat on the long leather couch in the lobby, waiting for her husband to pay the hotel bill. She counted the six whale-colored pieces of luggage again, and then lifted the top of the plaid case in her lap to check her make-up in the mirrored lid. The shuttle to the airport would come along in another twenty minutes, the bellman had said, and he would be back to help them with their luggage.

Her husband, frowning as he put on his dark glasses, joined her. They were both the same age, but he looked much younger. During the ten years of their marriage she had gained four pounds each year, and the extra forty pounds, together with her size eighteen traveling suit, gave her a matronly appearance. Her husband, lighting a cigarette, shook his head when she patted the cushion next to her. He stuck the burnt match into a concrete urn filled with white sand, and leaned against the Alabama marble pillar.

"How much was the bill?" she asked.

"Seven-thirty."

"Seven hundred and thirty dollars? Isn't that a lot?"

He shook his head. "Not really. We used room service. We ate in the dining room a couple of times, and the bar bill is also included."

"May I see it?"

"See what?"

"The bill."

"It's okay. I checked it."

"Do you mind if I take a look at it?"

He took the folded bill, which was long and green on stiff paper, out of his inside jacket pocket and handed it to her. She took her reading glasses out of her purse, put them on, and examined the bill.

"They put the tax on every day, don't they?"

"Of course. They have to. The law requires it."

"I would've thought they'd wait 'til we checked out, and then add the tax all at once."

"What difference would it make? It would still add up to the same thing."

"I know, but . . . What's this for—M.S.G., thirty-four dollars?"

"I don't recall."

"M.S.G. Is that an abbreviation for 'message'? We didn't send any messages for thirty-four dollars."

"Here. Let me see that."

She passed him the bill. He looked at it and nodded.

"I remember now. That was for the massage boy."

"Massage boy? What massage boy?"

"On the seventh. That was the night you went out to dinner with your mother."

"And you refused to come with us."

"I didn't *refuse* to go with you. I said I didn't want to go with you because all she ever talks about are the dead and dying people I don't know from your old neighborhood."

"So let's talk about the massage boy."

"He wasn't really a boy. He was in his early twenties, I'd say. I wasn't very hungry, so all I had was a hot roast beef sandwich with potatoes and gravy in the coffee shop. I'd planned on watching TV in the room, but there was nothing on. Then I started looking through the Yellow Pages."

"Why? For a massage boy?"

"No. You can learn a lot about a city by looking at the Yellow Pages, that's all. I noticed the ads for massage, and I called the number. He came over and gave me a massage. It relaxed me. I went to sleep, and I don't even remember when you came back to the room."

"Thirty-four dollars for a massage?"

"Actually, it was twenty-five. I gave him a nine-dollar tip. I'd intended to use my VISA card, but he didn't have the device you use for the card, you see. So I charged the massage to the room. The hotel paid him, and then I paid the hotel. It's no big deal."

"I think it is. A nine-dollar tip is a lot. It must've been some massage."

"Nine dollars isn't too much. He had to drive over here to the hotel. I imagine he had to pay a parking fee, too. And he gave me a good massage."

"I'll bet he did."

He put his cigarette out in the urn of sand, and looked at his wristwatch.

"Is the bellboy going to come back to help us with the luggage?"

"He said he would," she said.

Two tears oozed from her wet eyes and rolled down her powdered cheeks, leaving tiny furrows.

"What's the matter now?" he said.

"You realize," she said, "that after this, our marriage will never be the same again. . ."

He sighed. "It never *was* the same." ◉

# One Hero to a War

MY FIRST meeting with Nelson V. Brittin was somewhat strained—for both of us. Officially, as Noncommissioned Officer-in-Charge of the Information and Education Section, Headquarters, 24th Infantry Division, Kokura, Kyushu, Japan, he was my new chief, my NCOIC. I had six stripes on my arm at the time, and he only had four. So I minded—but I never did anything about it.

I had just given up—which I realized many years later—the best job in the entire world, the first sergeancy of Company A, 19th Infantry Regiment, to take on a weird but challenging unmilitary assignment as Station Manager, WLKH-AKAS, Kokura, an Armed Forces Radio Station. And the radio station, together with the Division newspaper, the printing plant, and the Education Office, were all separate subsections under Staff Sergeant Brittin's supervision. He was also Information NCO for Hq and Hq Company, 24th Infantry Division and, as Division Hq I&E "sergeant-major," he was responsible for the correspondence flow, including I&E program reports between the three regimental I&E offices, Division artillery, his office and on up to Headquarters, Eighth Army.

Complicated? You bet.

Brittin had a nasty, thankless job, but my new position as radio station manager was the easiest duty I had ever had during fourteen years (at that time) of military service. As a conscientious NCO, I never lost completely the feeling of uneasy guilt that waxed and waned for the year and some months I served as Station Manager. With six stripes all I had to do was say that I wanted Brittin's job, and I would have had it. But I did not covet his miserable overload of work. For the first time in my military career I had a soft snap and besides, I rationalized, any other job in the world is a comedown after a man has been a first sergeant anyway. A rifle company top-kick, with anywhere from 150 to 265 men under his direct, immediate control, has more status, more prestige, and more raw power than the President of the United States.

These thoughts entered my mind as I looked at the unimpressive Staff Sergeant Brittin. There was something paradoxical about him though, even at my first look, and I was unable to tag him and file him away as I usually did when I met another soldier. He looked exactly like what he was—a headquarters clerk, a typical ball-bearing WAC, as we used to call them. He was bald and getting balder; he was underweight and undersized for his grade and staff job. He only weighed about 145 pounds and, despite his stiffly erect carriage, he stood only about five-six in his thick-soled combat boots.

The door to his office was open, but I stood quietly in the doorway watching him type. I have seen some fast typists, but Bitter Brittin was the first man I had ever seen who could type, without mistakes, more than a hundred words a minute on a standard machine. He had developed a rhythm system of his own invention that was comical to see. As his shoulders jumped up and down, performing Old Howardish bumps and grinds to the clicking on the platen, his long skinny fingers danced over the keys with an eye-biting blur.

But what struck me as paradoxical about Brittin was his tailored uniform: it was sharply pressed, spotless, and his sleeves were rolled down and buttoned. His combat boots were shined. A clerk in a division headquarters with an immaculate uniform is as rare as a clerk who hasn't just this moment gone down the hall for coffee. Brittin also wore a Purple Heart ribbon, with a bronze oak leaf cluster, and a Combat Infantry Badge above his buttoned khaki shirt pocket. Knowing that he had had combat experience softened my attitude. He was a line soldier in a clerk's job—at least we had this much in common.

As things turned out, we had a good deal in common.

After he finished the letter and tossed it into his out tray, we left the office and went to the NCO Club for coffee. The

NCO Club bar did not open officially until 1700, but if a man was on good terms with the steward, it was possible to get a matutinal Coffee Royale. Brittin was on excellent terms with the steward.

"I've talked to the I&E Officer," I said, "and all he told me to do was to ride herd on the eightballs he got stuck with at the station."

Brittin frowned and shook his head. He was twenty-eight years old at the time, a year younger than I was; but when he frowned, deep lines creased his forehead, and even deeper lines darkened the sharply angled creases that led from the wings of his nose to the stern inverted U of his mouth. As a consequence, he looked at least ten years older than me. In all fairness I had been in the Army since my sixteenth birthday, and he had been a banker in civilian life. Having led the good Army life for almost as long as I could remember, and never in the position where I would have had to turn down some poor slob for a bank loan, my face was as smooth and cherubic as a child's; my face didn't begin to disintegrate until I had been out of the service for several years.

"No," he said, "they aren't eightballs, Saryent Willeford, they're mostly musicians. When they broke up the Division Band during the economy drive, we were able to get four of the bandsmen, the best of the lot, for the radio station. They're merely civilians in uniform. Let them go their own way, and they'll do a good job. What we needed you for was to handle the paperwork."

"Fair enough." I nodded grimly. "But I just came from the station, and the man on the control board was wearing a black beret, a dirty white T-shirt, OD slacks instead of summer khakis, and, when he made the station break, he mispronounced 'WLKH-AKAS,' 'Kokura,' 'Kyushu' and 'Japan.' "

Brittin didn't laugh; he never laughed or smiled. "That was probably Fred Mah, the Chinaman, he used to set type on a Chinese newspaper in San Francisco, so naturally he was assigned to I&E. But the division paper is printed in English, so we made him a radio announcer."

"That's what I call good personnel work."

"You're lucky to have him. The T.O. calls for twelve men, but you've only got six. There are no replacements in sight, and I&E has no priority on new men coming in. With the division down to less than fifty percent of full strength, the regiments are crying because they don't have enough men for guard duty."

"I know. I just came from Beppu."

"What do you know and what do you want to know about the functions of I&E?"

"Well, we had the weekly *Information Hour* on the Company level. I usually used the hour myself to lecture my men on V.D."

"That isn't the purpose of the *Information Hour*."

"I realize that but, every time a man got a case of V.D., I had to write a letter to the regimental commander explaining what I had done personally to prevent it. And he, in turn, has to explain the same case and what he did to prevent it to the commanding general."

"But you shouldn't have used I&E time for V.D. lectures. I handle the *Information Hour* for Headquarters Company, and it's compulsory for every man, including your radio station personnel. For those who can't make it on Saturday morning I hold a make-up period—when I can—during the week."

"I'll see that my men are there, Saryent Brittin."

"I know that you will. I brought it up because I had a little trouble on this score with the previous station manager. He transferred back to the Air Force on the last chance regulation, and they deserve him. Except for the *Stars and Stripes*, which carries very little world news, the *Information Hour* is just about the only contact the company has with the outside world. And this is my responsibility."

There was more shop talk, and Brittin managed to get across the idea that he was a conscientious NCO and that he was as good in his field as I was in mine. Nor was he self-conscious about it; he was merely efficient, and he took his job seriously. I appreciated these soldierly qualities, and I was reassured that we could work out a reasonably symbiotic relationship between us without the difference in grade making any valid difference. And it worked out that way.

Although Brittin didn't have nearly as much service as I had, we had many other things in common. We had both fought in Europe, we had both been wounded twice and, when the war had ended, we had both been able to wangle three-month college courses at the post-war GI universities set up in Europe after V-E Day. He had attended the university in Florence, because of his interest in Byzantine mosaics, and I had gone to the Biarritz American University to study painting and playwriting.

I think it goes without saying that not many professional soldiers are keenly interested in the fine arts. Brittin was the first soldier I had been able to talk to about painting since I had arrived in Japan. It was our mutual interest in art, as much as anything else, that cemented our friendship. After I got to know Brittin better, I trusted him enough with my secret to give him a copy of my book of poetry, *Proletarian Laughter*, that had been issued a few months before by the Alicat Bookshop Press. He did not like the poetry (nobody did, as far as I know), but he told me that I was fortunate to have a John Edward Heliker cover illustration. He was familiar with Heliker's painting, and I had never heard of the artist. I had been of the opinion that the publisher, Oscar Baron, had given the cover job to an unknown artist. Although Heliker is certainly a well-known painter today, he was not so well-known in 1948—outside of New York at any rate. I mention this to show that Brittin's interest and knowledge of art were not confined to the Byzantine period.

In the weeks that followed, I found out how dedicated Brittin truly was to his Information & Education duties—but I cannot say, in all honesty, that his enthusiasm was contagious. I helped him when I could, of course. When he wrote a skit on the Bill of Rights for the *Information Hour*, I took an actor's part in it, and I assigned him two of my radio announcers—an ex-trumpet player and an ex-percussion man—as alternating paragraph readers of the Bill of Rights. The captive audience that attended this *Information Hour* was bored stiff.

Brittin's preparation for his weekly lectures was, in my

opinion, ridiculous. The man-hours of labor that he put into preparation were certainly not justified by the results. The Army sent a good deal of informational material to the field, but none of it was inspirational. There were booklets called *Army Talks*, for example, which were written on such an infantile and boring level that they put the troops who audited them asleep. The booklets were not supposed to be read aloud; they were issued as guides. But most I&E NCOs at the company level, instead of extracting a paragraph here and there as a factual filler, read the book aloud in its entirety during the compulsory *Information Hour* instead. It was easier that way, much easier than to prepare an hour's lecture. But the upshot of the monotone readings was that the auditing troops developed a deadly hatred of the entire I&E program.

With the help of *Time* (after he had extracted the factual data from the slanted propaganda, which was no mean task in itself) and surface editions of the *Sunday New York Times*—which was always a month or so old by the time it reached Kokura, Japan—as well as monitored notes culled from the Tokyo APRS radio station's short-wave broadcasts, *Army Talks* and other special I&E material that came in from time to time, Brittin wrote out an organized full hour's lecture every week. If he had been content to read this lecture aloud and let it go at that, he would have had the best weekly *Information Hour* in the entire Army. But he carried it a step farther: he *memorized* the script every week! Every week he memorized these slowly gathered, but swiftly typed, bits and pieces of news, facts and opinions. In the evenings, after chow, he sat on the edge of his bunk reading his lecture through again and again until he had his talk down verbatim.

"Why?" I asked him. "Nobody expects you to knock yourself out on this *Information Hour* crap."

"There's no other way, Will," he told me. "I've tried reading the lecture, but when I read it, I couldn't look the men straight in the eyes as I talked. This way nobody goes to sleep on me—and the word has got around that I memorize the lecture. The mere fact that I have taken the trouble to learn it by heart makes the troops listen with more attention. They figure it's important, you see."

I couldn't quarrel with his logic, theoretically at any rate, except to say that it didn't work out that way. The attention span of the average infantryman is as short as his memory. Brittin was a dynamic speaker, with a rurally free delivery, and he practiced his gestures in the latrine mirror when he ran through his speech for sound on Friday nights. All the same, he put some of the troops to sleep. But thanks to his memorization, they did not enjoy their slumbers very long. He was able to spot a sleeper almost instantaneously, including those experienced professional privates who had learned how to sleep through lectures and training films with their eyes open. Brittin would roar the sleeper to his feet, and the poor devil was forced to assume the position of a soldier at attention for the remainder of the hour. The opinion that I passed on to Brittin was that it was the fear of standing at attention more than the memorization of his lecture that caused the troops to be so attentive. But he did not agree and continued to learn his lectures by heart.

I still don't know the answer to arousing the interest of troops in world and national affairs and issues of the day. The American soldier is, beyond a doubt, the most politically naive individual in the world—including, alas, general officers like MacArthur, Eisenhower and Dean (who led the 24th Infantry Division in its disastrous early days of the Korean War).

I have already gone into greater detail about the pre-Korean War overseas I&E setup than I intended, but when it is compared to the informational system of the Russian army—where a civilian politico well-grounded in ideology is assigned full-time to every platoon-sized unit—our efforts to make our troops aware of the big outside world seem feeble indeed. Brittin, I fear, was well over the heads of the troops who listened to him. Few college students can deliver a lucid explanation of capitalism or discuss intelligently what is meant by the Hegelian dialectic; is it any wonder that an intellectual like Brittin—who ran into a stony-eyed wall of indifferent ignorance every week—became so bitter that we, his close friends, nicknamed him "Bitter" Brittin?

To be fair there were a few of us who appreciated his lectures, and I was one of them, although I did not admire his wooden, unrelated, Bea Lily-like gestures. His explanation of Lenin's rise to power was a beautifully organized job of exposition, but from the comments I overheard afterwards, few troops were able to follow him because of the difficult Russian names (even though he wrote them on the blackboard as he went along). By the time a man is old enough to be a soldier, it is much too late to give him the historical background he needs to understand the ever-changing present.

Accidentally, although my conscience remains clear on this matter, I was instrumental in causing Brittin to be considered as a genius by the officers and men stationed in Kokura. I think that it may have hindered his work to some extent after the word got around he was the brainiest man in the entire United States Army, but perhaps it didn't make any difference at all. But after the word got out, officers, as well as enlisted men, acted as though they were afraid to talk to him.

One afternoon Brittin visited me at the radio station wanting to know what I could do by way of spot announcements to get more soldiers to sign up for USAFI courses. The U.S. Armed Forces Institute is the best educational buy in the world. For only two dollars (at that time), a serviceman could take a course in almost anything. And if the Institute didn't have the course the soldier wanted, they would find the college or trade school that did and pass along the information.

But there were a lot of girls in Japan and, for most of the year, the weather was pleasant on the island of Kyushu. It is one thing to take a correspondence course when a man is stationed in Newfoundland, but there are more interesting things to do with spare time when a man is stationed in Japan.

I broke out the office bottle, and we discussed the USAFI problem over a few straight ryes. The idea—a brilliant idea—came to me after only three drinks. Thanks to a publicity conscious club steward, the NCO Club gave WLKH four hundred dollars a month to use for a weekly quiz program, a program I MC'd via a remote hookup from the main ballroom at the Club. We had named the program *The Money Bucket*, and every week I filled an actual wooden, straw-lined bucket with a hundred dollars in small bills. By keeping the questions simple, I managed to give away the hundred dollars to four or five contestants during the allotted half hour the program was on the air, distributing it as equally as I could. The program was popular with the audience of NCO's and their wives at the Club, although it must have sounded more than a little dull to those who listened to it in the barracks.

"We'll put you on *The Money Bucket*," I said, "during the first break at the end of fifteen minutes. As a member of I&E, you can't appear as a contestant; but when the break comes, I pretend to spot you in the audience and invite you to come up on the stage where I can introduce you. Then I'll ask you some tough questions, some impossible questions. But you'll have the answers memorized in advance, you see, and you can rattle off the answers and amaze everybody by your erudition."

"What's the point? How will this help USAFI?"

"After we get through the questions, I can express my unbounded admiration for your vast store of knowledge and ask you how you learned all these things. All you have to do then is to say that yon learned them by taking USAFI courses in your spare time. If you want to, you can then give the audience the info on how to sign up for them at the Education office."

Brittin was delighted. We went to the library and dug out some truly offbeat technical questions and answers from the encyclopedia. Brittin was able to memorize all the answers easily, of course. I don't remember all four questions we decided upon, but one of them concerned the explanation of the steps it took blood to form a clot after a man was wounded. There were at least fifteen or twenty biological terms and chemical changes that took place in clotting, as I recall, and when Brittin glibly rattled these off on the night of the program, there was a rapt, open-mouthed silence from the audience of NCO's and wives.

Brittin and I kept the secret, but the audience reaction after he finished delivering his brief spiel on USAFI courses was certainly unexpected. For one thing there was no applause, and when he descended the steps from the stage and threaded his way through the tables toward the bar in the back of the ball-room, there was a stunned, awed silence as every bulging eye marked his passage.

Of course this unsophisticated reaction was due largely to Brittin's personality. He was a deadly serious man; he had never been known to laugh or smile, and no one who knew him would ever expect a man like him to pull a gag of this sort. But the fact he was willing to go along with the idea proves he had a sense of humor. To put the matter simply, the audience had believed him and in him. Apparently there was no doubt in anyone's mind that, not only did he know the answers to the impossible questions I had sprung on him, but that he would have been able to answer any other difficult question put to him. (And remember, this was in 1948, several years before the quiz scandals came to light on network television.)

Knowledge is a strange and peculiar power. It is a power even if one does not have it yet people *think* that one has it. And the NCO's thought that Brittin had it. They were all afraid to get into an argument with him. But when an argument arose in the bar—usually a stupid one like who was the best fighter, Joe Louis or Jack Dempsey—Brittin was appealed to for the decision, and his decision was accepted without question. It is to his credit that most of the time he refused to make a judgment. In most cases he merely shook his head and signaled the bartender to bring him another whiskey sour, his favorite drink.

Brittin was a sad, unhappy man, but why he was so unhappy, I do not know. I knew very little about his pre-service personal life except that he was born in New Jersey and had moved with his family to Philadelphia. One day while I was in his office, the company commander telephoned and ordered him to report to Hq & Hq Orderly Room. I walked over with him, and the captain told Brittin he had a letter from the Pentagon with umpteen indorsements on it wanting to know why he (Brittin) had not written to his mother. ". . . and I have to answer this today telling them that you have written home."

"No, sir," Brittin said, "I'm not writing anybody. Just

indorse it back stating that the soldier does not desire to write his mother."

"I can't say that," the captain said unhappily.

"Give me the correspondence." Brittin held out his hand. "I'll type the indorsement for you."

"That isn't what I mean. I'd still have to sign it."

"Yes, sir. Say anything you like, then, but I'm not writing anybody."

"But you have been told. Officially."

"Yes, sir." Brittin saluted, and so did I.

After we got outside, I asked him what the trouble was between him and his family. It was none of my business, but I was curious about family relationships having no family of my own.

"No trouble," he replied. "It's just that I've given up that way of living for this way, and I don't want to be reminded of it."

He had been raised by his mother and two sisters. Before he was drafted for World War II, he had been a banker in Philadelphia, and he had returned to the bank as soon as he was demobilized. Walking to the bank one day, he told me, he had passed under the big blue recruiting flag and realized he had liked the Army better than he had ever liked working in the bank. He took off his Homburg, threw his hat and briefcase under a parked car, climbed the stairs and re-enlisted in the Regular Army. This was on January 7, 1948, and after a short course in Information and Education work, he had been posted to Japan.

It had taken his family several months to find out what happened to him because he had never written or told them that he had re-enlisted. Whether Brittin ever wrote home or not I do not know. I like to think that he did—it makes me feel better to think so—but I doubt it. Brittin needed someone to love him, and I believe that his family loved him but took him for granted. I saw it happen many times: "Welcome home, the war's over, hurry down in the morning and get your old job back and start supporting us again." Some ex-soldiers can make this readjustment to civilian life without any trouble, but others join the American Legion where they can pretend that they are soldiers again—and they never miss a meeting.

No, Brittin was not, by any stretch of the understanding, a sentimentalist. He was, however, like most Regulars, a man without any "religious preference," to use the military jargon. No professional fighting man who has devoted a large portion of his life to becoming a competent soldier can believe that a personal or impersonal god is taking sides in anything as nasty as war. To do so would destroy his combat effectiveness and relieve him from the strong sense of responsibility he must have for the soldiers under his command and protection. I hesitated to mention here that Brittin was an atheist because so many Americans have the peculiar notion that atheism and immorality are synonymous. Brittin was the most highly *moral* individual I have ever known. And anybody who ever suggests to me that he was immoral because he was an atheist has discovered an indirect but foolproof way of finding himself with an upper lip full of teeth.

As New Year's Eve 1948-49 approached, Brittin got a little excited about the big costume ball the NCO Club was going to have. A new Club had just been constructed, and the members were going to celebrate New Year's and the new Club at the same time. Brittin liked the idea of wearing a costume, although he couldn't think of what kind of costume he wanted to wear for several days before the event; that is to say, he couldn't decide what he wanted to be. He had a dozen new ideas a day, discarding them one by one.

We had to improvise our costumes, of course, and I decided to go as Superman. Long olive-drab underwear, GI combat boots, a makeshift letter "S" sewed to the front of my drab sweatshirt and a dirty OD towel as a cape, and I was ready.

I had a hunch, however, that the costume ball was going to be a flop. We had hired an excellent ten-piece band, but there were not going to be enough women. Because of the puritanical attitude of the American dependent wives, single NCO's were not allowed to bring their Japanese girlfriends. It was to be a night of free whiskey as well, and I had a premonition that those NCO's who did have their wives in Japan with them would not risk bringing them to what might turn out to be a drunken brawl.

To some extent I was right, although there were about twenty-five dependent women present in the beginning. When the dance began to get a little rough around 2200, most of those wives—who were well into the spirits themselves—were taken home by their husbands whether they wanted to leave or not. But that was all right. There were at least two hundred NCO's present, and we danced with each other. The music was excellent, and a dance is a dance. The trick is to find a partner who will let you lead, and these were at a premium.

Brittin did not dance. Moreover, he had made himself up as a schmoo, that fabulist creature invented by Al Capp. One look at a schmoo, and the schmoo swoons over backwards and dies for you out of love. And here is where Brittin ran into a little trouble. I knew that he was a schmoo because he had told me that he was a schmoo. To the other NCO's he was merely a drunk soldier wearing a white mattress cover filled with dirty laundry. He had cut holes in the mattress cover for his arms and legs, and he bulged all around inside the cover with strange lumpy shapes. He had drawn black charcoal streaks on his upper lip to make a schmoo moustache but, frankly, he didn't look like anything. He resembled a schmoo as much as I—with my topkick's paunch—resembled Superman.

I got high myself, and the more I drank the more desirable a young medic became as a dancing partner. He was wearing a borrowed nurse's uniform, white cotton stockings, plenty of makeup and lipstick and a lacquered mop head as a fright wig. He was a superb dancer, too, but I could never dance with him for a full minute without some desperado cutting in on me.

I gave up the chase and, for a while, watched Bitter Brittin make an ass out of himself. Imitating the schmoo, he would come up to some unsuspecting NCO, holler "Schmoo!" at the top of his powerful voice and then flop over backward on the dance floor and play dead. It was bound to happen: after Brittin had "schmooed" in some guy's face for the third time in a row, the man got sore and took a swing at him. The fight was stopped before the guy got in a second swing. Brittin wasn't hurt, but he hadn't fought back either. He was a little stunned by the idea that anyone would get mad at a poor little schmoo. About 0230 I managed to get a taxi, and we returned to our quarters.

Hindsight, you see. Perhaps I am more perceptive than I used to be, and I wonder why I didn't see it at the time: Brittin wanted to love somebody—almost anybody—or he wouldn't have made himself up as a schmoo; and he wanted someone to love him, as well. But all he got for his pains that night was an awkward, drunken right to the side of his head.

A week later Brittin found himself a girl—Buttercup—a house in the suburbs of Kokura and a new bicycle. I don't know where he found Buttercup, but somebody had certainly lost her purposely. I don't mean to make any disparaging remarks about the Japanese, but the fact remains that it takes the average soldier at least six months in Japan before he can tell the difference between a pretty Japanese girl and an ugly one. But Buttercup, Brittin's unlovely mistress, would not be considered as a pretty girl by any racial standards. Her yellowish upper front teeth stuck straight out like a shelf of piano keys. She was tall for a Japanese girl, an inch or so taller than Brittin and, as we say in the south, she was so bowlegged she couldn't have caught a pig in a trench.

She laughed a lot, whether the remark was funny or not, and her command of English was negligible. But she was able to carry on a lively conversation with what she had, and she used the soldier's catchall adjective with insouciant aplomb. There is no doubt in my mind that she loved Brittin; she adored him, as well she might. He supported her, of course, and paid the rent on their house, but he did not have a fixed monthly payment arrangement with her the way most "shack-jobs" demanded.

Brittin's house was approximately five miles away from the main gate, and I only visited him once, for dinner, going out by taxi. His house was well above the ground on stilts, and there was a pleasant breeze coming through the opened windows. But the mosquitoes were fierce, and I left as soon after the meal as I politely could. I suppose that Buttercup was a fair cook, but I have never been fond of the Japanese practice of boiling meat with sugar. Brittin slept on the floor, Japanese style, but he had rigged up a GI olive-drab mosquito bar above the bare *tatami*, and he had chiseled some chairs and a card table to sit around. Very few Americans can spend an entire evening squatting on the floor. I found the atmosphere depressing. His small house was as ascetic as a monk's cell, and I would have had to be a desperate man indeed before I would have even entertained the idea of pedaling a bike five miles each way, every day, to share such a place with a girl like Buttercup.

After Bitter moved in with Buttercup, I rarely saw him anymore except in line of duty, which was seldom. His lectures were as carefully planned as ever. He practiced them beforehand on Buttercup, I supposed, substituting her smiling face for a latrine mirror. He was euphoric enough—if that is the word—to re-enlist for six years before the end of January 1949 and, with part of his huge re-enlistment bonus, he bought a lot of junk for Buttercup in the Post Exchange.

One Saturday afternoon I ran into Brittin in the downtown P.X. He was already loaded down with snack stuff—potted meat, crackers, and the like. Unlike married men, single soldiers living with Japanese girls were not allowed commissary privileges. Brittin was buying a dozen cans of orange juice when I tapped him on the shoulder.

"That's a lot of orange juice, Bitter," I said.

"Buttercup doesn't drink beer," he explained.

"This relationship, to be brutally frank, has lasted much longer than I expected it to."

"Will," he replied seriously, "I hope it lasts forever. I intend to stay in Japan from now on."

I grinned. "Perhaps, one of these days, we'll have to stop calling you 'Bitter'."

He shrugged. "I like it here." He nodded solemnly. "And I've already fixed it up with Personnel not to order a replacement for me."

"Want to go to the Club for a cold one?"

"No, I've got to go home."

I walked him outside, waited while he transferred his purchases into straw bicycle saddlebags, and waved to him as he pedaled off down the potholed street. Five miles, each way, ten miles a day. I couldn't get over it. A few months of that and his legs would be as strong as steel springs.

I had only one more serious conversation with Brittin after the P.X. encounter, and it is one I well remember. I was half-heartedly celebrating the final decree of my mail-order California divorce in the Club, and I was leaving Japan in a few days. I told Brittin I had decided not to re-enlist—I was fed up to the teeth with the Army—and the service was stifling my creativity. He listened patiently and, to all this, he replied realistically.

"Willeford," he said, not unkindly, "you are an ass. They'll kill you out there—don't let them do it to you."

I paid no attention to him, of course. Like Willy Loman's son, Biff, I was thirty years old and still trying to find myself—an absurd, neverending quest.

In June 1949, I returned to the States and was discharged in San Francisco. For the next few months, I followed the Goliardic trail with Romantic variations. I wrote an unsale-able novel and studied acting with Eddy Rubin in Dallas. For two solid months I painted nude Indian girls at the Universita-ria de Bellas Artes in Lima, Peru, and then flew to New York where I got a couple of small parts in television. One cold, miserable day in November, I started across Times Square to an appointment with a producer to try out for a part—which I wouldn't have got anyway—in a new play called *The Man*. The U.S. Army and Air Force Recruiting Station was on an island in the middle of Times Square. I went inside and re-enlisted as a Technical Sergeant in the U.S. Air Force. Civilian life, I had learned, stifles an artist's creativity.

A year and some months later I had my sixth stripe back, a pretty blonde wife and a very cushy job as a Liaison NCO with a Voluntary Air Force Reserve Training squadron in Santa Barbara, California. It took me almost a full hour every morning to get through with my paperwork, and I spent the remainder of my office day following the Korean War—then in full swing—in the *Air Force Times*, the *Army Times*, the daily newspapers and weekly newsmagazines. I wanted to

write some of my former friends in Korea for firsthand information, but it would not have made them very happy to read
a letter from me while they were fighting on the line and I was
sitting around in a new blue suit in a resort town like Santa
Barbara.

Brittin's award of the Medal of Honor was duly reported in
the *Army Times*, but the following is quoted from the official
citation, General Orders No. 12, 1 February 1952:

> Sergeant First Class Nelson V. Brittin (Service
> No. RA32271499), Infantry, United States Army, a
> member of Company I, 19th Infantry Regiment, dis-
> tinguished himself by conspicuous gallantry and intre-
> pidity above and beyond the call of duty in action on 7
> March 1951 in the vicinity of Yonggong-ni, Korea.
>
> Volunteering to lead his squad up a hill, with
> meager cover against murderous fire from the enemy,
> he ordered his squad to give him support and, in the
> face of withering fire and bursting shells, he tossed
> a grenade at the nearest enemy position. On return-
> ing to his squad, he was knocked down and wounded
> by an enemy grenade. Refusing medical attention, he
> replenished his supply of grenades and returned, hurl-
> ing grenades into hostile positions and shooting the
> enemy as they fled. When his weapon jammed, he
> leaped without hesitation into a foxhole and killed the
> occupants with his bayonet and the butt of his rifle.
>
> He continued to wipe out foxholes and, noting that
> his squad had been pinned down, he rushed to the rear
> of a machine-gun position, threw a grenade into the
> nest, and ran around to its front, where he killed all
> three occupants with his rifle. Less than 100 yards
> up the hill, his squad again came under vicious fire
> from another camouflaged, sand-bagged, machine-
> gun nest well-flanked by supporting riflemen. Ser-
> geant Brittin again charged this new position in an
> aggressive endeavor to silence this remaining obstacle
> and ran into a burst of automatic fire which killed him

instantly. In his sustained and driving action, he had killed 20 enemy soldiers and destroyed four automatic weapons.

The conspicuous courage, consummate valor, and noble self-sacrifice displayed by Sergeant Brittin enabled his company to attain its objective and reflect the highest glory on himself and the heroic traditions of military service. . .

"The poor silly schmoo," I said to no one in particular, "did he have to love us that much?"

The words *posthumously* and *killed* finally sank in and, for a while, my face was wet, but I'm not ashamed of those tears. After all, Bitter Brittin was a highly successful man. It happens that way sometimes: a very good man becomes a success because his particular talents suit his time and place, and this was a war that Brittin wanted to win all alone, as if to prove by his actions that he had meant every word he said during those dull *Information Hour* lectures.

A Medal of Honor winner is always a very special American, but Brittin was more special than other, more publicized winners. There has been no ballad sung about Brittin on our jukeboxes; Lowell Thomas hasn't written his biography; and it seems doubtful that Brittin's story will ever be seen on film. He was an intellectual, and he did not have to give up his safe job as I&E NCO at Division Headquarters to lead a rifle squad into combat. Unlike other reluctant soldiers, he knew what he was doing in Korea and why he was fighting there.

Do you? I know I don't. Perhaps, one of these days, I'll go back to Japan and ask Buttercup. Maybe she knows and, if not, I can at least thank her for giving Brittin a few months of happiness, the only real happiness he ever had. And come to think of it, that's quite a lot.

As Stephen Spender puts it, "Nostalgia isn't as good as it used to be." To go the old poet one better, I maintain that it never was any damned good, because every time I remember Bitter Brittin—which isn't very often—I weep.

Even now. . . @

## Behind Him Goes His Dream

MR. JORDAN started to come into my bar for a quick one about two years ago. He would drink one scotch on the rocks and then leave quietly. His face was narrow and there were deep, tragic lines running in furrowed cuts from the wings of a great blade nose to the corners of a thin mouth. The shiny redness of his face was not a whiskey tan; it was caused by long exposure to our California sun. A bartender knows the difference. He was always conservatively dressed in a $200 suit, and his only concession to color was a primary-colored tie.

But there was an air of mystery about Mr. Jordan. He parked his car in front, and it was always a gleaming convertible, but it was never the same car. Sometimes it was a Caddy, a Buick, or a Chrysler, but it was always a convertible. You get to wondering about a guy like that. How many cars did he own? What kind of business was he in?

On Saturday nights he came in fairly late, around twelve, drank his one drink and stared at the mirror behind the bar. His face was so sad at these times that I wanted to talk to him, maybe cheer him up a bit. But there was something in his eyes that didn't invite idle conversation. And anyway, Saturday night is my big night, and I always have plenty to do. Around 1:00 A.M. a girl would come in, smile at him, and off they would go in his convertible. But it wasn't always the same girl. It was a blonde, a redhead maybe, sometimes a brunette, but they all had something in common. They were always beautiful and always showgirl-sized — big and beautiful with full figures and that certain vacant expression most of the beautiful women have here in Southern California.

After two years of watching Mr. Jordan, I had built up a completely erroneous conception of him in my mind. I thought he was a big time movie producer or director. He was nothing like it. The guy was a used car salesman.

I found out last Tuesday night, and I suppose that is the last time he will ever come in here. No matter. It was late, after 2:00 A.M., and I was about to take inventory. The last customer had left, and I'd already pulled the shades and flipped the houselights. Mr. Jordan came in and his face was longer and sadder than usual. Before he asked for it, I poured his favorite scotch over ice and set it before him. He drained the glass and shook the ice for another. I refilled the glass to the brim.

"You know, Mr. Jordan," I said, "that's the first time you've ever had two drinks in a row since you been coming in here."

"You married, Harry?" He didn't mention the drinks.

"You bet," I said. "I've got two girls and one boy." I brought out my wallet and my file of photos of the wife and kids. He waved his hand and shook his head, and I put the wallet back in my hip pocket.

"Do you live in a project house?"

"As a matter of fact I do, Mr. Jordan. I bought out in Van Nuys three years ago. Got a three-bedroom plus den, a patio, a barbecue pit and carport. All on the G.I. Bill."

He shuddered violently and, for a moment there, I thought he was going to be sick, but he pulled himself together.

"Are you a member of the P.T.A. too?" he asked.

"Well, Mr. Jordan, I'm kind of tied up with the bar and all, but I've gone to a few meetings. My wife goes all the time though."

"You're a nice guy, Harry."

"Thanks, Mr. Jordan."

"I make between two-fifty and three-fifty a week. Is that pretty good money, Harry?"

"It's a lot more than I make," I lied.

"I've got a good job then, huh? Too good to quit."

"I'd say so, Mr. Jordan, unless you can get a better one."

"That's the American Way, isn't it, Harry? A man should always strive to better himself. Never down. Always up."

"That's the way it seems to be." I didn't know what he was driving at, but I listened attentively as he unfolded his story.

It was fascinating, and his voice was the most persuasive I've ever listened to.

Mr. Jordan was really a professional bum. He was a depression kid, and he had taken to the road when he was twelve years old. He loved it. The freedom, the constant movement from place to place in the early thirties was a way of life to him. And it was a way of life he never wanted to change.

He had ridden freight trains all over the United States and on most of the Canadian roads. He described his happiness in the mornings, the waking up in an empty boxcar and looking at open vistas, plains and fields, or maybe pulling into the yards of a strange city. He seldom knew and never cared where he was, and he said this was the greatest feeling in the world. He was hungry, true, almost always hungry, but he was an accomplished mooch, and within a few hours he would be eating in somebody's kitchen and talking to a housewife about how rough the depression was. When he was young he ate very well indeed, he said. The American people were kind to him, and he appreciated their kindness in allowing him to continue his way of life.

As he grew older he was forced to abandon neighborhood bumming. It was too easy to get arrested. People are often afraid of a grown man knocking on their back door, and they have a tendency to call the police. But he still managed to eat well. A restaurant will almost always feed a man who offers to do a little work, and nine times out of ten they won't make him do the work he has requested. And the wonderful Salvation Army was always good for a new pair of shoes or a pair of khaki pants.

Not knowing any other kind of life, you see, Mr. Jordan thought he had the best life of all. As he talked his face lighted with nostalgia, and he described the wonder of the night in a hobo jungle — a small fire with a couple of potatoes charring in the embers, the fragrance of boiling coffee, the stars overhead, the feeling of space and freedom.

"A man doesn't have that kind of freedom in the city, Harry," he said, remembering, "the cities are for wintertime. And the winters were bad, but they were the price paid for spring and summer, and I had patience in those days."

His misfortunes began in 1945, right after the war. He had spent four war years in the Army without leaving Georgia and was discharged there. After blowing his discharge money on a big drunk in Atlanta, he began to work his way west by hitch-hiking. He was picked up in Texas and, after riding a few miles at high speed, the man drove the car into a tree. When Mr. Jordan regained consciousness, he found himself in jail. It was a stolen car, and the thief who picked up Mr. Jordan was killed in the accident. Mr. Jordan took the rap and was sentenced to ten years in prison.

After four years in the Army, which was almost like prison to a professional bum like Mr. Jordan, the prison sentence was a terrible shock. But he had patience and did his time with a minimum of bitterness. He could have been paroled at the end of seven years, but that would have meant taking a job and reporting to a parole officer every week. Naturally, he refused the parole so that he would be free to travel when his sentence was served.

In prison he made his plans, poring over maps obtained from various chambers of commerce. It would be winter when he was released, and he would spend it in Los Angeles. Then in spring he would take the Poultry Route, up California through the Owens Valley, over the Donner Pass into Nevada and Utah, then down to Arizona, walking all the way. The hand-outs on the Poultry Route were the greatest. Plenty of fresh, green vegetables, cold milk, cider, and maybe a day's work once in a while to get a dollar for cigarettes. He would sleep in fresh-cut hay at night, swim in creeks and rivers, catch a trout for breakfast . . . The way he described it put a catch in my throat, and I knew exactly how he felt. But it didn't happen that way.

During the ten years he was in prison, the United States underwent a terrible transformation. Money became plentiful. Jobs cropped up out of nowhere. He couldn't believe what was happening to him; he was bewildered, dazed. It was like living a nightmare.

The day he was released from prison, he had hopped a

freight for California and found that he was the only bum on the train. When discovered by the brakeman he was taken into the caboose and fed instead of being cracked over the head with a brake handle. He was treated kindly by the train crew and, at the division point, the conductor got him a job driving a truck. He was paid ninety dollars a week just to drive a truck.

He didn't want the job, but it was hard to turn it down when it paid so well. He stuck it out for a few months and then quit when the gentle winds of spring reminded him of the Poultry Route. With more than $500 in his wallet and a tailor-made suit, he bought a ticket to Los Angeles. It was the first time in his life he had ridden the "cushions."

On the ride to L.A. he figured out a way to get rid of his money. He would get blind drunk in a Skid Row bar and, when he passed out, he would be rolled. It had happened to him before and, basically, it was a sound plan. But it didn't work that way. He had only reached his third drink in an East Fifth Street bar when a talent scout from Hollywood came in accompanied by two detectives. Along with three other bums, he was driven out to a studio and put into a movie Hollywood was making about slum areas. The studio paid him one hundred dollars for only three days' work. The detectives watched the bums to prevent their escape until all of the scenes were shot.

Richer than before, Mr. Jordan was now desperate to leave Los Angeles, and he decided to buy a secondhand car and make his getaway in it. That decision was his final downfall.

As soon as he stepped onto the gravel of a Crenshaw Boulevard used car lot, the dealer begged him to take a job as a salesman. At first he turned the job down cold, but the dealer insisted; and when he was guaranteed two hundred a week in commissions, he accepted. The American Way of Life had pinned him down at last!

And Mr. Jordan turned out to be an excellent salesman. His commissions were never below two-fifty, and he had made as much as $500 in a single week. So here he was, trapped. He had an apartment in Westwood Village, a television set, a

$1,600 hi-fi set, maid service, and his boss let him drive any car that happened to be on the lot. (That accounted for the many different convertibles I had seen him drive.) Women in Southern California were plentiful indeed to a man with his kind of money, and he was welded to the American Dream.

But lately Mr. Jordan had met a woman a little different, and he suspected that she wanted to get married.

"Then," Mr. Jordan said bitterly, "I'll have to buy a project house in San Fernando Valley, a pinto horse and a beagle hound. The first thing you know—children, P.T.A., Rotary, Kiwanis, civic organizations—" he shuddered, "politics. Boom! Governor of the damned state!"

The door opened then, and a small, rather plain woman of about thirty-five entered the bar. Her hair was a mousy brown, and she was at least twenty pounds overweight. She was smiling, and the only thing I can say about her smile is that it was determined.

"There you are!" she said brightly to Mr. Jordan. "I've been looking all over for you!"

"Hello, Martha," Mr. Jordan greeted her dully. He took the woman by the arm, and they started out. He let her out first, turned and tried to smile at me. It broke my heart.

"So long, Harry," he said, "I probably won't be dropping in anymore."

"Good luck, Mr. Jordan," I called after him, my voice cracking, and then I cried. I cried for the first time in twenty years. But why? What in the hell was I crying for? ◉

# An Actor Prepares

ALL DAY long I am up to my ears in noise. There is a clatter of dishes as the waitresses shove them, dirty, of course, into the big metal receptacle next to my zinc double sink. There is a shrill cry of tired voices calling in orders to the kitchen, the rasping growl of the chef as he replies, the swirl of steaming water as it runs into my sink, the clatter of pans and pots; and all day long, at intervals, I can hear the toilet flush through the wall. My sink is on the same wall, this side of the men's room. Lots of noise. All day. I make a lot myself, and I hear a lot. But no sound. I still haven't said what I mean. But I am getting a lot closer, I think, and maybe I had better start over.

I am a dish-washer. I am forty-nine years old. Single. Bald. In a way, I am kind of skinny, although I am beginning to get one of those little melon-sized pots puffing out below my beltline. My waist-size stays the same, however; thirty-two. I haven't always been a dish-washer. A few years ago I owned my own little Café. Six stools, one counter, a grill and a double refrigerator. I lost it. How I lost it doesn't matter now. I wasn't a good businessman, I suppose. I no longer care about the loss of my little Café. Now, even if I owned this nice restaurant where I wash dishes, it wouldn't have made any difference when I made the sound. The sound—that is what I mean. A small sound, and everyone wants to make one before he dies. I wish I were more articulate. Some people can come right out with it and say what they mean the first time and the listener knows exactly what they mean. But with me, it isn't that way. I have to think things over, weigh this against that, and even then I am not always sure. What does that make me? Slow-witted? Dumb? I don't think I am dumb, but sometimes people get that impression. Mr. Knowles was an exception. He didn't think I was dumb or slow-witted.

Mr. Knowles is a salesman who works two doors away from the restaurant. The Classy Men's Shoppe. He sells men's clothing, suits, pants, shirts, and like that. He comes to the restaurant for coffee in the mornings, and frequently comes in for lunch. That is how I happened to meet him. When things aren't too busy in the kitchen I sometimes go out front and cut myself a slab of pecan pie and sit down at the counter with a cup of coffee. The boss doesn't care. That's the way I met Mr. Knowles, at the counter. After we got to be friendly, he would talk to me about the little theater. That was his way, you see, of making the sound. The whole world is filled with people like us, not that I am trying to compare myself with Mr. Knowles; after all, he is the director of the little theater group. But he doesn't get paid for it. None of them do. The typists working in offices, the fellow who pumps gas for the Exxon station and who wants to play Hamlet some day, the white-haired old widow who pours coffee during intermissions at the plays, and so on through the whole little theater group. They don't get a dime for their work. We live in a small city and there are no Hollywood or TV scouts here to pick out a promising actor or actress for better things, so what do they all get out of it? I never knew until I met Mr. Knowles. I never even went to any of the plays. Amateurs, I thought, so why should I pay good money to see an amateur play when I can go to a movie for the same price and see two features?

That is exactly what I told Mr. Knowles.

"I suppose you're right, Jake," he told me. "Sometimes I wonder what I'm trying to prove myself. Our audiences are mighty small, and we don't attract the young people the way we should. Like you, they can't see the advantage of an amateur play over a double-feature, and maybe there isn't any. I don't know. But if we don't attract some of the younger people, what's going to become of the legitimate theater in the future?" He shook his head. "All day I stand on my feet in the store, and it's an effort, sometimes, to drag myself down to the theater at night for rehearsals; trying to coax passable performances out of actors who don't have to give, but then, there it is, opening night and, well, it's the only night I feel truly alive." His face colored slightly. "There's only one word for it, Jake. Magic."

I didn't say anything at the time. It wasn't as if Mr. Knowles had explained anything to me. He hadn't. But I realized that he had something I didn't have and he made me feel it. I returned to the kitchen and turned on the hot water tap. I thought about what he had said all day. And all day the next day. Soon; next week, next month, next year, maybe, I would be dead. And I hadn't made any sound at all. Not a single one. Never married. No children. I never made enough money to give any away. I had a paid-up burial policy and $187 in the bank. And that was all. I worked six days a week, got drunk in my room on Saturday night. On Sunday, I sobered up and did my weekly wash at the washeteria. The rest of the week I was in bed by eight-thirty every night, figuring that I needed the sleep because I have to get up at five-thirty A.M. Not much of a life, any way I looked at it.

The next morning I watched out for Mr. Knowles. When he sat down at the counter I wiped my hands dry, drew a cup of coffee, and sat beside him. I knew what I was going to say and I said it:

"Mr. Knowles, I'd like to help you out with your little theater, that is, if you can use me."

It was funny, but I held my breath while I waited for him to answer. By all rights he should have turned me down. After all, what did I know about the theater? What could I do?

Mr. Knowles nodded, rubbed his chin, and then he smiled. "We'd be glad to have you with us, Jake. How would you like to be in our next play? Just a walk-on, but an important part just the same."

"I don't know about that, Mr. Knowles. I hadn't figured on doing any acting. I never did anything like that. I thought I could be an usher, or sweep up or something."

"We're casting tomorrow night at the high school auditorium. Eight o'clock. Can you make it?"

"I'll be there, Mr. Knowles."

The next night I reached the auditorium on the dot. There were about twenty people already there, all seated around a large table up on the stage. Mr. Knowles introduced me around and they all seemed glad to see me. Not knowing anybody there, except for Mr. Knowles, I was surprised by the friendliness. I sat down and kept my mouth shut and Mr. Knowles explained to the group what the play was all about. It was a mystery play—*Things That Go Bump!* A college student had mailed it to Mr. Knowles and he liked it and wanted to put it on. No one objected, and he explained what my part was to be.

I was only in the first act. When the curtain went up I was seated at a desk with a lamp in front of me and I was supposed to be reading a letter. The rest of the set was in darkness. The door opened and a hand holding a pistol fired once and I was supposed to drop dead. Throughout the rest of Act I, until the curtain came down, all I had to do was stay slumped over the desk without moving. The rest of the play was taken up with a detective and the rest of the cast trying to figure out who killed me. Not a great part, maybe, but in a way it was the most important part in the play. If I wasn't killed, there wouldn't *be* any play. I accepted the part without hesitation.

I didn't have any lines to memorize, but I never missed a single rehearsal. I could have been excused every evening after I slumped forward dead over the desk, but I insisted on staying so I could get used to remaining in a still position for the forty minutes of the first act. I liked everybody in the cast and all of the backstage helpers. They were all younger than I was, but they treated me like one of the group. A man appreciates things like that. When it was my turn to make coffee or hustle down to Donutland for donuts they didn't skip me just because I was older than they were. And on the Sunday before the opening I was asked to come down and help paint flats and I did that too.

We had our dress rehearsal on Wednesday night and opened on Thursday; and we would play Friday and Saturday as well. Opening night, I had an attack of stage fright, but I kept it to myself and nobody knew about it. Mrs. Knowles was the make-up lady, and she put mine on because I didn't know how. As a costume, I wore my blue serge suit, a white shirt, and a red-bow tie. After I was dressed and made up I went out on the dark stage and sat on the desk. I switched on the desk lamp and took a good look at the finished and dressed set. With the curtain down it looked like a real room, a rich study for a wealthy man, and for a moment, that was me. I could hear the audience through the curtain, buzzing away, and the bang of the seats as they sat down. Tommy Norton, the stage manager, who works in the flower shop at 11th and Custer as a designer, checked the props and stage one final time, then slapped me on the shoulder as he went off-stage.

"Three minutes, Jake," he whispered, and I was alone on the stage.

It was a long three minutes. The curtain jerked up slowly as it was cranked from the wings and I was staring into darkness because the house lights were out. A brief but enthusiastic roll of applause came from the audience. I thought it was for me and I was startled, but I found out later that they were merely applauding the set. I opened the envelope on the desk, removed the letter and started to read . . . BANG! The blank was fired, the audience gasped, I clutched my chest and fell over the desk. The play went on, but there was some scattered, nervous laughter in addition to the collective gasp. The audience hadn't expected the shot, and every person out there was surprised into a reaction of some kind.

That was the sound I made. Me. Jake Sinkiewicz.

When the curtain came down on the third act, I took my place with the others in line, and we received three curtain calls. Lots of people came backstage afterwards to congratulate the cast, and I shook hands with several strangers. All of the cast had programs and we all signed each other's programs. I know I signed every one of them and I made sure that everyone, including Mr. and Mrs. Knowles, signed mine. I still have my program with all the signatures. My name is in print on the program, too:

*Sir Calvin Wardhouse* . . . . . . . . **Jacob B. Sinkiewicz**

I never acted in any more plays after that one. I didn't have to, because I had made my sound. It was a small sound, but I am a small man, not a big man. There are a lot of big men, bigger than me, richer than me, and louder men than me, who have never made any sound at all. ◉

## The Emancipation of Henry Allen

STAFF SERGEANT Henry Allen, U.S. Air Force (retired), completed his arrangement of the cigars in the showcase and looked approvingly at the contents of his new poolroom. The two ancient pool tables were shiny with new coats of polish, and their felt playing surfaces were carefully brushed. The snooker table was covered with a piece of brilliant red oilcloth purchased the day before for the "opening," and everything about the large room had a new look of clean but shabby elegance.

Satisfied, Henry selected and lit a fifteen-cent cigar, rang a NO SALE on the battered cash register and lounged in the doorway, blowing great clouds of uninhaled smoke into the fresh morning air. This was at seven-thirty on a Monday morning.

At nine-thirty a man wearing overalls entered the poolroom and purchased a box of matches. Henry Allen, Civilian, after twenty-five years in the service, was in business for himself.

At ten-thirty Jake Rauhaus, a bookie, entered and challenged Henry to a game of straight pool.

"Fine," Henry said, "want to lag for the break?"

"Go ahead. I challenged you."

Henry removed the pyramidal rack from the numbered balls, selected a cue stick, called his shot and made the first ball. Carefully, but in an effortless manner, he ran the table, lined the balls up again and continued to shoot without missing until he had made fifty points. He replaced his cue stick in the wall rack and turned to his bulging-eyed challenger.

"That'll be thirty-five cents."

Jake paid. He then put his unused cue stick away.

"I've been playing pool ever since I remember, but I ain't never seen shooting like that before."

"I once ran four hundred and seventy-three balls."

"I believe it."

"Some people don't, so I never say much about it, but I did."

"Know where the Southland Pool Hall is, over on Slauson?"

"Afraid not. L.A. used to be my hometown, but I been away too many years to know where anything is."

"The owner over there would like to meet you, I know. I'll bring him over."

"Fine. I'd be glad to meet him."

Jake left. Henry practiced trick shots at the table until hunger hit his over-sized paunch. This was at eleven-thirty, early chow time in the service. Locking the door, he put a makeshift OUT TO LUNCH sign on the door and jaywalked across the street to the New York Café. A crudely printed sign in the window stated simply FRY COOK WANTED. The printing was worse than his, he noted.

The Blue Plate Businessman's Special looked good on the menu. He ordered this and washed it down with three cups of coffee. The coffee, at any rate, was very good. Finished, he paid an aged waitress and returned to his poolroom. Jake and a stranger were waiting at the door.

"Been out to lunch," Henry said, and unlocked the door.

"That's what we figured when we saw your sign," the stranger said.

Introductions were then made by Jake Rauhaus. Jake discovered Henry's name, and Henry discovered Jake's name and the name of the stranger. The stranger's name was Melvin Thead, but nearly everybody called him Mel. Mel was a tall, thin fellow who peered at the world through a pair of rose-tinted glasses. He had a nervous habit of clenching and unclenching his long bony fingers.

Mel looked Henry over carefully. He took in Henry's bald head, paunch, blue sport shirt and GI black shoes with such an inquiring manner that he reminded Henry of an officer from the Inspector General's Department.

"Jake tells me you're a pool player." Mel said, flatly.

"I play at it," was Henry's reply.

The two men looked at each other silently for a moment, and Jake climbed into one of the high chairs against the wall.

"Ever bet?" Mel asked.

"Sometimes."

"I'll bet that you can't run a hundred balls in succession. If you do, I'll give you one hundred dollars. For every ball under one hundred that you don't make, you give me five dollars."

Henry thought this over. It sounded like a good bet but, on the other hand, maybe it wasn't.

"How about going over that again?" Henry asked.

Mel was more thorough this tine. He explained with such patience that a man more sensitive than Henry would have been irritated.

"All right. Here is an example. The balls are racked. You shoot. And you call each shot. If you keep shooting without missing and go ahead and make one hundred balls in a row, I give you one hundred dollars. Now, let's say you make seventy-five balls and, on the seventy-sixth shot, you miss. That leaves twenty-five balls. Twenty-five balls at five dollars a ball is one hundred and twenty-five dollars. You give me one hundred and twenty-five dollars, understand it?"

Henry nodded. "Is there any time limit?"

"No."

To stall, Henry got a cigar from the showcase and lit it. This was a serious bet, and he wanted to think it over. He had put almost every cent he had into the poolroom. He had some money left, but he was going to need it until the poolroom started to pay off. To run a hundred balls in succession was easy enough, but under pressure--suppose he missed? However, if it was such a good bet. . .

"Tell you what I'll do, Mel. I'll make you the same bet."

"I'll take it." Mel said. He removed his coat but not his rose-tinted glasses. He began to try cue sticks for straightness by rolling them on the table. Before he found one that suited him, he had tried them all.

Mel broke the balls and began to shoot. He was the most cautious player Henry had seen in a lifetime of playing pool.

It was almost ridiculous the way he studied each shot. He sighted each ball down his cue stick before shooting, looked over all possibilities and always selected the easiest shot. After an hour of this slow, cautious play, he was finished. He had made the one hundred balls in succession.

Henry wrote a check for one hundred dollars and gave it to Mel.

"You can shoot pool all right." Henry said.

"Want to get even?"

"Same bet?"

"Same bet."

Prior to becoming a Mess Sergeant, Henry had been a cook. A service cook is on a day and off a day. On Henry's off day he had played pool. This twenty-five years of practice, combined with a good eye and a steady hand, had made him a master. He selected a cue stick and broke.

Henry ran the table easily, the balls heading for the pockets just like they had eyes. He wasn't a fast player, but he could figure his shots out three or four in advance and knew what he was doing at all times. By making his hundred balls in less than half the time that Mel had taken, he figured he had called the challenger's hand in addition to getting his money back.

Mel passed the check back to Henry.

"How about coming over to my place? Can you close up for awhile?"

"Sure."

The three men got into Jake's car and motored to the Southland Pool Hall on Slauson Avenue. On the way over, Jake twitched in the seat. He was supposed to get something out of this but didn't know if he was entitled to it.

"How about our bet, Mel? Did I win or not?"

"We both made a hundred balls without missing, didn't we? Of course you didn't win."

"Who'd you bet on, Jake? Me or Mel?" Henry asked.

"I bet on you, but I guess it didn't do me no good."

Henry was pleased. Jake parked in front of Mel's establishment, and they went inside. It was an improvement over Henry's little pool hall. There were six tables for straight pool and two for snooker. It was also a lot dirtier, but there were several men playing and a great many onlookers. Mel had an office in the back that also served as his living quarters. The three went into the office, and Mel flicked the switch on his hot plate to heat water for coffee.

"How do you like my little setup?" he asked Henry.

"You've got a nice place here."

"I hire a kid to rack balls. Full-time."

"Is that right?"

"I got a day man, but I always take over in the evening."

"You must take in quite a bit."

"I do all right." The preliminaries were now over, and Mel got down to the issue.

"Henry, I don't know you from Adam, and you don't know me. But both of us have seen each other shoot pool. And both of us have given up most of our life to learning how to shoot pool. Am I right?"

"So far.

"Up to the time I saw you I thought I was the best pool shot in Los Angeles, if not in the whole world."

"I always figured I was the best myself." Henry said.

"And I can see why you thought that." Mel rapidly clenched and unclenched his fingers. "A guy gets that way after awhile. No matter who you play, you always win and, after awhile, you think you're invincible."

"That's right. I beat everybody I ever played."

The two great men sat thoughtfully, thinking of their greatness. Jake sat blinking at them, feeling the tenseness in the close room.

Mel broke the solemnity of the moment by clearing his throat.

"Henry. I've got to find out who the best is."

"I do, too."

"We could play here, but I don't think it would be fair for either of us to be under pressure from a bunch of kibitzer's."

"We can play at my place, and I can lock the door."

"Jake can be the referee, that is, unless you have somebody else in mind?"

"Jake will be fine," turning to Jake, "if it's all right with you?"

"Glad to," Jake said, and they left the office without waiting for the coffee.

On the drive back to Henry's poolroom, the details were worked out. Whoever made the greatest number of balls (without missing) in a two-hour time limit was the winner. The winner was also to win the loser's poolroom. Henry was well-satisfied with the bet believing himself to be the best shot. He realized, too, that Mel's poolroom was better than his modest establishment, but he thought that Mel's ego forced him to put up the larger odds. And the two-hour time limit was really a break as he remembered the slowness of Mel's playing.

Jake took his duty as referee seriously. He was going to see a game that would give him story material for many years to come. He pulled the shades down and switched the lights on above the two pool tables. He racked both sets of balls very tightly and placed a high chair in such a manner that both players could be observed.

Henry passed the talcum powder to Mel to pour over his cue stick and was thanked very kindly. He placed fresh cue chalk on each table. They were ready.

Jake watched the sweep-hand on his wristwatch and held his right arm over his head. "Go!" he said and dropped his arm. They both broke at the same time.

Henry had always been a methodical player and had never strived for speed, but now he tried because of the time limit. But he was wasting his time. Mel was a different man altogether. His cautious, careful, studied manner was gone, and he raced around the table like a madman. He barely paused between shots, made seemingly impossible combination shots, then rushed around the table to line up on his cue ball again. By the time Henry had made fifty balls, Mel had made a hundred. When Henry had made a hundred, Mel had made three hundred.

Henry replaced his cue stick in the wall rack without waiting for the time limit. He got his lease from the cash register, handed it to Jake, unlocked the door and left.

He cut across the street to the New York Café, took the FRY COOK WANTED sign out of the window, gave it to the owner and was promptly hired. This was at four-thirty in the evening. Just in time to get things ready for the dinner rush hour. ◉

# Some Lucky License

THE FIRST hour of waiting was bad enough; then I ran out of cigarettes. Any second now I would be called into the committee room where three serious members of the Board of Inquiry—the Honorable Police Commissioner J.D. Mathews, presiding—were determining my fate, my future, my life's work. I simply could not chance going downstairs to the cigarette machine. Instead, I tried to picture in my mind the order of brands in the machine from right to left across the glass-faced panel. I discovered to my surprise that I was unable to make an intelligent guess. Some detective you are, I thought in wry disgust; so much for your keenly developed powers of observation.

At this moment Chief Garland Carey ("Gar" to his friends, and I was purported to be one of them) entered the anteroom, lumbered over to the closed double doors leading into the chamber of deliberations, and paused with his hand on the doorknob to look at me. I rose, of course, as he entered, and the movement made it almost impossible for him not to acknowledge my presence. But he did the next thing to it. With his right hand on the knob, holding a slip of yellow paper in his left hand, he looked through me and said, "Sergeant." With that, he was through the doors. They closed quietly behind him.

Not "Bill" or "William" or "Hartigan," but the impersonal word "sergeant." And what was written on the little slip of paper?

It was my fault that Chief Carey was wearing his dress uniform this morning instead of his preferred costume, the sober charcoal gray suit. And, with silver eagles shining on his shoulders, he was more self-consciously my commander than he was my friend; or my supervisor, to whom a detective-sergeant addresses oral and written reports. I could sense that he didn't like me very well at the moment.

I still didn't know what was written on the slip of paper. I was tired of waiting, so I ran downstairs to the cigarette machine. I was back up the stairs, taking them three at a time, arriving in the antechamber just as Gar came out of the committee room. I held out the pack.

"Thanks." He took a cigarette, lighted up, turned his head away from me, expelled a thin column of smoke, and said, "The Brett kid died."

These four words changed the picture and the channel. Section 1277 of the Criminal Code was no longer an abstract paragraph to be learned and forgotten during one's stint at the police academy. It was a real live issue and, depending upon its interpretation by the board, could now be applied to me. In a way, however, I was glad that the Brett kid had died; now the issue would be resolved one way or another, once and for all.

Succinctly, Section 1277 states that any police officer who fatally shoots six persons—in line of duty or no—will be separated from the force, and will not be reinstated. The section is known unofficially among policemen as the "trigger-happy" rule. The mental processes by which the drafters of the Code arrived at the cut-off number of six defy reason. The idea behind Section 1277 was that if a police officer shot and killed six men he had somehow violated the laws of "chance" and he was therefore "trigger-happy." As an incipient killer, he should not be retained on the force. Logically, one can shoot a good many holes in the rule. Every time a police officer shoots and kills a man in the line of duty he must be cleared by a board of inquiry anyway, so technically, as long as he has been cleared each time, as I had been cleared on the first four men I had shot and wounded fatally in the line of duty, what difference did it make if I shot and killed ten, twenty, or even a hundred men? But the squeeze that put Section 1277 into the Code was determined by public and political pressure, not by the prescribed policeman's duty. On the other hand, perhaps a statute like this was needed; if not for me, perhaps for some policeman who was truly trigger-happy.

Now, with the death of the second kid, Tommy Brett, the three-man board deciding my future was being faced with a disturbing technicality that made their decision even more difficult than it had been before. If they followed the Code religiously, my case did not come under Section 1277. I had shot and killed Joseph E. Craig; I had *not* shot Tommy Brett. Brett had been a passenger in the stolen car being driven by Joseph E. Craig, and his death had been caused by the accident that followed, after the driver-less car zoomed into a giant elm shading the lawn in front of 1507 West Crescent Drive. Craig had died instantly when I shot him through the left temple. Brett had still been alive, without any bullets in him, when we pulled him from the wreck, and he had been kept alive for five dramatic days in the hospital—choosing an even more dramatic moment to cash out. The news of his demise in the hospital was the information Chief Gar Carey had scribbled on the note he had taken into the board before I dashed downstairs for cigarettes.

Would they or would they not count Tommy Brett as my sixth victim? If they did, I was through as a policeman. Certainly, mine had been a line of duty shot. We had chased Craig for fully five miles at high speeds; the fear-maddened youth in the stolen car was endangering the lives of countless innocent citizens; and I had fired two warning shots before sending the third bullet into his temple. But I knew, and so did Chief Carey, that the board was going to charge me with both deaths. Such is the irony of being an overly conscientious police officer. The citizens, those I had tried to protect, were clamoring for my badge; the newspapers had recapitulated all of my previous fatal shootings, and they were calling me William "Trigger-Happy" Hartigan. This pressure was being felt by the board of inquiry, and Brett's death made their decision tougher.

Joseph E. Craig had been fourteen years old when I shot him, and young Tommy Brett, his equally guilty passenger, had been thirteen. My fifteen years on the force, my excellent record of arrests, and my good name were being weighed against the ages of the two teenaged victims, not against their crime.

At any rate, being something of a fatalist, I decided to hope for the best. And the best I could come up with was that I would now be forced into half-retirement with about a hundred and fifty dollars a month, thanks to my fifteen years of honorable service on the force. Not only was one fifty a big comedown from my monthly salary of six hundred, but if I were forced into retirement under the trigger-happy law, I wouldn't be able to get another policeman's job anywhere. All I knew was police work. Somehow, I had to hang on for the next ten years to get my regular retirement pay of two hundred fifty a month for twenty-five years of service.

"Well?" Gar said, breaking into my dismal reverie. "Haven't you anything to say—about the Brett kid?"

I shrugged. "It's a tough break for me; what else should I say? Do you want me to say I'm sorry for him? He was a thief, just as much of a thief as Craig, so now there are two less thieves in town instead of one less."

"You talk to the board in that tone of voice and you'll be bounced out right on your ear."

"Don't kid me, Gar. I'm going to be bounced anyway illegally, but politically, and you know it."

"Maybe not. I just gave them an alternative way out. Play along with them when they call you in. Show some humility and contriteness whether you feel it or not, and they might just accept my suggestion. Lieutenant Morris did a brilliant job defending your record; so his recommendation, together with mine, should carry some weight with the board."

"What's the alternative?"

"If they accept it, you'll be told. Just wait and see. But I gave them a way out."

I nodded. "Don't worry, Gar," I said, softening. "I know how to perform for them. This is my fifth stellar appearance." I grinned.

"I know," he said grimly. "And if they take my suggestion, it will be your last."

Chief Gar Carey's so-called alternative was accepted. I wasn't keen on it, but the ugly moment of truth I had faced in the waiting room more or less forced me to accept the board's decision with an outward show of good grace. I even went so far as to thank the members of the board of inquiry.

I was still a sergeant, but I was no longer a plainclothes detective. I drew a sergeant's pay, and I was given an administrative position as "police force" jailer, a job that did not require me to wear a gun; in fact, I was now forbidden to wear a gun. I hated the job. There was nothing for me to do, and I had too much rank to be a mere assistant to the official city jailer, Mr. Malcolm. I was merely there, in Mr. Malcolm's office, in a "made" position.

I sat at a desk in Mr. Malcolm's office from eight to five. A precedent had been set for this sinecure several years before when an aging patrolman with arthritic feet had been allowed to sit quietly in the city jailer's office for three years to sweat out his retirement. Gar, playing on my good record, had sold the idea to the board.

However, I'll say this for Mr. Malcolm: he ran an efficient, no-foolishness lockup. He had everything down to a tight methodical schedule, and the simplicity of his system made the prisoners fear him. His impersonality toward the prisoners was deadly. He counted them six times daily, including Saturdays and Sundays, counted them as if they were cards in a newly opened deck; he wasn't concerned with their faces, only their backs and the accuracy of the count. Except for the trusty, Thomas "Mary Ellen" Wolgast, who cleaned the offices downstairs and waited upon us, I doubt if Mr. Malcolm knew any of the prisoners by name.

I had no paperwork to do. When I volunteered to help Mr. Malcolm with some of his, he merely shook his head. "No, there ain't that much."

A few days later, I offered to count the prisoners for him. He thought that over, and pulled on his nose. "No, Sergeant Hartigan," he said, finally. "It would upset my routine. I'd rather do it myself."

Mr. Malcolm needed the excuse of counting prisoners to get away from his desk several times a day. Most of the time we merely sat in the cramped little office, smoking and drinking coffee. We had tried to talk to each other at first, but neither of us was much for small talk. The trusty, "Mary Ellen" Wolgast, brought us coffee, cake, sandwiches, or ran errands, whenever we hollered for him, and the turnkeys, all of them well past middle age, needed no supervision.

The turnkeys were ex-police officers or ex-deputies. Obviously, Mr. Malcolm had selected them with great care. They were as silent and colorless as Mr. Malcolm himself. They did their work quietly, and treated the prisoners firmly but fairly. I snooped around a little, naturally, but none of the turnkeys was violating any of Mr. Malcolm's rules. The prisoners who had money on the books were allowed to send out for cigarettes, candy, and restaurant meals, and the turnkey who made the outside trip charged the flat rate of fifty cents for every delivery, whether it was a pack of cigarettes or a hamburger.

After three weeks of sitting in the city jailer's office doing nothing, I gained seven pounds. The following Monday morning I called on Chief Gar Carey in his office.

He grinned as I entered. "Morning, Bill. I expected to see you sooner or later."

"This isn't working out," I said bitterly. "It's worse than being a prisoner."

He nodded. "I know it's tough on an active man, Bill, just sitting over there. But you'll simply have to sweat it out until things blow over. The public has a short memory, and after a year or so—"

"A year or so!"

"I'd say at least a year. But if you're willing to wait it out, I'll be able to get you a rehearing, and—"

I shook my head. "Gar, I can't do it. If I sit in that office for a full year I'll be as stir-simple as Mr. Malcolm."

Gar shrugged. "Okay. You were officially cleared on the Craig and Brett shooting—"

"Craig only," I quickly reminded him. "Brett died as the result of an automobile accident."

He ignored my interruption. "—so you're perfectly justified to resign from the force at any time. You aren't quitting under fire, and if you want to leave I'll give you an excellent recommendation if you want to work on another police force in some other city."

"Thanks. Thanks a lot," I said dryly. "If I resign, what happens to my retirement?"

He raised his shaggy gray eyebrows in mock surprise. "You lose it, of course, as you very well know. You only get the half-retirement pittance when you're forced out because of circumstances beyond your control, on a line of duty basis, naturally."

"Fifteen good years down the drain, or another ten years sitting in the city jailer's office. This is some choice to give a man with my proven ability."

Gar's face reddened. "I did you a favor, and you grabbed it because you damned well had to! Don't come sniveling to me because you're drawing six hundred bucks a month for sitting out your time."

"I didn't mean it that way, Gar, and you don't have any call to get hot at me, either. I just thought . . ."

"All right, then, face the facts. In another year, I can probably get you a rehearing and a reinstatement on your old job. If you're turned down the first time, you'll get back on active duty the second or third year. These things blow over eventually; you have to give them time."

"Sure, Gar. I understand. Thanks for seeing me this morning, and thanks for the time."

In the slow days that followed, my mind worked overtime in an effort to find a way out. But the restrictions imposed by the board, I soon learned, went beyond the simple denial of my carrying a pistol. I called the commandant of the police academy, volunteering to teach a course to police cadets. He was delighted. An hour later he called me back to tell me he was sorry, but he had a full complement of instructors and couldn't use me after all. I got the idea. The board, as well as Chief Carey, wanted me out of sight and mind for the months it would take the public to forget about me; and they didn't consider me a good example for rookie cops, either.

There was only one sure way out of my problem, and that was to become a hero. And the only way I could become a hero was to make a spectacular arrest of some kind without, of course, having a pistol or firing a shot. But the regulations were particularly strict in this area; any policeman who made an arrest when he was unarmed would be suspended immediately, and he would then meet a board to see if he had enough marbles in his head to be retained on the force.

Then I got stubborn. I decided to do my time just like any other prisoner with a long stretch, one day at a time.

To keep my mind from going dull, I worked the daily chess problem in the newspaper each morning, and studied the rest of the day in preparation for the annual exam coming up for lieutenant. I was eligible to take the exam, and the idea pleased me. If I made the highest score on the exam—and I had a good chance, with nothing to do but study all day— the promotion board would be shaken up when they had to refuse a promotion to the brightest member of the force, a highly trained police officer who was doing absolutely nothing for his monthly salary. The irony of the situation cheered me up considerably, and each morning I arrived at the office eager to hit the books.

This was about as far as I could go in making a break for myself without any outside help. But when the real break came, I very nearly missed it.

At nine thirty A.M. I told Mary Ellen, the trusty, to bring me a ham sandwich and a cup of coffee from the kitchen upstairs. Mr. Malcolm ordered black coffee only. I had figured out the final move on my chess board by the time Mary Ellen returned with the tray. Two bites later my teeth bit into a piece of paper. I pulled out the slip of paper and tossed it into my wastebasket, making a mental note to chew Mary Ellen out later for being so careless when he made my sandwich. Not until I had finished the sandwich and started on the coffee did I realize that Mary Ellen would not be likely to make a mistake of that nature. He was too neat to leave a piece of paper on the ham.

Watching Mr. Malcolm out of the corner of my eye, I dumped my ashtray into the wastebasket, retrieving the piece of paper at the same time. Holding it in my lap, I read the faintly

printed message: SGT. HARTIGAN, IMPORTANT! MEET
ME DOWNSTAIRS JOHN DURING 11 A.M. COUNT.

The note wasn't signed, but it had to be from Mary Ellen
Wolgast; he was the only prisoner excused from Mr. Malcolm's count.

At five minutes to eleven, Mr. Malcolm and I left the office
together. I headed down the corridor to the men's room; he
had his clipboard, and took the self-operated elevator upstairs
to make his count. Wolgast was already in the latrine, swish-
ing a damp mop over the vinyl-tiled floor.

"Intrigue, Mary Ellen?" I asked.

He didn't smile; he was too frightened. Chewing nervously
on his lip, he leaned the mop handle against the wall and, with
difficulty, fished a folded twenty dollar bill out of his pocket.
He handed the bill to me and said, "I'm in a jam, Sergeant
Hartigan, a real jam."

"This isn't supposed to be a bribe, is it?" I grinned.

"No, sir. Not to you—to me; and I don't want any part of
it! Bert Gulick gave it to me to—to help him escape." Close to
tears, he ran his long fingers through his lank blond hair.

"Go ahead," I encouraged him, "tell me about it. And
don't worry about Gulick finding out you told me." I was
interested, keenly interested.

Wolgast nodded, and his bulging Adam's apple bobbed
convulsively for more air. "I didn't know what else to do. Bert
Gunlock's got a good plan worked out that will get him out
of here tonight, but he couldn't get away without my help. I
don't want to get involved and lose my good time. I only got
forty days to go," he whined.

"Get on with it," I said impatiently.

"But if you catch him, he'll beat me up. I know he will!"

"No," I shook my head, "I guarantee you that he won't
touch you. That's a promise."

"I don't have any choice, anyway. You know the corridor
from the elevator to the back door of the kitchen on the
second floor? After supper at night I usually get a volunteer to
help me bring down the trays. If nobody volunteers I have to
wash 'em myself, but I usually get somebody because it gets

a man away from the tank for an hour, and the cook always gives us a sandwich or something to take with us when we finish up. Anyway, the wire-mesh screen at the end of the corridor by the fire escape is only set in there with screws, and for the last three nights Bert Gunlock's been helping me, loosening up the screws while we wait for the elevator. Tonight, when we come down, I'm supposed to tell the cook I couldn't get any volunteer to help me. But Gulick'll come down with me, take off the screen and go down the back fire escape. He'll have at least an hour's advantage, but they'll know I had to lie and—"

"Never mind about that. You're in the clear already. What time do you bring down the dirty trays?"

"Well, we bring them down on the cart about six, but it'll only take Gulick a second to take out the screen and raise the window. The screws are just barely in there now."

"Doesn't a turnkey come down with you?"

"No. We're checked out upstairs when we get in the elevator. Without the elevator key, the elevator won't come down to the first floor; it's locked and set only to go to the second, so nobody needs to go to the kitchen with us. The turnkey, Mr. Conroy, has the key, and he unlocks the elevator when the cook goes home at night."

"Okay, Wolgast, I get the setup. And don't worry about it. I'll take care of things from now on. Just go ahead as you've planned it, and say nothing to Bert Gulick." I unfolded the twenty. "This twenty, and another one just like it, will be put on the books for you to draw on." I grinned. "If you spend a dollar a day, you can be flat broke when you're released."

"If Gulick ever finds out that I—"

"I told you not to worry. Your name won't be mentioned. Just go ahead with it, and keep your mouth shut."

At five o'clock I left the office, went to my car in the back lot, and got my pistol out of the glove compartment.

It felt nice and heavy in my hand. I smoked a cigarette, waved goodbye to Mr. Malcolm as he spluttered out of the lot on his ancient motorcycle, and looked through the windshield at the lovely darkening sky. It wouldn't be completely dark until well after six but, thanks to a low overcast of purple rain clouds, dusk would be darker than it usually was at this time of the year.

There was more than one way for me to handle the situation. For publicity purposes it would be much better for me to apprehend Gulick in the act of escaping than it would be simply to plug up the escape route and prevent a "possible" breakout. After I picked Bert Gulick up at the bottom of the ladder, I could then march him around the front of the building and make a dramatic entrance with him. My picture would be in the morning newspapers. There would be a photo of me around back, pointing up at the fire escape and the raised window and, with luck, there might even be a posed shot of me holding my pistol on Gulick in the downstairs outer office. The fact that I had picked him up without shooting him would carry a lot of weight with the board.

I was quite pleased with myself when I took my position in the shadowy recessed delivery doorway beneath the back fire escape. I didn't worry about Bert Gulick; he was a wife beater, not a strong-arm boy. Although he might be armed with a knife, he certainly didn't have a gun. I hoped he had a knife; it would be that much better for me when I took it away from him.

I didn't hear the noise of the screen being removed, but I heard the squeal of the tight window as he pushed it up. The rusty iron steps rattled and shook as Gulick backed down them as noiselessly as he could. I waited until he was midway between the second floor and the ground floor before stepping out of the dark doorway.

"Freeze, Gulick," I said sharply. "This is Hartigan."

He froze all right, not moving a muscle, with his back to me; and he was so frightened by my name that he clung there trembling and rattling the metal ladder. All I had to do now was to back him down a step at a time, put the cuffs on him, and march him around the building to the front entrance. With a spectacular arrest to my credit, I'd be back on my old job within a few weeks, doing what I wanted to do.

And what did I really want to do?

The realization hit me for the first time. I honestly hadn't known it until this very minute. I wanted to shoot and kill men like Gulick; that's what I really wanted to do! And with Bert Gulick as Number Six, I would be retired on a hundred and fifty a month for life. Why not Gulick? Why should I wait for someone else at a later date? Sooner or later I was going to get a sixth victim anyway. And because Gulick was my last free one, the last man I would be able to shoot legally before I lost my shooting license, my hand was never steadier as I squeezed the trigger. ◉

# A Matter of Taste

THE CAFÉ was called MOM'S, and it was about three blocks away from the downtown public library. I walked in and ordered a bowl of chile and a cup of coffee, black. There were eight stools at the counter, and a sign on the wall stating: WE CAN FEED 8,000,000 PEOPLE—8 AT A TIME.

My companions at the counter were an old hook-nosed man, wearing a filthy nylon windbreaker, and an equally old woman, who resembled Queen Mary. The cook-and-counterman was a thin, quick fellow with a glabrous skull, and quivering, mottled hands. He and the old man with the windbreaker were apparently old friends, because they kept talking to each other all the time I was in there.

The cook said:

"There was a guy come in here Monday morning, said he just got out of jail. They'd kept him over the weekend, and didn't feed him good. He ordered himself up a dozen scrambled eggs, four sides of ham, two bowls of grits and coffee. I just stood there lookin' at him, of course, till he put a ten-spot down on the counter. Well, I fixed it all up for him, and he ate every bit of it. And to top it off, he drank down a quart of milk."

"That's the way it is," said Hooknose. "No matter how much a man gets to eat in jail, the day he gets out he's always hungry."

"How'd you like a steady diet of swordfish?" I said.

The two men and the old lady looked at me.

"I got vagged once in L.A. back in the 'thirties," I continued, "and I was given three days in the Lincoln Heights jail. This was about the time that Zane Grey, the Western writer, was fishing off Catalina Island. He caught a bunch of swordfish and gave them all to the city, and for three days, morning, noon, and night, we ate nothing but boiled swordfish."

"That must've been pretty rough," the counterman said.

"They can't arrest a man for vagrancy now," Hooknose said. "It's unconstitutional."

"I know," I said, "but they could then, and it was rough. I was lucky though, because I only had to eat swordfish for three days. Those other guys who were still in there had to eat it for about ten more days."

The woman with the Queen Mary hat cleared her throat. "You would think," she said, "that a brilliant writer like Zane Grey would have better sense than to give all that fish to prisoners."

"I don't know," Hooknose said. "What with the depression and all, he probably thought he was doin' a good deed. A lot of those rich guys who mean well just don't use their heads. I remember one night—I dinged a guy in the street for some money. I wasn't hungry or nothing, I just had a few friends coming over to my room that night and I wanted to get some more dough for gin. This guy insisted that I eat, and he took me into a restaurant and ordered me up a big meal. I ate it, all of it, but it danged near killed me. But I didn't want to hurt the guy's feelings, you see. He thought he was doin' a 'good deed.' "

"You did right to eat the meal," I said.

"Hell, that's all I could do."

The old lady had finished eating now, and she lighted a Salem 100 Light. She waggled gloved fingers at the cook. "I don't usually say this," she said, "but that was the best hamburger I ever ate. In fact, I think that's the first time I ever seen one fixed that way."

The cook shrugged. "It's easy. I just smear mayonnaise on the bun before I toast it on the grill. That's what's called 'marination.' All good cooks know how to do it, but most of 'em just don't care."

"All I know," she said, "it sure makes a good hamburger."

She paid him and left.

After the door banged shut behind her, the cook laughed. "I sure wish I knew her name."

"Why?" Hooknose asked.

"Because she'll be back tomorrow or the next day askin'

for credit, that's why. I never seen it to fail. If somebody says something nice to you, they want something. She's gonna be fooled though, because I don't give no credit. If I gave credit to everybody who asked for it, I'd be broke in a week."

"Maybe she meant it," Hooknose suggested.

"How long you think I been behind a counter? She either wants credit or she's tryin' to cover up something." He was clearing away the old lady's dirty dishes. "Here it is! She burnt a hole in this here plastic plate. See?" He showed the brown spot to Hooknose, and then to me.

"That's it, all right," Hooknose said, nodding. "She was tryin' to pass it off by giving you a compliment."

"Of course," the cook said. "A hamburger is a hamburger. None of these people can fool me. I've been in this racket too long." He took my empty bowl. "Want some more coffee?"

"No, thanks," I said. "How much do I owe you?"

"A dollar for the chile, a quarter for the coffee, plus tax. . ."

I paid him, and headed for the door. He called to me. "How was the chile?"

"I've had better," I said, "and a hellova lot cheaper." I started down the street toward the library. I had decided to look up the definition of "marination." ◉

The following is the only existing material from an unfinished novel
Charles Willeford ultimately abandoned in 1975:

## The First Five in Line. . .

### PART ONE

*"Them that dies'll be the lucky ones."*
—Long John Silver

MEMO: (Confidential)
FROM: Doremus Jessup, Vice-President for Programming,
NBN
TO: Russell Haxby, Director of Creative and Special Programs
SUBJECT: "The First Five in Line. . ."

Dear Russ, this is merely an informal memo, on the eve of
your departure for Miami, to wish you Godspeed and to mention some other assorted shit that has been on my mind.

I'm not, for example, satisfied with the program title, even
though, at the present moment, it seems to fit, in an honest
way, with the theme and projected format. The ellipsis following the title implies that others will eventually join the line and
that this experiment is only the beginning of a long line of various titilating programs to attract more jaded viewers, but I'm
still not certain whether the ellipsis is a valid addition or not.
Do not waver in your thoughts for a better alternate title. We
(the Board and I) are very receptive to a title change, and you
should submit periodic alternates right up until deadline.

The Board is quite excited about the entire concept. In
ancient Rome it was possible for theatergoers to see actual
fornication onstage (including rapes), actual crucifixions and
ritual murders (usually with unwilling Xian actors), and it
does not seem unlikely to me that, in the not so distant future,

we shall see planned murders on our home screens as well as the unplanned, i.e., Ruby shooting Oswald, the colonel shooting the prisoner in Saigon, the female newscaster's on-the-air suicide in Sarasota, etc. And NBN may very well start the trend with our innovative *TFFIL*. . . The design is already apparent, with from 30 to 35 simulated murders per night on the tube, as if every network were preparing the viewer's minds for the real thing. The latest estimates indicate that the average viewer, by the time he reaches 65, will have seen 400,000 simulated murders and maimings on TV, discounting the murders and maimings he also has seen in movies. I saw the handwriting on the bloody wall as far back as *The Execution of Private Slovik*. The huge audience for this show was predicated on the sure knowledge that Slovik would, indeed, be executed before the end of the program. Such knowledge was foreshadowed by the revealing title, even for those viewers unfamiliar with Huie's book. That's one of the reasons I'm not too happy with *The First Five in Line*. . . as a title. *In line for what?* a viewer may very well ask, so keep thinking about an alternative.

But I also agree with you that real TV murders must be led up to gradually, if we are ever to see them at all. To jump right in with them without prolonged and careful audience preparation, even though the actors—victim and killer—were to sign releases, would still not absolve the network from the many legal problems that would surround such programs, at least initially. When the time is right, we shall have them, of course, and it will always be in keeping for NBN to pioneer in the most dramatic and exciting programming we can provide for our loyal viewers. As a possible title, however, just off the top of my head, for such a show in the distant future, what about *Involuntary Departures*?

But back to *The First Five in Line*. . . : The Board concluded that it must run for the full thirteen (13) weeks, not for just the six (6) weeks you and I had planned. This means, Russell, that you're going to have to come up with a good many innovative ideas to stretch out the series and without any watering down of the entertainment values. Suspense, of course, is the key—but then I don't need to tell you how to do your job. Money is no problem; don't worry about the money. We will have the sponsors, all right; and it will also mean extra money for the five volunteers even though they are not to know about *any* money in advance, which would screw up the statistical nature of the selection, as you know. At any rate, the go-go decision for a full 13 weeks puts us right up in there in the Emmy running for a new series, whereas a six-week miniseries would not. And I think we *do* have a No. One Emmy idea.

You will have to handle Harry Thead, the station manager of WOOZ, with kid gloves—a last minute reminder of this requirement. The program idea was his in the first place, which is why we have to originate from Miami instead of St. Louis, even though the latter was a much better location demographically-wise. But Harry Thead had no objections to you as the overall creative director, just so long as he could play an active behind-the-scenes part in the production. He wants the series credits, which he needs, and you may tell him that he will be on the credits network-wide as "Associate Producer for Miami." The credit is rather meaningless, but it will look good on the crawl, and I think he'll be happy with the title. The main thing is to keep Harry Thead informed at all times of what you are doing, so that he'll have the right answers for the WOOZ owners. You could also use Harry as your coordinator with the Miami office of Baumgarten, Bates and Williams, who will handle the national advertising. They are also very excited about the commercial possibilities.

Harry Thead did not have to come to us with his idea, even though WOOZ is an affiliate. He could have run the show as a local Miami show, which would have blown the idea for the network. So we have a lot to thank Harry Thead for. When he asks questions, answer them; he's behind us and the new program 110%, and he respects your creative genius.

I wish you had been present when I sold the idea to the Board. I won't bore you with it except to say that some of the reactionary reactions were predictable, ranging as they did from pretended shock to forced indignation; but we soon settled into the specifics, and your overall tentative plan (except for the addition of another seven weeks, which reveals their true enthusiasm) was accepted *in toto* without any major modifications. Mr. Braden, who was in favor of Miami over St. Louis all along, pointed out that the high crime rate in Miami has prepared the local audience there for violence better than St. Louis (excepting East St. Louis, naturally). St. Louis is quite religious-oriented, as Mr. Braden mentioned, whereas Miami has only a few organized religious groups, i.e., Hare Krishna, Unitarian, and a few other sects. The former isn't taken seriously in Dade and Broward counties, and the latter discredited itself with Miami businessmen several years ago when they—the Unitarians—protested putting up a cross on the courthouse lawn at Christmastime.

Another update factor, which comes as good news from a statistical standpoint: Unemployment in Miami has increased 3.7% since Harry Thead's original demographic study which, in turn, increases the predictable volunteers in Miami from 6.9 to 7.1. If I was apprehensive about anything, it was the 6.9 predictability; but the larger range to 7.1 insures the required five volunteers. (The new 7.1 figure includes the overlap into Broward County as well as Dade County.)

You, your staff, and the five volunteers, when you have them, will all stay at the Los Piños Motel. The third floor on the wing facing the bay has been reserved, as well as the third floor conference room. The motel is less than three blocks away from the 89th Street Causeway location of WOOZ. Billy Elkhart, the unit manager, is already down there, of course, and he has everything under control including rental cars. Phone him before you leave Kennedy, and he'll pick you up at the Miami airport.

One last item, and it is not unimportant: Harry Thead is a Freemason, with all 32 degrees. Before you leave the city, pick up a blue stone Mason ring (blue is the 4th degree, I think) and wear it while you're down there. Stop by Continuity and ask Jim Preston (I know he's a Mason) to teach you the secret handshake that they use. It will help you to gain rapport with Harry Thead (call it insurance), even though he'll be coopera-tive anyway.

From time to time, send me tape cassettes about your progress and don't worry about the budget. Simply tell Billy Elkhart what you need and let him worry about the budget. He has the habit of thrift anyway, and if he goes over, it'll be his ass not yours. You have enough pressure creative-wise; I don't want you worrying about money. *The First Five in Line. . .* is undoubtedly the greatest concept for a television series ever to hit the air in modern times, Russell, and we (the Board and I) have every confidence in you as the creative force behind it.

Good luck, and Godspeed!

ls/DJ


## VIOLETTE WINTERS

Ms. Violette Winters, 36, had short, slightly bowed legs, a ridiculously wide pelvis and tiny, narrow, hurting feet. She wore size 5-AAA shoes—slit at the big toe with a razor blade to relieve the pressure on her bunions—usually nurse-white with rippled rubber soles, and cotton support hose. So far she did not have varicose veins, but she lived in dread of their purplish emergence, and she hoped that the white cotton support hose would hold them in abeyance for as long as possible; but she was fully aware that varicose veins were the eventual reward of the full-time professional waitress. Violette's broad, blubbery hips and thick thighs—even with her girdle stretched over them—were mushy to the touch, and she bruised easily without healing quickly. Her ankles and calves, however, were trim. In her low-heeled white nurse's shoes, she was 5'4" but appeared to be taller because of her narrow-waisted torso, petite breasts (with inverted nipples), long neck and the huge mass of curly marmalade hair, which she wore with a rat piled high on top of her head. When she worked her hair was covered by a black, cobwebby net, which darkened her curls to an off-shade of dried blood. Her cerulean eyes were deep-set, well-guarded by knobby, bony brows and thick brown eyebrows. Any time a male got within seven feet of her person, her eyes narrowed to oriental dimensions. Her face had been pretty when she was a young girl, and she would have been handsome still if it were not for the harsh frown lines across her broad forehead and the deeply grooved diagonals that ran from the wings of her nose to the corners of her turned down mouth. Her *retrousse* nose was splattered with tiny pointillist freckles.

Violette always moved swiftly at her tasks around the restaurants where she worked—rarely made a mistake in addition—and her large white fluttering hands could deftly carry up to six cups of coffee on saucers without spilling a drop. A highly skilled waitress, when the time came for her to quit a job, every manager she had ever worked for regretted her departure. By all rights Violette should have made more money in tips than the other waitresses, if efficiency was a factor, but she was the kind of woman (and men knew this, as if by instinct) who would accept a miserly ten percent tip without making a fuss. Shrewder middle-aged men, after taking a sharp look at her, left no tip at all. As a consequence, she made much less in tips than the other waitresses.

At this midway point in her life—which frequently, at thirty-six, seems even more than a midway point to women than it does to men—Violette had had three husbands so far. By her standards, by anyone's standards, they had been losers to a man.

Her first husband, Tommy, was the same boy she went steady with all of the way through junior and senior high in Greenwood, Mississippi. They had moved in with Tommy's parents after getting married upon graduation from high school but, three months later, Tommy left Greenwood with a carnival that was passing through town, and no one had ever heard from him again. Two years after his departure, Violette got a divorce after giving Tommy notice in the classified section of the Greenwood paper for three weeks in a row.

At that time and in a less than liberal region, it had been embarrassing for a divorced woman to live in Greenwood, so Violette added the extra "te" to her name and moved to Memphis. She obtained a job as a roller-skating carhop at the Witch Stand.

After only three months on the job she was hit by a red M.G. that pulled into the lot at 55 miles per hour. Even so she would have been able to dodge the M.G. okay, the manager told the police (Violette was a terrific skater), but she had tried to save a tray full of cheeseburgers, double fries and two double choc-malts at the same time she tried to make good her escape from the vehicle.

During her stay in the hospital, Violette fell in love with an alcoholic named Bubba Winters who was recovering from double pneumonia. Bubba had passed out in a cold rain down by the levee and had almost died from exposure before being discovered by an early morning fisherman. They were married two days after their release from the hospital, and Violette went back to work—this time as a waitress at the Blue Goose Café—still wearing a cast on her left leg. She had to pay off both hospital bills and support them both as well, because Bubba's old boss at the Regroovy Tire Center claimed that Bubba, with his weak chest and all, wasn't strong enough to change tires all day.

To show her love for Bubba, Violette tried to drink with him at night when her work day was over, but she didn't have the head for it. Bubba, who had learned to drink in the Marines where he had served three years out of his four-year hitch in Olongapo on Luzon, had a great capacity for gin. In addition to ugly hangovers, Violette awoke one morning to discover that she had a tattoo on her right forearm, a tattoo she had assented to woozily the night before to show her devotion to Bubba. In addition to a tiny red heart pierced with a dark blue dagger, there was a stern motto in blue block letters below the heart: DEATH BEFORE DISHONOR. The twin to Violette's tattoo—although it was slightly larger, both heart and lettering—was on Bubba's right forearm and had been there since his first overnight pass to San Diego from Boot Camp. Somehow the tattoo looked right on Bubba, but it looked a little funny on Violette's forearm; and because the Blue Goose patrons made remarks about it all the time, she was forced to wear long-sleeved blouses to work. She never drank again.

When Bubba's unemployment checks ran out, and Violette was unable to keep him in gin because of the exorbitant doctor and hospital bills, so did Bubba. When Violette finished paying off her debts, she moved to Jacksonville, Florida. She didn't want to risk the possibility that Bubba might come back to Memphis.

Violette retained Bubba's surname, however, after divorcing her third husband—a civil service warehouseman (G-S 3) in the Jacksonville Naval District—because she had never gotten around to divorcing Bubba Winters before she married him. The warehouseman, Gunter Haas, who didn't drink or smoke, was a compulsive gambler. Every two weeks, when he got paid, he lost his money in the regular warehouse crap game before coming home to Violette. Violette, who worked as a waitress at Smitty's Beef House in downtown Jax, rarely had two dimes to rub together all of the time she was illegally married to warehouseman Haas.

One night—a pay night—after Haas had lost all of his pay, he brought three of his fellow warehousemen home with him at 1:00 A.M. to show them Violette's tattoo. Unbelievers, they had foolishly bet Haas five bucks apiece that his wife did not have a tattoo on her forearm. She showed them the tattoo so Haas could collect his winnings, but the next day she had left Haas and Jacksonville for Miami on the Greyhound bus. Except for his low I.Q. and penchant for gambling, Haas hadn't been a bad husband, as husbands go; but the insensitivity to her person in bringing three men into her bedroom, and her with just a nighty on, had been too much for her. Besides, as she wrote her married sister back in Greenwood, "we were only married in name only. Legally, I'm still married to Mr. Winters, even though I'll never love anyone as much as I loved Tommy."

Three sorry marriages to three losers had made Violette wary of romance. She suspected, wisely, that she could fall in love again and that she was susceptible to losers. So she solved her problem by staying away from men altogether except in line of duty as a waitress. Gradually, week by week, Violette was finally building a little nest egg for herself, depositing ten dollars of her tips each week in the First Federal Savings Bank & Trust Company of Miami.

In Miami Violette had found a job almost immediately in the El Quatro Lounge and Restaurant on the Tamiami Trail (Eighth Street). Because of its peculiar hours (it opened at 4:00 A.M. and closed at noon), the El Quatro attracted a unique clientele. The first arrivals, at 4:00 A.M., were mostly drunks who came from other bars or party diehards who had decided to carry on the party elsewhere. By 6:00 A.M. another group arrived, mostly hard-working construction workers who liked steak and eggs for breakfast. There were also large breakfast wedding parties two or three mornings a week. By 10:30 A.M., a good many secretaries arrived in twos and threes to eat early lunches. They would be needed to answer the telephones in their offices during the noon hour when their bosses went out for longer and much more leisurely martini lunches. As a consequence, Violette worked hard at the El Quatro and never quite got accustomed to the hours.

Violette rented a room with a private bath from a Cuban family on Second Street. She said very little to the members of the Duarte family because they made it a practice—a dying stab at the preservation of their culture—to only speak Spanish at home. Violette did not sleep very well, that is for any prolonged stretch at a time. The family was noisy, but that wouldn't have bothered her much; it was the peculiar working hours. Exhausted by the time she arrived home at 1:00 P.M., she napped fitfully, off and on, and watched television until it was time to go to work again. She ate two meals at El Quatro and rarely fixed anything to eat on the hotplate she had in her room. She ate a good deal of candy between meals, mostly Brach's chocolate-covered peanut clusters and chocolate-covered almonds.

On her day off (Monday), she took the bus to Key Biscayne and rented a *cabana* at Crandon Park. She would wander around the zoo, sit in the shade of her *cabana* looking at the muddy sea, and browse idly through the magazines she brought along. Her favorite magazines were *Cosmopolitan* and *Ingénue*, with *Modern Romances* a close third. She also subscribed to *The Enquirer*, but she read that at home. On these lazy off-days, Violette almost forgot sometimes that she was a waitress, but she always remembered to pick up her clean uniforms for the week on her way home.

Violette hated being a waitress, but she knew there wasn't anything she could do about it because of her astrological sign. She had read it in the *Miami News* when she checked her daily horoscope on her birthday: "An Aries born on this date will be a good waitress."

And it was true. Violette was a good waitress: she was waiting, and she was an Aries.

## TAPE CASSETTE

Whihh, whihh, wheee! Hello test, hello test. Okay. Note to Engineer. Please make a dub of this cassette for my file and mail the original to Mr. Doremus Jessup, Veep for Programming, NBN, New York.

Hi, Dory, this is Russell Haxby, and I want you to know first off that the quarters at the Los Piños are el fino, as they say down here in Miami. Harry Thead and I, you'll be glad to know, are getting along fabulously. In fact we already have a bond in Quail Roost, and Harry isn't into Scotch like so many TV station managers. So we drink Quail Roost and, thanks to you, the fraternal idea of being Masons together has worked out rather well. Incidentally, Jim Preston, in Continuity, gave me a pretty damned hard time when I asked him to show me the secret handshake. I had to show him your memo ordering him to give it to me before he came across with it. Don't reprimand him or anything like that, but I hope you'll bear it in mind when cost-of-living time rolls around. No man loyal to the network should put some sort of weird lodge on a level higher than the organization he works for.

Numero Uno. The soundproof glass boxes are being built

now at the station according to the specs. We plan to use the narrow parking lot behind WOOZ, which faces Biscayne Bay. This area is ordinarily the staff and V.I.P. parking area, but there is plenty of parking space out front, so Harry said to preempt it. A good part of the Miami skyline is in the b.g. so, for the interview shows, we can do them outside, putting the skyline in the background when the M.C. talks alone or goes from booth to booth. We will be able to hear the volunteers, but they won't be able to hear each other. The speaker in each box will pick up the M.C.'s voice and, for control, my mike from the director's booth.

Two. At Harry's suggestion, we are going to lodge the five volunteers when we have them—but not the staff—in a fairly large, two-story houseboat that's moored about fifty feet down the causeway from the studio property. The houseboat belongs to a friend of Harry's, and it will make everything much simpler. No transportation problems, and we can put the psychiatrist in there with them and station a couple of security men at the gangplank for absolute control. The staff will remain at the Los Piños. I told Billy Elkhart to work out some kind of fair rent deal with Harry's friend even though we were offered the houseboat gratis. It's better to lock up a rental contract at a minimum fee so he doesn't all of a sudden need his goddamned boat back in the middle of things.

Point Three. As it turned out, it was a good idea to select the resident psychiatrist down here instead of bringing one down from New York. Not only was it cheaper—twenty applicants from the Miami area answered our ad in *The American Psychiatrist's Journal*—but these Miami doctors are more familiar with Florida mental profiles than New York doctors. Dr. Bernstein, by the way, is enthusiastic as hell about the program. He thinks he'll get a book out of it, poor bastard. A New York doctor would have understood the release he signed, or at least have had his lawyer read it. I didn't tell Bernstein any different; I'll lay that bomb on him after he turns in his pre- and post-program studies. On the release he signed, he won't even be able to retain his notes.

Eliminating the other nineteen psychiatrists was simpler

than Harry and I thought it would be. The first five we interviewed had nasal Midwestern accents, so we let them go
immediately. Four others hadn't published anything in the last
two years, one of our main requirements. As you know, I
won't even go to a goddamned dentist if he doesn't write and
publish in his field. And three were against the program mor-
ally, or said they were, so I let them go. We narrowed down
the others on the basis of videotaped screen tests and their
publications. Bernstein's recent article in *The Existential Ana-
lyst's Journal* was the most objective and, if you want to read
it, let me know and I'll send you a xerox. He can also fake
a fairly good German accent that's still intelligible. He used
to imitate and mock his old man, he said, and that's how he
learned how to do it. He's photogenic, wears a short white
goatee, and his crinkly eyes will look kindly—with the right
makeup. Also, he has a full head of salt-and-pepper hair and
a little below-the-belt melon paunch. If it weren't for his bona
fides, he could've been sent over by Central Casting. In fact,
he looks so much like a psychiatrist, we're going to have him
wear a suit instead of a white doctor's coat when we go on the
air.

Problems. A few. And I don't mind suggestions. WOOZ
has got six camera operators. Five are women, and one is a
fag. Harry says the five women are all good, and he hired them
a couple of years back to keep the women's lib people down
here off his ass. The same with the fag, who's the secretary-
treasurer of the North Miami Gay Lib Group. The women
have degrees in communications, two of them with M.A.'s
from Southern Illinois. So there's no way we can fire any of
them for cause or incompetence. I talked to them, and none of
them object to the program idea. Why should they? They're
pros, and they have union cards. But—and here's the problem—these women and the fag, being women and a fag, might
faint during the operation scenes. They've never seen anything
like the stuff we've got coming up, you know. What I wanted,
and we discussed this in New York, were some ex-combat
Signal Corps cameramen who were used to the sight of blood.
These female operators sure as hell wouldn't stand for any

standby cameramen either. They want to do a network show, more for the prestige than for the extra money. Anyway, we've still got plenty of time and, if you have any ideas, let me know soonest.

Everything else is on schedule. We're working on the script for the TV spot announcements—to get the volunteers—this afternoon. Dr. Bernstein is a help here, more help than the writer you sent me, Noble Barnes. He can't seem to forget that he's a novelist and a black novelist at that. He's got to go. I've been around for a long time, Dory, and I've never seen a novelist yet who could do shit with a spot or a screenplay. Noble can't spell, and he leaves the esses and ee dees off his words as well. On a program as important as this one, I've got to have another writer. *The First Five in Line* isn't Amos and Andy for God's sake!

—Sorry, Dory. I know we have to have to have at least one black on the staff but, if we're lucky enough to get a black volunteer, I'm shipping Noble Barnes's black ass back to Harlem. How, I'll always wonder, did this fucker ever get through C.C.N.Y.?

Tomorrow we meet with the Miami account exec from Baumgarten, Bates and Williams who wants to discuss national accounts at this end. I'll send you a tape or a transcript of the minutes. The WOOZ engineer has rigged up the conference room at the Los Piños, and we're going to tape everything. It's quite possible that Mr. Williams himself might come to this meeting according to the account exec. A good sign, don't you think?

Some possible alternate titles from my notes: *The Five Who Fled*; *The Finalist Quintet*; *The End of the Line*; *Doctor, Lawyer, Indian Chief, Cowboy and Lady*; *Five Fists Full of Dollars*.

I'm not crazy about any of these titles, but they're on the record so you can kick 'em around.

Ciao, J.D. And that's a ten-four.

## JOHN WHEELER COLEMAN, Col., A.U.S. (Retired)

A good many men in America, if they had to do it at all, would have rather done it John Wheeler Coleman's way than the more conventional method; but Coleman had always felt cheated by the failure of his father to get him into the U.S. Military Academy at West Point or, failing that, into the Virginia Military Institute where General Marshall had matriculated. In other words, despite Coleman's distinguished military career, he had never managed to become a Regular Army officer.

His failure to become RA had colored his life brown.

Coleman had obtained his commission as a second lieutenant at the Infantry School at Fort Benning by attending Officer's Candidate School, and he had served his country well for twenty-four years. He had retired as a lieutenant colonel with a "gangplank" promotion to full colonel on the day before his retirement from the A.U.S.—Army of the United States instead of the United States Army (U.S.A.).

The difference between A.U.S. and R.A., in Coleman's case, would have made all the difference to his career. As a Reserve officer on active duty—instead of being a Regular Army officer on active duty—Coleman's active duty status was in jeopardy every single day of the full twenty-four years he served. Every Reserve officer on active duty knows this, but Coleman had never been able to adjust to the idea of sudden, peremptory dismissal. There wasn't a day that went by that the possibility of a letter, informing him that he would be "riffed," would land on his desk. The term "riff" is an acronym coined by Louis Johnson during his tenure as Secretary of Defense from "R.I.F.," Reduction in Force. Many thousands of officers were able to stay the full distance for twenty years and retirement, but many more thousands were riffed; and when an officer was riffed, there was no way that he could find out the reason if, indeed, there was a reason other than a further reduction in force.

Coleman often thought bitterly (never voicing it, to be sure) about General Douglas MacArthur's fatuous remark, "There is no security, there is only opportunity."

Sure, a man who was R.A. could say that, and MacArthur had gone to West Point; but if MacArthur had been a reserve officer, he would have whistled a different tune.

Serving in Korea and Vietnam as a combat officer, Coleman had been decorated with the Distinguished Service Cross; the Silver Star, with one Oak Leaf Cluster; the Bronze Star, with V Device; and two Army Commendation Medals. As a reserve officer Coleman had always tried harder than regular officers of the same rank, but the positive knowledge that he could be booted out of the service any day—without a reason, unlike R.A. officers—and without getting a dime in severance pay, either, had affected his decision-making ability. Coleman never hesitated about making a decision, of course (if he had, he never would have lasted the full twenty-four years), but his decisions were always determined by thinking first what kind of decision his immediate superior officer (the officer who made out his biannual Effectiveness Report) would have made in the same situation.

He had been very successful at this kind of thinking although, as a consequence, the overall pattern of his career made his record a somewhat eccentric mixture of inconsistencies. A brilliant record, to be true, but a strange one if examined closely because it reflected the thinking of more than 100 different superior officers. Despite his "superior" effectiveness reports—with only one "excellent" report to mar his record (the time when he was a First Lieutenant and Supply Officer for Company "A," 19th Infantry, and someone had stolen ten mattress covers from the supply room)—Coleman had served under a good many officers who had made dumb decisions. His decisions under dumb officers had been equally dumb— but that had been the game he had had to play if he wanted to stay on active duty.

With his daring combat record as a junior officer, Coleman, by all rights, should have been a full colonel with his own regiment at least five years before his retirement; but he had performed so brilliantly in Command and General Staff School at

Fort Leavenworth, he had been marked down for staff work. Without ever getting into command of at least a battalion, he was doomed to staff work from then on; and no matter how brilliant a staff man happens to be, he is always considered a No. Two man, which means he is passed over for command more often than not.

The key year for an officer with reserve status on active duty is his eighteenth year of service. If the officer is allowed to serve for eighteen years, he cannot be riffed (except for a very serious cause) until he has served twenty years and is eligible for retirement. But even after Coleman passed safely through his eighteenth year and then his twentieth, he was still unable to relax his vigilance. He tried even harder, in fact, feeling now that there was still a chance to make R.A. before his retirement and then stay on for thirty years. If he could stay for thirty, or until he became sixty-five, those extra years would make the possibility of becoming a general officer a certainty. But he never made it. He languished as a regimental S-3 and was finally riffed after serving twenty-four years.

One morning as he had been expecting for all of those years, a letter riffing him from the service appeared upon his desk.

If a man is single—and Coleman had never married—a colonel's retirement is sufficient to live on providing his needs are simple. He lived frugally in the Bide-A-While Mobile Home Community in Homestead, Florida, and did his shopping in the Homestead Air Force Commissary. He fixed his own meals and did his laundry at the common laundry room at the Bide-A-While Rec Center. Once a week he visited the officers club at Homestead Air Force Base on Bingo Night. The rest of the time he watched TV or took long nature walks in the nearby Everglades State Park. He drove a Willy's Jeepster and sometimes drove to the Keys just to have somewhere to go.

After a few months of this boring retirement, he took a course in real estate, like so many other retired officers living in Florida, and passed the examination for agent. During the long hot days after getting his license, he sat in empty houses for eight hours a day and sold at least one house a year. His commission was usually $1,200 for each house he sold, and he added it to his savings. His savings, more than $100,000 in Gold Certificates, were kept in the Homestead Air Force Base Credit Union at eight percent. Sitting in empty houses gave him something to do, and he considered the commissions he made as hedges against future inflation.

Coleman had made few friends in the army, and he found it even harder to make friends on the outside. He was a lonely man, and he was ashamed of his military career, which many men would have been proud of—for one reason.

Despite his combat decorations for bravery under fire, Coleman felt as if he had never been tested. Coleman, who had never known any real joy, had never known any real pain either. He had never been sick a day in his life. He was trim, athletic, and ate with small appetite. Nor had he ever been wounded in combat or even hurt. He had never known the joy—or pain—of marriage and fatherhood. In short, by normal standards, many men would have considered him to be a lucky bastard all of the way 'round. Though he kept his hair in a brush cut, with white sidewalls, he had even retained his hair.

But when a man has never been tested, truly tested to the limits of his endurance, how does he know that he can meet the test? There is only one way, and that is to take the test.

Coleman thought about this a lot, especially during the long days when he watched the soap operas as he sat in empty houses, considering the emptiness of his life.

## TAPE CASSETTE

Hi, Russell, this is D.J. I'll be sending this tape down with Ernie Powell who'll also bring along some notes, including the comments from Doctor Glass of Bellevue. Ernie's been hired by the unit manager as a production assistant for *TFFIL*, but he's really a procurer. He has a rep in the trade, in case you haven't heard of him, of being able to get any prop—or anything else for that matter—within twenty minutes. He worked for seventeen years as a stage manager in summer stock, so you know how valuable he is. Ernie's worked with Billy Elkhart before, so I know Ernie'll be glad to have him on the staff.

First, those titles you reeled off were terrible! I'm putting a couple of Columbia grad students on the title. They'll be working free at NBN for two weeks for two college credits, and they might as well learn something about TV the hard way. It will give them some incentive. I told them that if they came up with a usable title, great, but if they didn't, I wouldn't recommend them for the two college credits. It's obvious from your last tape that you don't have time to think creatively about an alternative title, and I want your mind to be free for all of the things you have to do.

We're paying Dr. Glass a bundle, and you'll see by his notes that he's finally come up with some valuable stuff, except it's about two months too late. The gist is that the last three weeks in August and the first week in September would be the best time of the year to get volunteers. Our predictions show, as I said in my memo, a possibility ratio of 7.1 for volunteers counting the new Miami unemployment figures. But in August, plus the first week in September, Glass claims that ninety percent of Miami analysts, psychologists and psychiatrists go on their vacations to North Carolina. This means that there are approximately five thousand or more neurotics stumbling around down there without a doctor to turn to for advice. At loose ends, these analysands would undoubtedly boost the probability factor for volunteers. Now don't think I'm worried, but it's just too bad that Dr. Glass's information was a month late and, as L.B.J. used to say, "a dollar short."

We also need a black man as a volunteer or, failing that, a Cuban. But Glass said we would never get a black volunteer, never. They're too practical, he said; but at least they won't be able to holler discrimination when we're playing this game straight and can prove it. So you'll be stuck with Noble Barnes as a writer. At any rate, Glass's figures will be helpful if we get another season out of the show—and next time, we'll go to St.

Louis where there is a bigger percentage of blacks.

Re the women (and fag) camerapersons: no sweat here. Hustle their ass over to the emergency ward at Jackson Memorial Hospital and make them watch a few emergency operations from the car wrecks. There will be amputations aplenty, so make them watch a few. If any of them pass out, you can replace them before rehearsals begin, and they can't squawk to the union. Anyway, hire at least one ex-Signal Corps cameraman, as an advisor only, and have him stand by for emergencies during the actual programming. Too bad we decided to do this live instead of on tape, but we do need the immediacy that a live show engenders.

Are you getting any, Russell? If not, ask Ernie, and he'll have a broad in your room within twenty minutes. It'll be good recreation for you, and you should do it anyway—even if you aren't interested—just to see Ernie work. Here he'll be with this tape and the notes—right from the airport, and in a strange new city—and I'll bet you a case of Chivas to a case of Quail Roost that he can get a broad in your room within twenty minutes. And a free one, too. It's rather uncanny when you come to think about it.

I called the Los Angles office, and it's firm: Warren Oates will be the M.C. We might have to work around his movie schedule, but that'll be Billy Elkhart's problem not yours. You *will* have Warren Oates as your M.C. Warren used to work a live game show with Jimmy Dean back in the early fifties, and he did a lot of TV work before going into films. He'll be a great M.C., and he has a positive image for this kind of thing. The only snag in his contract is that he gets to wear his dark sunglasses on the show. I had to concede this point, but you may be able to talk him out of it. By the way, when Warren comes out there from Hollywood next week, do not—do not under any circumstances—ask him what he's carrying in that burlap sack he lugs around with him. He's very sensitive about this point, okay? Okay.

This is D.J., and a ten-four and Godspeed.

## LEO ZUCK

At 82, Leo Zuck (*nee* Zuckerman) was a dapper dresser even by Miami Beach standards, although sartorial standards on Miami Beach are not very high. Leo owned a white gabardine suit and a burnt orange linen suit which, in various combinations, gave him four different changes. He possessed two white-on-white, drip-dry-never-iron shirts and twenty-five pink neckties. (He had had the neckties made to order out of the same bolt of cloth at a bargain price.) He also owned a red silk dinner jacket with a ruffled pink shirt and maroon bow tie to go with it, as well as blue-black tuxedo trousers and cherry red patent leather pumps to round out the costumes. He did not, unhappily, have any underwear, and he had only two pair of black clock socks left in his wardrobe. The white suede shoes he wore with his suits-sports outfits, although they were clean enough, were very bald.

Leo Zuck, living in very reduced circumstances, was mostly front. Leo had lost his job as the M.C. at the Saturday night pier dance, and he did not know what he was going to do for the little luxuries that extra ten dollars a week had provided him with: a daily cigar, Sen-Sen (for his notoriously bad breath) and an occasional Almond Joy. But now he had to give up these small luxuries.

If Leo had learned or invented some new material each week, he could have, in all probability, kept the M.C. job indefinitely. Abe Ossernan, who ran the weekly dances (admission 25 cents) and owned the pier concessions on South Beach (as South Miami Beach is called), was not a mean man. Abe had hinted to Leo more than once that he should brighten up his faded material, but Leo paid no attention to Mr. Ossernan. Leo loved his material, and he had it down ice cold. Leo had purchased his act in 1925 for $150—when $150 *was* $150—and he had sharpened and refined the material to perfection on the Keith-Orpheum vaudeville circuit for fifteen years. An excellent mimic with a rubbery, if deeply lined face, Leo did accurate and extremely funny imitations of Charles Ray, George Bancroft, Emil Jannings and Harry Langdon. He was also able to sing "I'm a Yankee Doodle Dandy" raucously out of the side of his mouth in a near-perfect imitation of George M. Cohan. This act of Leo's had wowed the hicks in the sticks for years, but the material was so old now, it baffled even his nostalgic audiences at the pier dance on Saturday nights.

Leo had a large scrapbook filled with yellowed clippings from every large city and from most of the small cities in the United States and Canada attesting to how good his act was—or had been—and, in Leo's opinion, the act was still as good—if not better than ever. Except for minor alterations in timing, the only addition to Leo's act since 1925(a socko finish!) was made in 1945. In this cruel year, Leo had had his remaining teeth removed and was fitted with a full set of upper and lower white plastic choppers. Because of his thick, fairly long nose and pointed, rather long chin, Leo could perform a reasonably accurate imitation of Popeye the Sailor by removing both plates. Except for elderly persons with very keen memories, however, Popeye the Sailor was the only imitation most audiences recognized.

When vaudeville died out forever, as it had in 1940, Leo had been fortunate enough to get into the U.S. Army Special Services during the war—joining various variety companies as they were put together in New York—and he had entertained troops in the South Pacific, England and, eventually, Italy. Between overseas tours, he had made the rounds of stateside Special Service shows as well. G.I. audiences are not critical, and they had applauded his old gags and imitations of long dead movie stars with cheerful tolerance. They especially liked his introduction:

M.C.: *And now, straight from the Great White Way, the famous star from the Keith-Orpheum vaudeville circuit, Leo Zuck!*
*(Enter Leo Zuck)*
*Zuck: Suck what?*
*Audience: (Laughter, and so on. . .)*

When the war and his teeth were finished, Leo obtained summer employment in the Catskills and Pocono's at third-rate hotels on the Borscht Circuit. Social directors did not care greatly for Leo's act, but he was a great success with the old ladies, mostly widows, who sojourned at these cheaper mountain hotels. Leo had never married, and single men were at a premium in the mountains.

In his red satin dinner jacket under a pink spot, Leo was distinguished-looking on stage. He knew how to apply makeup for maximum effect, and his full head of blue-white hair reminded many old ladies of Leopold Stokowski. Leo sported a well-trimmed, white toothbrush mustache, and it was almost as white (except in the center where it had turned brownish from cigarette tar and nicotine) as his flashing false teeth.

Except for his own act, which was practically engraved on his brain, Leo's memory was not consistent. But no one in the Pocono's minded when, in his M.C. capacity, he put on his reading glasses and introduced the various acts by reading the names and remarks off three-by-five cards with a flashlight.

In the mid-1960s, however, Leo had been unable to get any more work—even in the Pocono's—and he had retired to South Beach to a residential hotel. He drew the minimum in Social Security benefits, of course, because, like many entertainers, he had preferred to be paid in cash for most of his theatrical life; but the minimum had been enough to pay for his room and meals for several years. From time to time he had also supplemented his meager income by playing a few dates at parties and social functions. Leo had been interviewed twice on WKAT radio (for free) and once on a late-night talk show on Channel 4. (When the host on the *Channel 4 Talk Show* introduced him, Leo said automatically, "Suck *what?*") Because of three irate phone calls, Leo wasn't invited back to the TV station, but he was still a kind of celebrity to the retired old people who make up the general population of South Beach.

With inflation, Leo's Social Security check was barely enough to cover the rent of his hotel room and, when the rent was raised again—which it soon would be—he would have to find a cheaper room, although there were no rooms cheaper in South Beach than the one he had. After paying the rent there was no money left over to eat with, and he had to be satisfied with the one free noon meal he got each day at the Jewish Welfare Center. The loss of his M.C. job at the pier—and the tax-free ten dollars that went with it—was a disaster for Leo and, for the first time since 1940, Leo Zuck—the old trouper—began to doubt seriously that vaudeville would ever come back. . . ◉

# The Tupperware Party

BOB, THE airline-pilot, called me:

"You going to John's Tupperware party?"

"Yeah. I guess so. When he asked me, I didn't know how to get out of it."

"Well, I'm not going."

"Why not? It's something to do."

"He didn't ask me, that's why, but even if he had I wouldn't have gone, so I suppose that's why he didn't ask me. He knew I wouldn't go, that's all. But he still should've asked me, anyway, even if he knew I wouldn't go. It's a stupid thing, an all-male Tupperware party."

"Maybe so, Bob, but I'm going. I said I would so I am."

I think Bob was hurt because John hadn't asked him to the party. John should've asked Bob, knowing that Bob was certain to find out about it. Down at the Embassy Bar, where we go for drinks at night, that's all everybody was talking about. But then again, I guess John didn't ask Bob because he didn't want any flak about the party, which he knew he would get from Bob, whom anyone could predict would think the idea a little crazy.

Well, I was going. I said I'd go, so I would go, but that didn't mean I would have to buy anything.

Eight guys showed up. They were all bachelors or recently divorced men, and they all needed Tupperware, John told me, because they didn't have much of anything in the way of kitchen stuff. The divorced guys lost all their stuff to their wives when they moved out, and the bachelors, or those guys who'd never been married, didn't know what to buy for their kitchens, anyway. John was right about that much, anyway. And that's why it's so important when a man decides to get married that he pick a widow or a divorcee so he doesn't have to buy anything—not sheets, or furniture, or silver, or dishes, anything. All he has to do is move in with his dirty laundry.

John had asked more than 20 guys, but he had figured most of them wouldn't show. It was Saturday afternoon, and there are other things more interesting to engage a man's time than a Tupperware party on a Saturday afternoon. No one called to say he wasn't coming, either; although all 20 had said they would be there. Men are like that.

In fact, I doubt very much if John would've come to a Tupperware party himself if someone else had given one, although he would've promised to come because he is a very amenable guy except when he has been drinking heavily throughout a long afternoon and evening. Then he gets a little surly, and says that as soon as he can amass a small stake he's going to leave Miami, and move back to Appleton, Wis.

Sharon, John's girlfriend, was the hostess for the party. The party was really her idea, not John's, and she had already given one party that morning for a group of women in a condo apartment down in Perrine. That's what Sharon did for a living: give Tupperware parties. She was a buxom young woman, around 25 or 26, and her eyes bulged, too. She was a little nervous around all of these men, I thought, and it didn't help, when she started to make her introductory remarks, that John sent her out to the kitchen to get fresh beers for everyone.

When we all had fresh beers, and were gathered around the coffee table, which held weenies in blankets, pretzels, potato chips, and celery stalks stuffed with pimento cheese, Sharon told us that it took five people to have an official, or legitimate Tupperware party, and with eight present, counting John, we might as well start. She then passed out little capped cups with notes inside, and with numbers on the base. She told us not to open them. At the end of the party, she said, she would draw a number, and that number would get a door prize. If the person who won a door prize would give another Tupperware party in his home, he could then open the little cup and get another prize.

"What about the games, Sharon?" John reminded her.

"They don't look like they want to play any games. Do you all want to play a game?"

There was mumbled assent, so she passed out the catalogs and order forms and ballpoints.

"Just write your answers on the back, blank side of your order forms," she said. "All right, list ten parts of the body that only have three letters."

This was a difficult test. I got six right, which was about the average in the room but then she said that none of us—and we all had them—could count "ass" and "tit" as parts of the body. The proper name for these parts were "buttocks" and "breast," she claimed. I had "ear" and "lip" but never thought of "hip." Inasmuch as no one got all ten, no one got a prize, and the prize was a Tupperware ice bucket with a lid. There was some grumbling that the test was too hard, and that no one could be expected to get all ten words like that, but when she read off the answers, it merely revealed that we hadn't been given enough time. Given enough time, we agreed, we would've gotten them all.

She also showed us how to wink the tops. At one time, Sharon said, they used to call it burping the lid to get rid of the excess air, but now the company wanted people to call it winking instead because winking is politer than burping.

Eddy, a full-time professional fund-raiser, who had already downed three beers and was working on his fourth, burped loudly.

"Excuse my wink," he said. We all laughed, including Sharon. It was funny if you were there, but it doesn't sound funny now that I write it down.

Altogether, I bought $11.40 worth of stuff, which John would get from Sharon later and deliver to us the following week. For giving the party, and the use of his apartment, John got a free ice bucket, two containers with lids, and a tube of some kind. He got all of that free, just for giving the party. But because all of us had had at least three beers apiece, he didn't come out ahead; and he had to furnish the food, too.

Sharon then made another big pitch for someone else to give another Tupperware party at his apartment, but none of us was interested. In fact, everybody we knew who might come to a Tupperware party was already at this one, and we all had enough Tupperware now to last a lifetime. Just as the party broke up, and a couple of guys were leaving, Dick arrived. Dick is a big guy who used to play college football about ten years ago. He couldn't believe it when he saw all of Sharon's Tupperware stacked up on the dining table. He shook his head. "You really meant it when you said a Tupperware party. I thought you were kidding."

We laughed at his bewildered expression. Sharon took Dick to one side, got him a beer, and gave him a private pitch and showing. Dick ordered about $20 worth of stuff, even though he didn't get to play the three-letter body game.

Sharon called out number four. This was my number on the bottom of my little cup, so I got the door prize. The door prize was a pair of lidded containers about an inch deep. They are too small for food, but I decided I could keep stamps in one of them, and, perhaps, paper clips in the other. I don't know what else to do with them, but I kept them because they were free.

Later, when I got home, I called Bob, and told him about the party.

"You really should've been there," I told him. "It was fun, and we all had a good time and several beers."

"I wasn't asked," he reminded me. "Do you have this Sharon girl's phone number?"

"Sure," I said. "She gave us all a card in case we wanted to order something else, or changed our minds about giving our own Tupperware party."

"That's what I'm going to do," Bob said. "I'm going to get her to give a party at my house, but I'm not going to invite John. D'you want to come?"

"Why not?" I said.

I'd be a fool not to: I kept the list of ten three-letter words for parts of the body, and I'll be able to win a Tupperware ice bucket. ◉

## The Gardener and the Princess

MARIELITOS, INSOFAR as I have been able to determine, are adjusting very well to the broader aspects of American culture. On the other hand, when it comes to nuances (or "nuancles," as General Haig prefers to call them), it's a different story altogether. And although I have always considered inchoateness as a cop-out, my success in explaining nuances has been negligible.

For example, Fernando, the *marielito* who mows my lawn twice a month, recently faced with his first tax return, now requests cash instead of a check on his bimonthly visits. He is aware that he must file an income tax return next year, too, and if his income is lower his taxes will also be lower.

On the nuances, however, despite our long talks every two weeks, I simply haven't been able to answer his questions satisfactorily, or to provide him with answers he considers reasonable or logical.

Take the sugar substitute: A couple of months ago, after he finished the yard, I invited him in for sweet rolls and *Café con leche*. He was genuinely puzzled when I put a sugar substitute into my coffee instead of sugar. I was embarrassed by the question, too. I could not very well persuade him to believe that the substitute had fewer calories than sugar, not when the pastries alone had enough calories to provide a construction worker with his daily needs, so I hemmed and hawed.

Finally, I said:

"It's like the Greeks, Fernando. Before they pour their wine they spill a little on the ground. That's to placate the gods, you see, and that's why I use a sugar substitute. It's a kind of sop to our Protestant God, our Puritan heritage."

He touched the religious medals dangling from his neck, and nodded solemnly, *"Religioso!"*

"Something like that," I muttered, "only not exactly."

How does one explain the Puritan conscience to someone who has never heard of Plymouth Plantation, Melville, Hawthorne, Emerson, or the new Canaan?

Nor did I get anywhere with the white socks, either. Fernando invariably wears white socks. When we became friendly enough, I explained that Americans did not wear white socks unless they were playing tennis or some other appropriate sport. He did not believe me.

"You know Paul Newman, the actor?" He pointed to his brown eyes.

"Of course. The blue-eyed actor."

"Is he rich? Is he American?"

"He is indeed a rich American."

"I saw the movie, *Fort Apache, The Bronx*—and in this movie, Paul Newman wears white socks!"

I tried to explain the difference between the character Newman was playing and Newman the real person, but because there really isn't a dime's worth of difference between the parts Newman plays and the man himself, I was merely wasting my breath and time. Fernando, who admires Newman more than he does me (a view I share, incidentally), continues to wear white socks.

Fernando, who also takes care of some of the lawns in and around Kendall Lakes, is puzzled about the many dentists and lawyers who live there. "Why," he asked, "with all the money they make, do they drive these little Volvos?"

"Television," I explained. The TV ads say that an intelligent man drives a Volvo, so they buy one. They save on gas."

"Do you think I'm intelligent?"

"Of course. Your English is improving every week, and your lawn business is thriving. In fact, considering the short time you've been here, you've done very well."

"I am buying Trans Am."

"Don't do it, Fernando, they use too much gas. What you need is a Luv truck. You could use it in your work, and it's small enough to take out dates at night."

"A man who drives a Volvo cannot prove he's intelligent to

me. If I drive Trans Am, everybody will know I am intelligent enough to buy Trans Am."

"That's conspicuous consumption. Veblen has written a book about it."

"What kind of car does Veblen drive?"

"He was a professor at the University of Chicago making five hundred bucks a year. I doubt if he ever owned a car. He couldn't afford one. He's dead now anyway, so it's all academic."

"I like Trans Am. When you drive the Trans Am, people know you're driving *something.*"

"It isn't practical," I protested.

"Then why do you live in a four-bedroom house?"

"When you get through with the back lawn, see if you can sweep up the big leaves under the seagrape tree. Last time you forgot."

That was a month ago.

Last week Fernando drove up in his new Trans Am, and unloaded his lawnmower from the trunk. He was visibly excited, and wearing a wide grin. Shyly, he handed me a Polaroid snapshot. The photo was of a blonde young woman. Her hair was on the frizzy side, and she was wearing a gold circle pin on the left side of a blue mohair sweater.

"My fiancée," Fernando announced proudly.

"Where does she live?"

"Miami Beach."

I cleared my throat nervously. "You haven't asked her yet, have you?"

"*Si!* We're engaged."

"What kind of car does she drive?"

"Volkswagen. Gray, like elephant color. A little bug. She has a big plastic flower on radio aerial, and rainbow decal in back window."

By this time I was quite concerned. I like Fernando, you see, and he didn't know what he was getting into. My hands began to tremble.

I spoke slowly, enunciating carefully. "With an 'i' on the end, is her name Alli, Debbi, Kati, Sandi, Candi—?"

"Candi! You know Candi?"

"No, but I know who she is. You can't marry this girl, Fernando."

"Why not?"

"She's a princess."

"No, she's not princess. Her father is dentist."

"I suspected as much. Didn't you tell me that you had a cousin in New Jersey? Maybe if you get on a plane for Jersey, and stay with him for a year or so, you can get out of it."

"I don't want to get out of it," he said angrily. "I'm in love."

"OK. I guess it's none of my business, anyway."

I went back into the house and poured three fingers of Wild Turkey. There are some fine points about American culture that simply cannot be explained to a *marielito*. You have to be born here. ◉

# The Laughing Machine

SMILEY MASON opened his eyes and blinked them a fraction of a second before the alarm clicked preparatory to ringing. He reached out a lone bony index finger and touched the alarm knob. The stretching finger and clicking sound synchronized, and no bell rang. Four-thirty P.M., time to go to work. For a moment Smiley lay there, fully awake now, his mind ticking away in time with the cheap alarm clock on the night table, trying to make up his mind: Grand Central Station or Penn?

Shuddering with cold and apprehension in his underwear, Smiley threw off the covers, sat up in bed, and swung his skinny legs to the floor. What difference did it make? The fuzz was on the lookout for him in both stations anyway. Trying to work the locker dodge and dodge the dip detail at the same time became a more difficult task with each passing day. He made an indifferent decision: Yesterday had been luckless at Penn, so today he would try Grand Central.

Smiley lit a cigarette, inhaled the two deep drags he dreaded, and snubbed out the cigarette just in time. The coughing fit was a terrible ordeal to undergo, especially the first one on waking, but he stoically endured the routine several times daily. His frail body was racked with convulsive ripples, his sunken chest heaved, his long arms and legs were extended stiffly, and they trembled violently. After a few choking moments he panicked in spite of himself, as he often did of late. Was this the time? How long could he go on this way? Was this the day when the coughing wouldn't stop?

The paroxysms grew longer and more painful with each fresh spell, and he lived in daily fear of the time when the coughing would go on and on and on without stopping, until the last fragment of his remaining lung was ripped out of his heaving chest once and for all. But at last he stopped, slowing down gradually, like a wheezing donkey engine running out of gas. Briny tears burned his eyes. A sweet weakness enveloped his body like a wet warm sheet, and he maintained his sitting position on the edge of the bed by a determined effort of will. He wanted more than anything else in the world to flop backward on the bed again and remain there, warm under the covers, forever, to fall into a deep unconscious sleep that would never end with another alarm click and the necessity to inhale two murderous billows of smoke into the empty cage of his chest.

He had coughed up nothing but the smoke; perhaps there was nothing left to come out? In some ways, he thought, the smoke was at least something to bring up. It gave reason to his coughing spells. The smoke was a goal, so to speak. Getting rid of the unwanted smoke made his coughing purposeful, if nothing else. He hadn't hacked up any blood or sputum for months now, but the coughing itself hadn't stopped, and he needed the smoke as an excuse for his misery.

Barefooted and gently rubbing his sore, hairless chest with the tips of his fingers, Smiley padded to the dresser and examined his solemn face in the cloudy mirror. The small fly-black eyes in the mirror searched his face without apparent recognition, but they noticed, all the same, that this pale face would have to be shaved today. His beard grew slowly, but three days was the limit without a shave; on the fourth day his beard was a noticeable salt-and-pepper bas-relief on white parchment.

A single bar of black eyebrow lay like a strand of dyed false hair across his bare sloping forehead, and his large hooked nose made his eyes appear more deeply recessed into his skull than they were. His mouth was a frugal crescent; the tightened corners pointed sharply and disapprovingly downward at all times. Emphasizing the stern set of his lips, two deep, almost black, lines formed sharp angles from the wings of his nose to the corners of his lips, as if they had been intaglioed into the white glove leather of his face with a razor blade.

For almost as long as he could remember, Smiley Mason had been called "Smiley." The last person who had called him

"Alexander"—except for officials entering his name from time to time-served—had been his mother, and he had never seen her again after being sentenced to the reformatory the first time. Even as a kid at the reformatory, he had gone by this moniker, and his fellow cons had continued to call him Smiley (when they had talked to him at all) during his three stretches at the state prison. It is common enough in America to call a man who never laughs or smiles "Smiley" or "Happy" or "Cheerful," and, at one time or another, Smiley had answered to all of them. What he was called was an indifferent matter to Smiley; he knew that the man who never laughs or smiles has a greater chance of getting such a name than an idiot who chortles and giggles constantly—and that was all there was to it.

With a face like his, and Smiley had pondered this idea more than once during his criminal career, he should never have embarked on a professional life of crime. As an actor, or even as a politician, his face would have been an asset to him instead of a liability. People who saw Smiley's face remembered it. In fact, they sometimes remembered his face when they had never seen it before. The liquor store salesman who had put the finger on him in the lineup when he got his last three-to-five had never seen him before. And even the cops, who knew that Smiley had never carried a gun in his life, were well aware of the bum rap—but a case cleared up was a case cleared up . . . and Smiley simply had that kind of a face.

All of the amorphous guilt of the city had accumulated there, and no conscientious policeman had ever let Smiley walk past him without shaking him down for a concealed weapon. Smiley's contempt and hatred for the world was nakedly apparent in his embittered features. To look at him was to return his hate; to look at him one knew that he had a pistol in his pocket; to look at him one also knew that if one were in his place, the pistol would be pointed and fired in revenge before the day ended. So Smiley had never carried a weapon. The pettiest of petty criminals, he had never averaged more than $1,200 a year from his criminal activities (although, to be fair to him, fifteen of his thirty-four years had been spent in confinement).

After dampening a red sponge in the hotel bathroom, Smiley returned to the mirror and methodically scrubbed Panchromatic No. 27 greasepaint into his sickly white face. The pink makeup, designed for juvenile roles, did not remove any years from Smiley's face; it merely changed his death-like pallor to the concealed pallor of an embalmed corpse made up for a final boxed appearance before relatives. Smiley smoothed rouge into his cheeks, blended it with the No. 27 with circular motions of his fingers, and then powdered his face evenly with beige powder. He patted the puff well up on his naked head, put down the powder puff, and opened the tube of spirit gum.

His nose wrinkled at the acrid smell, and he held the tube away from him, afraid of another coughing spell. He squeezed gum onto a forefinger and then dabbled the mixture onto his naked skull at one-inch intervals until his head was a mottled pattern of brownish spots. With difficulty—it took three tries—Smiley snapped an iron-gray, crew cut toupee over his knobby bald head. The hairpiece, which Smiley had discovered in a suitcase stolen from Penn Station two months before, had been made for a head much smaller than his; as a consequence, there was a full inch gap of bare skin at the back of his head, a white beach of pale skin between the iron-gray of the toupee and the dull brownish fringe of Smiley's ring of back hair. Nevertheless, from the front Smiley had undergone a miraculous transformation. With the makeup and hairpiece, he no longer looked so angry; he resembled a man who has had a few drinks too many, enough to flush his face and to allow him to accept his place in the world with bitter resignation.

A dark suit, white button-down shirt and conservative blue tie completed Smiley's disguise. The only concession to his preferred attire was the pair of black, pointy-toed shoes. With black socks, however, even the shoes helped his impersonation of whomever it was he represented instead of the flashily dressed Smiley Mason the dip detail men were looking for. Smiley scooped his last six quarters off the dresser, dropped them into his jacket pocket, and left the hotel room without bothering to snap off the light.

Twice on the short two-block walk to Grand Central, Smiley stopped to cough. Once he hung limply, his right arm encircling a lamppost, barking at the people on the sidewalk as ineffectually as a Pekinese dog. During the second spell, he coughed feebly against a building, holding his bobbing head away from the wall with his palms pressed flat against the bricks. If passers-by noticed Smiley and his coughing spells, they gave no sign as they hurried along the pavement.

When Smiley entered the station, his bearing changed. From some inner resource he drew enough wiry strength to hold his slim body stiffly erect. He walked quickly and purposefully across the terminal, looking neither right nor left, a man preoccupied, a man with a train to catch, and without much time to catch it. When he reached his favored row of banked twenty-five-cent lockers, he opened an empty and dropped in a coin pocketing the key with a swift, practiced sureness. The movement of his right arm was a fuzzy arc of dark-blue sleeve. A moment later, a newspaper before his face, Smiley leaned against a nearby wall. A tiny hole, cut through the paper with a fingernail, gave him a perspective for locker-bound prospects.

An old woman, loaded down with a shopping bag and a bulging cardboard box tied with string, was looking for an empty locker, but Smiley ignored her. Her things were too unwieldy. She would probably want to help him, and even unsuspecting assistance invited detection. With a feeling of loss, Smiley watched her stuff her belongings into an empty locker. She lip-read the directions three times before she could decipher the simple method of locking the door and getting the key. She dropped the key into her scuffed black purse and shuffled off tiredly toward the coffee shop.

Perhaps she had been the big one? One of these days (and this was the dream that kept him going) Smiley was going to get safely away with a suitcase—and it could very easily have been that cardboard box of the old woman's, so tightly tied with twine—and find it filled completely with lovely green money, all in small bills. And when that big day came, he would take the twenty thousand dollars (the dreamed-for sum was always twenty thousand, no more, no less) and fly away to the hottest hot country in South America. Until the last dime was spent, and twenty thousand would be more than enough to outlast his remaining years, he would lie out all day in the tropical sun, tanning his pale body to a golden brown, and drink ice-cold orange juice until it bubbled out of his ears——

Swiftly, but unhurriedly, Smiley folded his newspaper and slipped it under his left arm. A sweating, red-faced, middle-aged man was heading toward the lockers, and a huge black suitcase banged him on the leg with every step. He kept looking about him as he walked, his blue eyes goggling at the crowd. Smiley's timing was perfect as he intercepted the perspiring stranger three feet away from an empty locker.

"Here," Smiley said firmly, clutching the handle of the suitcase so deftly that the owner's fingers were dislodged before he could protest, "let me give you a hand."

The bag was uncommonly heavy, but Smiley opened the door with his left hand and allowed the weight of the bag to assist him as he swung it back and up into the empty locker. He wheeled abruptly, holding out his right hand, palm up.

"Quarters," Smiley said impatiently. "It takes quarters."

"Oh, sure, sure," the stranger said amiably, and he dug into his trousers and came up with a handful of change. Smiley picked out a quarter, turned back to the locker, raised his left arm slightly, and his newspaper fell to the floor. As if on signal the stranger bent down to retrieve it. Smiley locked the locker, pocketed the new key, and held out the switched key to his empty locker before the innocent traveler straightened up with the newspaper.

Smiley nodded a curt, indifferent acknowledgement to the "thanks" and, unfolding his newspaper, turned away. The man grasped the sleeve of his coat and smiled.

"Where do they hide the pay phones around here?"

Smiley hesitated, as if to ponder the question. "Well, there're some behind the coffee shop over there, but you'll never get an empty booth this time of night. Your best bet, probably, is to take the down escalator to the concourse"—he pointed—"and turn right at the first level. Then try for an empty booth on your right past the shoeshine stands. You can't miss 'em."

"Thanks. Thank you very much."

A taxi deposited Smiley and his heavy acquisition across the street from the alley entrance to his hotel a few minutes later. He entered the basement door, which the janitor left unlocked between five and seven every evening for a monthly gratuity of ten dollars, and rode the service elevator up to his floor. Although he had lugged the heavy suitcase a relatively short distance—from locker to taxi, from taxi to elevator, and from the elevator down the corridor to his room—Smiley was damp with perspiration. He breathed through his open mouth in short controlled gasps, forestalling a coughing fit, and rested for fully five minutes, sitting in the straight chair beside his bed.

This five-minute rest was a period of delicious anticipation for Smiley. Every suitcase, paper sack, shopping bag, cardboard box (and even the occasional serviceman's duffel bag) that Smiley stole and smuggled into his room was a treasure trove, a cause for excited anticipation. And the longer Smiley could delay the opening, the better it was when he opened the surprise package. To Smiley a locked suitcase was like a Christmas present and, despite the hazards of his occupation, he celebrated Christmas morning almost every night. He liked to savor the opening of his finds; he patiently untied the hardest knots when a suitcase was hound with twine or rope. And best of all, he liked a difficult suitcase lock—although he had never encountered a locked suitcase that could not be opened with his prized collection of assorted keys and odd pieces of wire.

Rested, breathing audibly but a little easier, Smiley admired the enormous black suitcase on his bed. He rubbed his palms together, unsnapped the two side clasp locks simultaneously, and tentatively pressed the silvered push-button beneath the black leather handle. With a solid clicking sound the top popped unlocked, and Smiley raised the heavy lid.

This was no ordinary two-suiter; it was a case for a machine

of some kind. A shiny black enameled panel confronted his
eyes instead of heaped clothing, a complicated instrument
panel dotted with black knobs and little glass-faced meters
above most of them. There was a huge glass-faced meter in the
center of the panel, and there were additional meterless knobs
labeled "Vol," "On," "Off," "Treb," "Bass," "Comp," and
others in combinations of upper case letters. Other mysterious
knobs were identified by numbers in serial, running from three
figures to five. Evidently, Smiley concluded, this was some kind
of high-powered radio.

He confirmed this hasty guess by unlatching the snaps on
each side of the instrument panel. The front wall of the case
fell forward exposing two cloth-covered speakers and a center
jack-nest with a half-dozen male and female sockets. There
was a pullout cord, and Smiley pulled it out and plugged it
into the wall socket beside his bed. He turned the "On" knob
as far to the right as it would go and started when the panel
flooded suddenly with light and the machine hummed angrily
into life. He turned down the "Vol" and the humming sub-
sided to a barely audible undertone. Never, never had Smiley
found anything as unusual as this—whatever it was—and he
pulled his chair closer to the bed to study the machine carefully.

Berkowitz would surely give him at least a hundred bucks
for this beauty, although it would be best to start the haggle
at two hundred to be on the safe side. Smiley reached out and
tentatively turned one of the small metered knobs to the right.
A dry cackling noise came out of both speakers. It stopped. A
moment later the cackle broke out anew, stopped again. An
unpleasant cackle, the jeering laughter of an old crone, false,
ingratiating, insincere.

Smiley listened to the dry cackle three more times before
turning the knob back to zero. He tried another knob, and
this twist produced a hearty belly laugh, a deep, masculine ho-
ho-ho brought up from the jellied depths of a fat man's stomach. The third knob was a silly schoolgirl's foolish giggle, a
trilling tee-hee-hee ascending to high C and on into an even
higher register. Smiley switched it off quickly, before the voice

could giggle again.

There was a different laugh on each track, and Smiley tried each of them singly, in turn, before trying them in various combinations. The machine was simple enough to operate, once he got the hang of it, and finally he turned on all of the knobs and left them on. He twisted the main volume control to the last notch, and his small ascetic room rocked with wild laughter. The uncontrolled laughter reverberated from the walls with an overpowering, insane, helpless burst of merriment.

With a curse, Smiley turned off the machine and pulled the plug out of the wall. He opened the door a crack and listened for a moment, but there were no footfalls in the corridor, no complaining voices. He locked the door and sat in his chair, facing the machine on the bed. It was a laughing machine—that was what it was, all right—but what good was it? Who would want it? Berkowitz would know, of course, what the machine was for and how much it was worth, down to the last penny. But he would probably—most certainly—lie about the value of the laughing machine. Instead of starting to haggle at two hundred dollars, Smiley decided to ask five hundred right from the beginning. A lot of work had gone into the designing of this curious machine, to say nothing of finding all of those people with their different kinds of crazy laughs to go with it.

Smiley called Berkowitz on the phone and told him to bring plenty of money with him. Waiting, nervous now as he waited for the fence to arrive, Smiley lit a cigarette to induce a coughing spell ahead of time in the hope that he wouldn't have one during Berkowitz's visit. The hope was in vain; Smiley began to cough the moment the fence entered the room with a cigar clamped in his teeth.

"Sorry, Smiley," Berkowitz said, stubbing out his cigar in the ashtray on the dresser. "I forgot about your cough. Now, what's so great that you wanted me to bring *money* instead of just money?"

In reply, Smiley plugged in the machine and gradually controlled his breathing. He turned on the machine and twisted the second knob—the big belly laugh came through the speakers. The second time the laugh boomed, Berkowitz joined in himself, and Smiley switched off the machine.

"Every knob makes a different laugh," Smiley explained, "and they all work. You can make 'em all laugh at once or one at a time. This machine's worth a lot of dough, Berkowitz, and I don't feel like arguing all night about how much either."

Berkowitz chewed pensively on the wide end of his dead cigar. He studied the machine without touching it. He stared at the corner of the room for a moment then turned his gloomy eyes on Smiley. He shook his head and started toward the door. With his hand on the knob, he turned.

"D'you know what that thing is, Smiley?"

"Sure, it's a laughing machine. What else?"

"That's right, Smiley. But what's it for?"

"For laughs, what else? A guy's unhappy, he needs a few laughs, he buys himself a laughing machine, that's all," Smiley said quickly, alarmed by Berkowitz's signs of departure.

"Nuh-uh." Berkowitz shook his head. "This thing's a TV laughing machine; and with only three networks, it's got to belong to one of them. A hot laughing machine is too damned hot to handle, Smiley. They use machines like this instead of an audience when they tape TV shows. You've seen these kind of shows, Smiley. A woman from next door comes into her neighbor's kitchen with a cup. She says, 'Can I borrow me a cup of sugar?' Quick, then, the TV technician with the laughing machine—like this one—throws in a few chuckles or maybe a couple of giggles on the tape. A real audience don't laugh when somebody asks for a cup of sugar, so they got to use a laughing machine to put some fake laughs on the tape. I couldn't give you even a dime for it, Smiley, because I couldn't get rid of it. It's too hot."

"It's still worth a lot of dough no matter what it's used for," Smiley protested.

"That's right. Especially to the network man you copped it off of, but I ain't sticking my neck out for any TV network. Your best bet is to get rid of it—and fast." Berkowitz opened the door.

"Just a minute." Smiley pushed the door closed. "What about a reward, like jewels and insurance? We put an ad in the paper the way you do with hot ice. 'Will whoever it was who lost a laughing machine contact box so-and-so. All replies confidential.' Then when the network answers the ad, we make us a deal like with jewels and insurance companies. They pay us a reward, no questions asked, and they get back the machine—"

"No. With jewels, Smiley, money is involved. Real money. But not with something like this machine. They got TV technicians at the networks who could throw another machine like this together in maybe two or three hours. There isn't enough money in it to fool with it, not with the risks involved." When Berkowitz reached for the doorknob again, Smiley stood aside and let him out.

"Later, Smiley. But thanks for giving me first crack at it, anyway."

"Later, Berko."

Smiley closed the door and bolted it with the chain lock. He returned to the machine, twisted the first knob and was rewarded with the same unvarying, dry, insincere cackle. He pulled the plug, closed the lid and refastened the clasp locks. Berkowitz was right: the valuable machine wasn't worth a dime. It would be pointless to call another fence; he would get the same kind of turndown. He looked at the clock—eight o'clock. Too late for another crack at Grand Central. Besides, the basement door was locked, and if he did get anything, he would have to come through the main lobby, and the night clerk would raise hell with him again.

Smiley fished out his five quarters and juggled them in his hand. He already had a locker key, and five quarters were enough for another night. He only needed four quarters for change, in case he ran into somebody with a dollar bill, and that left two-bits over to buy a bowl of lentil soup. He was chilled clear through now that his excitement had passed, but he wasn't hungry—not hungry enough, anyway—to leave his warm room again. Not tonight.

Without warning, the cough began again, and this time it

was truly bad—the worst ever. He stretched out prone on his bed beside the laughing machine, gasping and crying as the dry hacks tortured his thin body. By the time he stopped, he was so weak and dizzy he whimpered. Smiley ripped off his tight toupee and tossed it on the dresser. He soaped off the makeup in the bathroom using water as hot as he could stand on his face. He removed his jacket and dropped it on the floor on his way back to the bed.

He flopped on the bed beside the machine. He would have to get rid of the machine, but not tonight—tomorrow. He began to cough again, a high squeaky noise this time, like some kid jumping up and down on one of those rubber dolls with a whistle in the back. This was really the big one—he knew it—but no, he stopped, and just in time, too. His room was full of stars. It was bad enough to be dizzy when he was on his feet and coughing, but to get dizzy lying down was too much for a man, too much for anybody.

Barely breathing through his open mouth, Smiley sat up and swung his feet to the floor. He leaned forward and held his head in both hands. As blood filled his head, the dizziness gradually disappeared. He dropped forward to his knees on the floor, pulled his jacket toward him, and took the locker key out of the pocket. He got to his feet, crossed to the ugly Monterey desk beneath the window, and took a hotel envelope out of the drawer. He scratched "F.B.I." on the envelope with the gummy hotel pen, dropped the key inside, and licked the flap. He centered the envelope on the desk and began to flip through the big Manhattan telephone book. When he found the F.B.I. emergency number, he lifted the phone and gave it to the switchboard operator.

"Listen once and listen close," Smiley said slowly, when the connection was made and a deep male voice answered, "because I ain't going to repeat anything. Now. My name is Smiley Mason—Mason—and if you don't believe what I tell you when I'm through, you'd better check my record out with the dip detail. According to them people, I'm capable of anything. I just planted a time bomb in Grand Central Station. It's in a two-bit locker, and I mailed you the key. It's set to go off in two hours, or maybe three; it's homemade, and I'm not sure which—" Smiley quickly racked the phone.

Somehow the lie made him feel a little better. Smiley returned to the straight-backed chair beside his bed, sat down and stared glumly at the huge laughing machine. Now that it was closed, it looked like a large but quite ordinary suitcase. He probably should have gone down to the lobby and used the pay phone. If the agent hadn't been too excited about the time bomb, and if the operator happened to remember the number, they could trace his call. Maybe they could, and maybe not—but in the meantime, all hell would be breaking loose down at Grand Central as they tried to clear people out and find the time bomb that wasn't there. . .

In slow motion, the downward arrows at the corners of Smiley's mouth made a looping curve and pointed toward the ceiling. His lips and face broke into contorted wrinkles of pain and pleasure and, from deep inside his chest—who knows where it had hidden so many years—a giggle escaped. The foolish giggle changed abruptly into a dry cackle; the thin cackle dropped manfully down the scale and almost developed into a mature, rumbling ho-ho-ho before the coughing started. But this time, when the coughing stopped, so did Smiley. ◉

## The Man Who Loved Ann Landers

PO BOX 33143347
Miami, Florida 33143
June 3, 1975

Dear Ann Landers,

Attend this closely: If you are one of Ann Landers' eight secretaries or letter readers, do not turn the page. Check the envelope again and you will see that it is marked *Personal* and *Confidential*. What this means, together with the Air Mail and Special Delivery stamps and the pasted-on certificate stating *Certified*, is that this letter is for the eyes of Mrs. Landers only—not for you, young woman, no matter how much you are trusted by your employer, who is probably the most trusting woman in the world.

Do you understand that, dear?

Very well, then, *do not* turn the page.)

Dear Ann,

Please excuse the sharp tone of the preceding page, but I have a secretary myself, Louisa Hawkins (who is *not* typing this letter, by the way—I am), and it took me many months to persuade Louisa not to read any of my mail that was marked *Personal* or *Confidential* or even *Addressee Only*. Not that I ever get that much personal mail, or mail that is clearly marked *Personal* on the envelope, but there have been a few letters over the years (I'm only human, ha, ha), even though I have been married for 21 years and in the lumber business for 14. I'm sure you will understand. No one, it seems to me, understands the human condition any better than you do, or as well, especially the American human condition, which is even more important, as we enter our Bicentennial Year, 1976.

I find it difficult getting into this letter, probably because I do not wholly trust the secretary of yours who undoubtedly opened this letter, even though it is addressed to you personally, and clearly marked.

(If such is the case, please stop reading, Ms.—, and turn this highly personal letter over to your employer at once.)

I have never written a letter to a newspaper or to a columnist before. You don't realize, or perhaps you do, how many letters to you begin this way, but I do, and the reason for so many firsts is that people love and trust you, and they turn to you as a last resort for relief from their anguish, pain, and in search for a loving, understanding heart, and know that you will be there with your wisdom, kindness, and comfort.

By now you have guessed, haven't you? But I'll go ahead and say it, anyway: "I love you, Ann Landers!"

But I didn't know how much I loved you until this morning, even though I've been reading your column every day for at least 18 years.

Here in Miami, if you don't receive your home delivery of the *Miami Herald* by 6:30 A.M. or the *Miami News* by 5:30 P.M., you call 350-2111, inform the girl on the switchboard, and a paper is delivered by a special messenger within a very few minutes. I take both papers, you see. I read your column in the morning *Herald,* and your sister's column in the afternoon *Miami News.* I won't go into comparisons (they are always odious) except to say that you invariably give heartfelt advice, and your sister mostly prints letters that allow her to say, "Thank you for writing; you've made my day."

This morning, however, when the *Herald* arrived, your column was not in the "Living Today" section. I looked carefully again, and then searched through the rest of the paper, thinking that perhaps your column had been switched to another section, to "Real Estate," or even "Sports." But it wasn't in the paper—anywhere. I called the *Herald* immediately, of course, but it was too early for the "Living Today" editor to have come in (she works from 9:30 A.M. to 6:30 P.M., the *Herald* being a morning paper). She finally told me, when I called her later from my office, that the column was somehow squeezed out of the Monday "A.M." paper because of a "jump" story from the "Living Today" front on how to cook a tuna casserole. She seemed to be as devastated as I was about the omission because, as I told her, and as friendly as I could under the circumstances (and please excuse the French) that any a—h— could certainly cook a tuna casserole without instructions but, you must realize that "Living Today" is merely a euphemism for what the *Herald* used to call the "Women's Page." Apparently, nowadays, what with the high rate of unemployment, inflation, and so on, the *Herald* is doing its part in calling attention to various ways that housewives, or "home-makers" as the "Living Today" editor puts it, can save some dough on their weekly food bills by fixing inexpensive meals.

But just sitting there, in the breakfast nook this morning, without your column to read with my coffee, it was like a blow to the heart not to find you in the paper. My wife sleeps until 10:30, or sometimes 11:00 A.M., and I have prepared and eaten my breakfast alone, except for you to communicate with (thank God) for most of my married life. I like it that way. I fix a four-minute egg (no trouble on my electric egg-cooker, because it comes out exactly the same every morning), a slice of very dry, almost melba-ed rye toast, and drink two, sometimes three, cups of instant coffee while I read the paper. Usually I can get to the bathroom for my daily-daily on two cups, but sometimes it takes three, and I always save the "Sports" section for the John, you see. Meanwhile, my wife pounds my ear in the bedroom (we have separate bedrooms; I want you to know this, because we haven't slept together since Kathy, my daughter, left for college two-and-a-half years ago).

I'm going to mail this now. I've broken the ice and you'll hear from me very soon again (how wonderful it is, for a change, to talk to a warm, reasonable, understanding and loving woman!), but I have an appointment right now with a man (he's in the waiting room now) who wants to buy at least two loads of siding. And business, especially the construction business, being as slow as it is today, I can't let this man get away from me. But I know you will understand.

The important thing is that I have told you that I love you, and this letter is not for publication. It is personal and confidential, and you don't have to reply if you don't want to, except to say that you have received it okay, and I have enclosed a stamped, self-addressed envelope for that purpose. There will be more, a good deal more, about my wife later.

All my love,
Mort Springer

PO Box 33143347
Miami, Florida 33143
June 5, 1975

Dear Ann,
(If you are a secretary, read no further. I am Mort Springer, and I am a personal correspondent and friend of Mrs. Landers, as is so plainly and clearly marked on the envelope.)

Dear Ann—I haven't heard from you yet, which isn't surprising because I only mailed my first letter to you yesterday, and Chicago is a long way from Miami; but all day yesterday, and well into the evening, I was walking around in a state of euphoria, sheer joy, and I knew it was because I finally had the guts, or the gall if you like, to tell you of my love. It truly made my day.

Finally, last night about eleven, unable to sleep because of my excitement, I took one of those non-prescription Nytol's and dropped off in a hurry. I don't remember ever taking drugs to get to sleep on before. I usually put in one "hellova" day down at the lumber yard, and then, after I get home and argue with my wife for two or three hours, I'm exhausted and ready for the sack. You see, I don't love my wife, Ann, I only love you. But the way things are, I am kind of stuck with her and can't think of any way to get out of my marital situation. I read your letters and replies (I've told you that already) and I know that you advise couples to stay together, no matter what, or to seek marriage counseling or psychiatric help or to join Al-anon; but, you can't squeeze blood from a turnip.

Not that my wife is a turnip; what she is is a drinker, not an alcoholic; a hypochondriac, not an invalid; and a whiner, nagger and, ever since she went through the change, a bitch on wheels. And, I've told her so.

"Myrna," I say, "you're a bitch on wheels." And she laughs at me.

She spends every dime I make, sometimes more than I make, and there are times, more frequently of late, when I feel like I'm working my ass off for nothing. It just so happens that I like the work, my work, and I hate to go home at night. I guess that is the only thing that has kept me going lately, knowing that for eight, more often ten hours, a day I can be busy at the lumber yard, although business recently hasn't been all that good.

In fact, business has been pretty bad, what with construction falling off all over Dade County. I'm still making it, however, but by going after the smaller accounts, and so far I haven't had to let anyone go. When a man quits, however, which doesn't happen often, I don't replace him, that's all.

It's not my purpose to bore you with business matters, but I want to set the record straight. I know almost everything there is to know about you from your daily replies to the letters you get, from the articles and pieces I've read about you in magazines and newspapers. Perhaps you don't realize how much of yourself you have given away to the keen and interested reader over the years. You haven't driven a car for 15 years, for example, which is another endearing feminine trait you have. My wife, of course, drives like a demon. When I bought her an M.G. on her birthday three years ago, she totaled it two days later. Unhappily, she didn't get a scratch, although she was shaken up a little. The doctor gave her a sedative; she slept for twelve straight hours, got up, and bugged me for a new car immediately, still in her nightie. I replaced the M.G. with a second hand Volks and she is not allowed, naturally, behind the wheel of my Imperial.

But there have sure been some wailing arguments about that Volks, as you can well imagine, especially about the color, a kind of brindle brown, to use a euphemism.

But you know so little about me, it's hard to begin to tell you. Finances are important. I have to meet a payroll of 15 employees, formerly 18, but I still clear about 75,000 a year. I've done better than that, but I'll do as well this year. Also, unbeknownst to Uncle Sam, I've got 22 thousand stashed away in a numbered account in Nassau, 26 minutes away by air from Miami, and I've been adding to this account for the last few years, knowing, or realizing, that if I was ever lucky enough to get a divorce, I could get cleaned out of, at least, half of everything I've got and, perhaps, a little more than that. So no one, other than you now, knows about my Nassau account.

I also own two points in a Palm Beach condominium, and not even my accountant knows about those two points; and I've been negotiating for two more points in a retirement complex in Ft. Myers, which is now the fastest growing real estate area in the U.S. (I pass this info on in case you want to get a little action and tax break in Florida). The rest of my money is clear and aboveboard, with some outstanding loans from banks for business purposes. In the lumber business, in any business, you use borrowed money, not your own. But then, I suspect you know all that.

My house, on a canal in Southeast Miami, was built ten years ago for $60,000; today you couldn't touch it for $150,000. But you and I can scratch the house from our future, because my wife would get that if we ever, you and I, get it on, which I know we will do, eventually.

I've enclosed a recent photograph. I thought it would be easier than to try and describe what I look like. As you can see, I'm almost six feet tall (that palm tree I'm standing next to is in my back yard), and I'm 220 lbs. I started a diet, however, and I'll be down 10 or 12 lbs. by the time we get together. It doesn't show in the photo, but I wear contact lenses; my eyes are blue. As you can see, I'm being honest with you. I didn't have to tell you about the contacts, but every man who passes 40—50 at least needs reading glasses. Last year I had a mushy prostate, but that's been taken care of, thank God, and I'm okay in that department now, which is something else you're entitled to know. I don't know why I feel so embarrassed, talking about myself this way, my physical self, I mean; but, my self-image is positive and there is no point in trying to disguise what I look like. To be completely honest, Ann, dear, I'm in pretty good shape physically for a man of my age. I used to run the 440 in college (University of Florida), and I still play tennis twice a week, Tuesday and Thursday evenings, with my accountant, a CPA, and a close personal friend as well. We only play two sets. I would rather play three and push myself a little more, but two sets is all he is up to for one evening. He frequently wins the first set, but I always win the second because I have more stamina.

That's enough for this letter, I guess. But you just write though, and ask me questions, anything you want to know about me, no matter how personal, and I'll tell you. When I love a person, and I do love you, I want everything to be aboveboard, on the line, and let the chips fall where they may.

Please write soon. I truly love you.

All my love,<br>Mort Springer

June 10, 1975

Dear Ann,

(PERSONAL AND CONFIDENTIAL—FOR ANN LANDERS ONLY. MORT SPRINGER.)

Once again, Ann, dear, excuse the abrupt message, above, in Caps; but, so many days have gone by now without my hearing from you I have been wondering whether you got my other two letters. I should have heard from you by now. After all, I've been sending my mail Special Delivery—Air Mail, which should indicate to you that an urgent reply is needed, and even if you do get 4,000 letters a week, how many of them are marked Personal, Confidential, and Urgent? We have got to do something about our lives, you and I, and although you have said in your columns many times that you are happily married to Mr. Landers I can read between the lines as easily as the next person.

You were very understanding when your daughter got her divorce, I thought, but I could also tell by the tone of your writing that you were teed off as well, and I don't blame you. But you and I are mature individuals, and we are entitled to at least a halfway decent love life in our declining, but golden, years.

With your husband off on business trips all the time, and you, lonely, rattling around all by yourself in that big, rambling apartment on East Lake Shore Drive, I know that your marriage is not as happy as you pretend it to be in your columns.

When you and I start living together, Ann, my little darling, believe me when I tell you that I'll never let you out of my sight. If you want to keep on with your column, if that's what it takes to make you happy, I'll fix up an office for you next to mine down at the lumber yard. But that's another matter we can discuss at some length when I have resolved my marital situation and you have done something about yours.

Meanwhile, it is very difficult for me to carry on this one-sided correspondence when you haven't answered any of my letters. If you feel the need of a secret code, or something like that, work it out, and I'll use it too. Or you can phone me: 305-443-9946. But I would rather that you didn't call me at home (my phone may be bugged). I'm not ready as yet to make my move. I need a written letter from you first, a confirmation in writing, of your love for me.

If you need any more details about me, want to know more, like my hobbies or something, you just write and ask away. Otherwise, I'm afraid of boring you with such things. I've told you the main things about myself as a person, but the primary thing is that I love you!

All my love,
Mort

June 20, 1975

Dear Ann Baby, it's Mort. Still no personal letter, although I finally caught on. You were very clever, and it was stupid of me not to see the code at once. But I had to read the column three times before it dawned on me. The obvious clue came in your reply to the woman with the snoring husband, and after that it was easy to break. If I hadn't been alert for a sign of some kind from you I would have missed it altogether. So you do love me—thank God! Fair enough. I realize that you've got to work out the problems with your husband first, as I still have to do with my wife, but now it will only be a matter of time before we're together forever!

From now on it will also be dangerous for us to correspond, or for me to write, but I'll watch your daily column, and when you give me the final word, I'll make my move. Then I'll write and give you the details on the final plan.

To this end, to speed things up a bit, I cultivated a Cuban paste-up man who works for the Herald. He will give me your columns in advance (xerox copies of them) as they come in. They arrive well ahead of time in batches of six, with the Sunday column coming in separately, as you already know, I suppose (ha ha); after all, you're writing them. I still can't get over that clever, absolutely brilliant, reply you gave me in the guise of a reply to the woman with the snoring husband. Wow, as the kids all say. How you knew that about me, I'll never know, unless you tell me. I know I never mentioned it in my other letters I sent to you.

Anyway, by getting your columns a week in advance of publication, I'll have more time to study the secret code, and you will hear from me earlier as well. Oh, my darling, darling, darling little girl, you are absolutely brilliant!

     All my love,
     Mort OOOXXXXXX(3 hugs, 6 kisses)

June 28, 1978

Dearest Ann,

There is no abrupt epigraph this time, because this letter
will be placed in your sweet little hands personally by a man
or woman wearing the uniform of the Quicksilver Messenger
Service, Chicago. When I got the word, I knew that ordinary
correspondence, even Registered—Special Delivery, would be
much too dangerous, and a phone call absolutely out of the
question. I'd have to give my name to get through to you.

I was overwhelmed, to put it lightly. In fact you bowled
me over by the outrageous boldness of your reply. I read the
xeroxed column again and again, and the tone of your message was exactly, precisely, right and in good taste. No one,
other than myself, will ever suspect that you are divorcing
your husband to come and live with me. Your column to your
readers was most discreet, and even if the truth comes out,
they'll all be on your side. And I can also understand that,
until you have actually met me, and have been in my loving
arms, you will still have a few reservations about my love for
you, too. But read on. What I have to tell you, if any more
proof is needed, should certainly persuade you.

After I picked up the xeroxed columns from the paste-up
man and gave him his fifty bucks (the best fifty I ever laid on
anybody), I read them through in The Oak Room at HoJo's,
drove to my office and read them again, at least a dozen
times.

Then I made my plan.

I called in Bob Coleman, my foreman, and told him that my
wife and I were going to New York City for two weeks on a
second honeymoon. That was clever, wasn't it? Because after
I return to work after being with you a couple of weeks, my
radiant expression will make me look as if I have been on a
honeymoon (ha ha)!

Bob can only handle things for about two weeks. If some
major problem arises, he has a tendency to panic; what he is is
a good No. 2-man, you know.

I went home at 5:30 as usual, and my wife had had two

martinis already. I was just as friendly as I could be, and I drank right along with her, although I made my drinks very light and loaded hers. She passed out at 10:00 P.M. I smothered her with a pillow and buried her after midnight in the backyard, right under the palm tree which is in the photo I sent to you. I made a small cross of laths and put it over her grave (it took me until 2:00 A.M. to finish the job) because she was a Catholic. If anyone ever says anything about the cross, I can always say that I buried a dog there. There's a city ordinance against burying dogs in your yard, but it isn't enforced, and almost everybody does it.

Then I sat down to write this letter to you. I'll be leaving for the airport in a few minutes, and will post the letter to the Quicksilver Messenger Service in Chicago with instructions and a signed $10 traveler's check. By the time your column announcing your divorce from Mr. Landers comes out in the papers all over the U.S.A., you will be with me in Nassau, at the Paradise Beach Hotel and Casino, Suite 312 (the reservations were made and confirmed by phone before I sat down to write this letter to you here in my study). We'll be able to talk, make love, swim, gamble if you want to—but most of all, talk—I've got a million things to tell you; and, we can make our plans for the future. If you want me to, I'll even sell my business and move to Chicago. But, I'm sure you'll like it better in Miami than you do in Chicago. The weather here is so much better.

Well, I have to pack now, and seal this letter, and then write out the instructions for the Quicksilver Messenger Service.

I'll be waiting for you in Nassau, my own sweet love—so be prepared for the happiest years in your entire life! I love you, and I'll be waiting.

     Your own dear Mort


XOXOXOXOXOXOXOXOXOXOXOXOXOXOXOXOXOX
AND A MILLION MORE!

# How Warren & Lee College Came to Florida Instead of Some Kooky Town in Southern California (Where it Belongs)

DURING MY last year in college I evaluated the teachers I had admired most and concluded, not surprisingly, that my best teachers had been either ex-actors who had lost their nerve or ex-preachers who had lost their faith. If, I remember thinking, a teacher should come along some day who filled both of those roles, and with a new idea, he would be rewarded with overflowing classrooms—if not money.

When I met Dr. William C. Childress one night at a crowded Florida West Coast tavern on U.S. 41, I finally discovered that teacher. "Bill" was in his mid-fifties, and he perspired freely. His face, as well as his bald head, looked as though it had been sponged with Campbell's tomato soup, and his tailored seersucker suit must have set him back at least 200 bucks. He had acted in New York; he had preached in California; he had been a high school principal in West Texas; and he was now a brand-new college president in Florida. There are no dates listed here because I didn't take notes, but readers interested in the statistics on Dr. Childress will find a detailed biography on the educator when the first college bulletin of Warren and Lee is issued.

Bill had just completed a survey of Florida for a location to establish the physical plant of the new two-year college of Warren and Lee. His salary, a modest $25,000 per year, would be increased, he said, as soon as the college was operative, the faculty hired, and paying students enrolled.

"Florida was a poor choice," I opined, "for a private two-year college. We've got 30 some-odd junior colleges in Florida already, and your new college will have keen competition for our low community college rates."

"Warren and Lee," he said, "is not a community college. It's a college for investigators. We will offer terminal degrees to those dedicated men and women who plan to devote their lives to uncovering the truth about the Kennedy assassination."

As Dr. Childress explained his plans for the new college I was skeptical, and some of my questions were probably impertinent.

"Who," I asked, sneering, "would be stupid enough to sign up for a school like that?"

"Well," he replied calmly, "without any publicity, we've had more than 300 inquiries already."

"That only proves there are a lot of nuts loose in the world. And to start a new college a huge endowment is needed, and—"

"Warren and Lee has an endowment of more than a million, and matching funds have been promised by three foundations as soon as we open."

My interest was aroused, and I signaled for more beer.

"The school will be small," Dr. Childress continued, "and we'll screen all applicants to keep out the 'nuts' you mentioned. As you may not know, there are more than 75 fulltime unofficial investigators now in the field who have promised to devote the rest of their lives to uncovering the truth about the assassination. Some of these investigators are professionals; others are amateurs performing substandard work.

"We will attract many of the latter, but we're counting heavily on drawing our students from the disaffiliated, the hippies, those young Americans who need worthwhile lifetime goals. Our college, which requires 60 credits for graduation, will be successful because it's needed—and traditional colleges aren't meeting the need. For example, instead of a summer do-nothing vacation, there'll be field trips to New Orleans, Dallas, Mexico, and Cuba for the purpose of following Oswald's Goliardic trail. Each student-investigator will be required to write a thesis on a new theory of the case, based upon his personal investigations. The student's senior thesis will determine whether he will receive his diploma and his lifetime investigator's certificate."

"Just a moment, Dr. Childress: why're you telling me all this, a stranger you met in a bar on a warm night? This stuff sounds like restricted, if not secret, information—"

"Until today," he laughed, "it was restricted. But now it's a relief to discuss the college with a friendly outsider."

"And why today?"

"Because today I've finally selected the site. Vizcaya, in Miami—"

"Vizcaya! That's one of Miami's prime tourist attractions! They'll never sell it to you."

"We won't close it down, son. The sight-seeing revenue from this estate will be another part of our environment. There'll be no difficulty in buying Vizcaya. Miami welcomes new industries, especially clean industries that don't burn oil or coal. Besides, Miami won't lose a tourist attraction, it will gain a sorely needed college. But to answer your earlier question, the selection of Vizcaya, together with other information about Warren and Lee, will be released to the wire services as soon as I've made my report to the trustees in Dallas."

"Who are the trustees?"

He smiled. "Their names are classified at present."

As he finished his beer I said, "Why did you pick on—I mean, choose—Florida? With your trustees all in Dallas, it seems to me that—"

"You should listen more carefully. I didn't say that my trustees all lived in Dallas; I said that I would report to them in Dallas."

"All right. But Dallas still seems like a better location for your kind of college."

"At first thought, yes, but with our two-year curriculum, and with our students living in the same city, they'd become too well-known to Dallas residents. And, in Dallas, there might be some police resentment. We've already decided not to enroll any ex-policemen from Dallas, nor will we accept former members of the CIA or FBI, even though they claim to be disgruntled defectors. Do you know what happened to the Communist Party when it opened its ranks to so-called defectors from the FBI?"

I nodded. "About how many students do you expect to have?"

"That question gave our planning committee a lot of headaches. A national survey was made, of course, and we were able to formulate a plan for our first three years. We'll matriculate 300 students a year, but we'll only graduate about 150 investigators per year. We learned from our survey that the American economy will only absorb about 150 new investigators per annum at a standard, middleclass wage."

"Do you mean that your graduates will be able to earn a living by fulltime investigation of the assassination?"

"Of course! By the publication of their findings, by television appearances, by renting the films they make, and so on." Dr. Childress shook his head and frowned. "Americans do not invest time and money in an intensive two-year training course if they can't make a living from it afterwards. There'll always be a new audience for assassination articles and books, television programs, and films. And, of course, there will be fresh and exciting new evidence uncovered by our skilled graduate-investigators.

"There'll be high and low information years, granted, but sensational discoveries will offset unyielding low-information years. But as I said before, our national economy will only absorb about 150 new investigators a year. As time passes, together with the development of new investigative techniques and new equipment, the day will surely arrive when Warren and Lee will become a four-year college."

"What are your curriculum plans—in general?"

"First of all, there'll be daily seminars for all students on the 56 volumes of the Warren Report. We've borrowed this pedantic practice from parochial schools. We want our graduates to know the Warren Report, chapter and verse, down to the most minute discrepancy. Then there'll be regular courses in investigative techniques, symbolic logic, abnormal psychology, and required courses on the standard assassination textbooks—"

"What standard texts?"

"Epstein's *Inquest;* Mark Lane's *Rush to Judgment;* Weisberg's *Whitewash.* Surely these basic texts are familiar to you?"

"I guess so, but I thought you meant something like Manchester's *Death of a President.* "

"Don't worry," Dr. Childress said grimly, "the Manchester book will be studied, but as an example of amateurism! It's an unhappy fact of education that even spurious works are valuable to learning: to understand Romanticism, one must, regrettably, read McPherson's *Ossian.* "

Although I had read and enjoyed Manchester's book, I decided not to say so. "How'd you decide on the name 'Warren and Lee'?" I asked.

"For the associative values. We feel that Warren and Lee will be associated in the public mind with Washington and Lee—two great Americans. But, as you know, there's already a college called Washington and Lee."

"Bill," I said casually, "I've got another question. What will happen to your college when one of the graduates discovers the actual truth behind the Kennedy assassination?"

"I've been expecting that one!" he said triumphantly. "And I'm going to answer you with another question. Why—think carefully—did Leon Czolgosz assassinate President McKinley?"

"I don't know."

"Well, think on it for a moment, bearing in mind that McKinley initiated our 'open door' policy for China." Smiling, Dr. Childress excused himself and headed for the men's room.

I paid the bar bill, his and mine, dropped a quarter in the juke box, punched the button three times for *Eleanor Rigby* and left. I was quick, but not quick enough. Dr. Childress caught up with me in the parking lot and hit me up for a donation to Warren and Lee. I handed him ten bucks and drove away fast, happy in a way that I had gotten off so lightly. ◉

## The Listener

THE FIRST time I saw The Listener, I was a Private in the United States Army stationed on Airstrip #37 near Stephenville, Newfoundland. And it was through a lucky accident that I happened to see him at all that night.

Actually I didn't mind being in the Army, and on the night The Listener appeared on television in the Day Room, I was thirty-seven years old with only two more months to go for discharge. In many ways I was lucky to have been drafted at thirty-five, so I could get my military service over with while I was still a young man. Back in 1960, when war was outlawed, one of the first things the Democratic administration did was raise the draft age to thirty-five, and even then they didn't take men into the Army unless they were married and had two or more children. As a consequence, it isn't really peculiar that I was the youngest man stationed on Airstrip #37. I enjoyed the life; I was away from my wife for two years, and all we had to do was a little close order drill in the mornings. I didn't even have to carry a rifle; being six feet tall, they made me the platoon guidon bearer.

In civilian life I had been an editor for the Farnsworth & Farnsworth Publishing Company, working mostly with novelists, and the two years in Newfoundland gave me an opportunity to work on a novel of my own. As an editor I had always (secretly) desired to be a writer instead. A writer has it all over an editor insofar as occupations are concerned; all he has to do is write a book and send it in to a publishing firm. But the poor editor has to decide whether it will sell or not. If he guesses wrong, the editor is in danger of losing his job; and if he guesses right, the best he can do is choose one book out of ten that will achieve a decent sale. But either way, the writer at least has his advance royalties to spend, whether his book has a decent sale or not. With only two months to go I was anxious to finish my novel. I had three completed chapters already, and I had only been working on the book for twenty-two months.

Corporal Baldy Allen stopped me in the hall after supper. "Les," he said. (My name is Lester Vitale.) "I was on the way to your room to get you. They've got some new tapes to show on TV tonight, some new shows that were flown in from the States this afternoon."

"I don't know, Baldy. I was going to work on my book tonight."

"Tomorrow is another day."

Unable to think of a counter-argument to refute his statement, I accompanied Baldy Allen to the Day Room. Everybody was there already, the entire platoon, all thirty of us. The first sergeant, a cranky old man of eighty-five who had been recalled to active duty from the Old Soldier's Home in Washington, D.C., sat at the dials of the television set. The first program of the evening was *The Listener*.

There were no sound effects, no music, and there wasn't any accompanying voice on the sound track. Merely The Listener, a man in his early forties, partially bald, with alert, keen eyes staring back at us, and a broad, understanding smile on his lips. Everybody waited, and when nothing happened, somebody called out to the first sergeant: "Put the sound on, Top!"

"It is on!" the first sergeant replied waspishly.

Everybody could see that the old sergeant was about ready to burst into tears, so we kept quiet, sat back and watched The Listener. I hadn't paid much attention to the title of the show, *The Listener*; if I thought of it at all I probably figured it was the beginning of a new family series. But the absence of commercials was a real shocker.

After the superimposed title faded out, the program opened with a close-up of The Listener's wonderful face. When the camera dollied back for a medium shot we all looked at The Listener, and he looked back at us. Wearing a black tuxedo, he sat relaxed in a large easy chair smoking a cigarette. Directly in front of his chair was a tall circular cigarette table holding a fresh package of Dream Girl jelly-filter cigarettes and an octagonal glass ashtray. The Listener was smiling, and his smile made me glow all over. I smiled back, and when I happened to glance around the room I noticed that all of the other soldiers were smiling at him, too. The Listener had such a nice, kindly, benign smile I felt like I knew the man, not as a friend, but as a brother. Later on, after I had watched him for a few weeks, I liked to think that The Listener was really my father. Not my own father, but my real father, a stranger back in my mother's past. I know how terrible it sounds to say such a thing, but I wasn't the only person who felt that way; a few months later there were millions of us who had similar daydreams about The Listener.

For the full half-hour, The Listener sat quietly in his chair smiling at us and, occasionally, nodding his head. When he finished one Dream Girl jelly-filter, he would light another, but it was plain to see that he was actively listening for what we had to say. He listened sincerely as if he wanted us to talk, to pour our troubles into his ear. I knew subconsciously that I could tell him anything and he would understand. Nobody made a sound during the program; we were in silent communication with the great man, and it was a truly wonderful experience.

There was no music, no announcer breaking in, and the production setup was simplicity itself, just switchovers from medium shots to close-ups.

When the program was over, the spell was broken of course. After war was outlawed, the networks were forbidden to show guns on any programs, and we sat through three new adult, weaponless programs. And they were above the average for adult westerns; Steve Allen in *The Tender Trapper*; Ed Wynn in *Camp Cook*, and Thelma Ritter in *Pale Face, Pale Rider*. But after watching *The Listener* for a glorious half-hour, the adult westerns weren't funny anymore.

"What did you think of The Listener?" Baldy Allen asked me as we started down the hall to the latrine after the Day Room closed.

"I'm not sure, Baldy. I know it sounds silly, but I wanted

to talk to the man and tell him about my novel. But the program's on tape, so it would be sort of foolish to talk to him."

"Nothing foolish about it," Baldy disagreed. "I wanted to talk to him myself. Some of the last few letters I've got from my wife have struck me as kind of odd, and I wanted to tell The Listener about them. D'you know what I mean?"

I nodded, and then a peculiar thing happened. I didn't smoke at the time, but I had an overwhelming desire to smoke a Dream Girl jelly-filter cigarette. "Say, Baldy," I said. "You smoke jelly-filters. Have you got an extra one on you?"

I thought I knew Baldy Allen. He was a used-car salesman in Queens back in civilian life, married, with five kids. We had been close friends for almost two years, and I really thought I knew him. But Baldy pulled his package of Dream Girls out of his pocket and counted them.

"I'm sorry, Les," he said firmly, "but I can't give you one. I've only got seventeen jelly-filters left, and I need them for myself." He left me standing in the hall without another word.

The next morning the Post Exchange sold out of Dream Girl jelly-filters at 9:00 A.M. The demand was so great a special planeload was flown up from Airstrip #18 in Chicago the same afternoon. Luckily I was able to buy two cartons, and I've smoked the same brand ever since.

Before *The Listener* appeared the following week, we signed a petition demanding individual television sets for our rooms so we could talk to The Listener in private. For a while it didn't look like we would get them, and then the sailors got—perhaps I had better explain.

In 1963 the Department of Defense finally achieved complete unification. As a consequence every camp, post and station and every ship at sea had the same complement of personnel and separate, but equal, facilities. On airstrip #37 where I was stationed, there were three officers: a Navy lieutenant commander, an Air Force major, and an Army major. There were thirty sailors, thirty airmen and thirty soldiers. The airmen did what little work there was to be done, servicing the few airplanes that landed on Airstrip #37 by mistake. The sailors, who didn't have any boats, tied knots all day and, as I said before, the soldiers did close order drill. In many ways complete unification was a real mess, believe me. Perhaps you remember Pete Martin's article in *The Saturday Evening Post*: "I Call on 186 Sailors, 186 Airmen, and 186 Soldiers Aboard the Nautilus Beneath the Polar Icecap"?

But the moment the sailors got individual TV sets, we got them, too. I had been waiting all week to ask The Listener one question, and it was the first question I asked when the program appeared.

"If I finish my novel, it'll be terrible, won't it?"

The Listener smiled and nodded his head, and I ripped the MS.—that's short for manuscript—of my novel into a dozen pieces and threw them into the wastebasket. There was a knack to asking The Listener questions; there wasn't anything negative about him at all. He never shook his head; he always nodded instead. And, of course, he never frowned; his wonderful smile was always on his sweet lips.

During the next few weeks, while I was waiting for my discharge date, The Listener confirmed a great many things for me that I had only suspected before. I learned that my brother-in-law would never pay me the ten dollars he owed me. I discovered that the dentist who charged me six hundred dollars to straighten my children's teeth made a profit of more than four hundred dollars! And I was really shocked to find out that my first wife was married again. I don't know why, but a man always thinks that—well, what difference does it make?

At last I was discharged, and my wife met me at La Guardia. (This was really Airstrip #48, but everybody still called it La Guardia Airport.) Naturally, the first thing I asked my wife was: "When does The Listener come on in New York?"

She had wonderful news for me. The demand from sponsors and public was so great that The Listener was now appearing for two solid hours every night!

"If we hurry," she said, "we'll be home just in time for his program!"

After being away from home for two full years, it was truly great to be home again, sitting in a comfortable chair and being able to watch The Listener on my own television set. And besides, the two-hour program had expanded in scope. It was a far cry from the half-hour weekly shows we had seen on tape over the Armed Forces Television Service. For the first time I was seeing The Listener on a live program!

The opening was unchanged, a close-up of The Listener's smiling face. But when the camera dollied back, there were dozens of commercial items on display. And during the two-hour show, the star managed to use them all in one way or another.

For instance, instead of smoking one Dream Girl jelly-tip, The Listener held a different brand of cigarette between each of his fingers, and a cigar between his thumb and forefinger. He would inhale from each brand, in turn, with evident enjoyment; and every time he took a puff, the sales of that particular brand skyrocketed all over the country.

But no matter what the sponsors made him do, The Listener's beautiful smile was constant. He still nodded his head now and then, although he was forced, by the nature of his activity, to sometimes take his understanding eyes away from the camera. That first two-hour program remains vividly in my mind.

After smoking for a few minutes, he crushed out the cigar and the cigarettes in an ashtray. He snatched a pogo stick from the floor, mounted it and bounced across the studio floor to a shiny new refrigerator. He opened the door, and as I remember, accidentally closed it on his fingers. Shaking the fingers of his injured hand, he sat down on the tiny seat of an Easy-Hay tricycle and pedaled across the studio again, this time to a brand new V-16 convertible. He patted the new car a couple of times, smiling into the camera, and then turned to a clothing rack that had been shoved onto the set by unseen hands. He slipped into three new overcoats, putting one coat on top of the other, shucked out of them quickly and let them fall to the floor. He ran a Dust-Down vacuum cleaner over the coats a few times, picked up a Nocry-Alldry Baby Doll and cradled it in his arms as he crossed the studio to another rack featuring women's Fourteen-Sixteen-Eighteen Petite Apparel. Dropping the doll to the floor, The Listener placed his left hand on his hip and modeled several of these dresses, holding them to his chest with his free hand. After discarding the dresses he pushed a Magneticsweep push broom across the floor on his way back to his easy chair. By this time there were several brands of toothbrushes and toothpastes on his low demonstration table and a small but compact shoe polish dauber and polisher. While brushing his teeth using a mixture of all the toothpastes, The Listener shined his shoes as well. That's the way the program went for the full two hours. The Listener demonstrated, touched or smiled and nodded at every one of the products sponsored, and all of them sold out the following morning as soon as the stores were opened.

Within a few weeks, the two networks opposite The Listener during the period he was on cancelled their opposing programs completely. With zero ratings no matter who they put against him, they found it much cheaper to have dead time. And besides, they had a difficult time finding performers willing to go on anyway. Who wanted to be doing something on an opposing network when they could be watching The Listener?

After two weeks at home, I went back to my old job as junior editor for Farnsworth & Farnsworth. And I was smart enough to get The Listener's okay before accepting any novel manuscripts for book publication. During the day I prepared short synopses of the MSS. submitted, and I read the synopses aloud to The Listener during his evening program. If he smiled and nodded when I finished the reading, I okayed the MS. for publication. If he smiled but didn't nod, I returned the MS. to the author with a printed rejection slip. My selection of novels with excellent sales leaped from a pre-The Listener average of one out of ten to a new high of six bestsellers out of ten. My salary soared from $10,000 a year to $35,000 a year, and with every bestseller that hit the lists, I received a large block of F & F stock.

Six months later, The Listener was on the television screen for twelve hours daily from six to six. I could do my work in the office, talking the problems over with The Listener on my office television set. I had a standing order with the Reliable TV Service to send a repairman to my apartment every afternoon to check my home set to make certain it was working properly. One evening when I got home, I found a note from my wife. She had fallen in love with the TV repairman and run away with him, taking both of the children. That was a brutal blow to the heart, all right. I lost the best TV repairman any man ever had!

The daily newspapers were filled with items about how The Listener had changed various persons' lives for the better. But there was very little personal information about the great man himself. *Time* magazine ran his picture on the cover every week in addition to a weekly cover story, but even *Time*'s best research editors couldn't dig out more than a sketchy background on his life. The way The Listener got started in television was another fabulous example of The American Way of Life.

He had been employed as a janitor by a local television station in Dallas, Texas. One night the old movie failed to arrive on time for the Late, Late All-Star Playhouse. Except for the technician on duty, there was no one else in the studio except The Listener, who was busily mopping the floor. The technician, with one of those brilliant flashes of inspiration that only happen to a man once in a lifetime, hustled The Listener into a tuxedo and trained a camera on him. That was his initial program, and he sat quietly in a chair, smiling and nodding into the camera for two solid hours while the technician fed canned commercials to the audience every fifteen minutes.

The response from the Dallas audience was so great that the Listener was kept on after that as a nightly Late, Late show. Three months after his first appearance a major network signed him up, and the rest is history. None of his fans knew anything about his personal life, but we didn't want to know anything about it. All we wanted to do was look at him, talk to him, and *love* him!

The next two years were truly The Age of The Listener, and the President issued a proclamation to that effect. On the day the three networks merged—and The Listener appeared on all three networks twenty-four hours a day—Congress declared a national holiday. I still remember the slogan: *Stop, Look, and Listener.*

I liked to watch him sleep at night. He smiled in his sleep, snoring away on a double-sized Bodyfirm mattress, wearing bright red Gallant Knight pajamas. They had to relax the rule about sound effects at night. He slept so peacefully that people got frantic, and the networks received so many panicky telephone calls from viewers who thought he was dead that they ran his snoring on the sound track. Sometimes during the night, when I awoke suddenly full of unknown fears, all I had to do was close my eyes and listen to his gentle snoring for a few minutes, issuing from the television set at my bedside, and I knew that everything was all right with the world. Within a few moments I would fall asleep again, back to the deep peaceful sleep of my childhood days.

And then the inevitable happened. Small groups of people began to band together all over the United States. The movement was small at first and, in New York, we blamed the Communist Party. Down in the southern states they blamed the N.A.A.C.P., but nobody knew for certain how the movement to eliminate The Listener began. They called themselves The Talkers, and they met in deserted garages, theaters and baseball parks just to *talk*, they said. But this was a dirty lie! What they really wanted was to *listen* to somebody else talk instead of talking to themselves or talking to The Listener!

The Talkers were definitely a minority group, less than ten percent of the entire population, but that fact was in their favor. The Talkers sent a delegation to the United Nations requesting the abolition of television. They were a clever group, all right. Not once was The Listener mentioned by name. But as a minority group they had the power under the World Constitution, and the United Nations passed a law abolishing television forever. The majority of the American public didn't even know there was such a group known as The Talkers. All of the time they were agitating, we were engaged in watching and talking to The Listener. Out of nowhere brutal F.C.C. men appeared in our homes, our offices, our bathrooms, all of them armed with axes. They smashed our sets to pieces before our astonished eyes.

The Age of The Listener was over.

Like all of the businesses, the publishing business picked up quickly as the writers began to write and submit manuscripts again. A lot of people don't realize it, but without writers, publishers would soon go out of business altogether. Psychiatrists who had been selling apples on street corners during The Age of The Listener were doing a land office business again. All across the nation, Americans were rolling up their sleeves and blinking their eyes in the unaccustomed sunlight as they went back to work.

No one knew what had happened to The Listener. He dropped completely out of sight now that television was gone, and within a few weeks everybody was too busy to think about the great man.

More than anyone else I felt his loss keenly. I had leaned on The Listener more than I realized, and I found that it was impossible for me to make a decision on any of the MSS. that were daily flooding my desk. And that's the only thing an editor is paid for: making a decision. I returned two hundred manuscripts in a row to their authors with printed rejected slips. Mr. Farnsworth, Sr. paid one of his rare visits to my office.

"Listen, Les," he said sternly. "You've okayed some good books in the past, and I know you can do it again. But you can't reject every MS. that comes in. Word gets around, you know, even to the writers in Kansas. The first thing we know we won't be getting any MSS. to reject at all. Now get busy! Work with these novelists! Make changes in their books whether they are needed or not so we'll have something to publish! We need new books for the Fall season, and we need them now!"

I was crushed by his angry logic. In desperation I picked up the first MS. my fingers touched on the desk and handed it to him.

"Here," I said. "Publish this."

The book became a bestseller, mainly because of a misunderstanding in the advertising department. The title of the book was *How to Mount Butterflies*, and it was written by a young fellow in Tujunga, California, named G. B. Shaw. The advertising department stated in their ads that it was a posthumous play by George Bernard Shaw. But that wasn't the only reason for the great success enjoyed by the little book. Now that television was gone, everybody was embracing a hobby of some kind to kill their evenings, and there isn't a more pleasant way to spend an hour or so than by mounting butterflies.

The slow months passed, but I never regained my former confidence. I selected books for publication by closing my eyes and picking one up from the desk, the way editors have been doing since the invention of movable type. And again I was back to the same standard of one best-selling book out of every ten published.

And then one fateful morning, Baldy Allen called me on the telephone. I hadn't seen Baldy since I left Newfoundland, and I agreed to have lunch with him and then go to a movie in the afternoon. He was unemployed and wanted to catch the show at the Paramount before the prices changed at 1:00 P.M. We didn't have much time to talk over old times because we really had to hustle to get to the theater on time.

I didn't particularly care for the movie. When television was abolished the motion picture industry had purchased all of the old television tapes and films and, as a consequence, there hadn't been a new movie made in years. The movie at the Paramount consisted of three old Jackie Gleason *Honeymooner* scripts spliced together with the commercials deleted. The newsreel was just as old, although it was very popular and was being featured all over town. Two-thirds of the newsreel was taken up by F.D.R. at his second inauguration in Washington. Without commercials, movies lack continuity. The management tried to make up for it by stopping the show in the most exciting spots and parading nude girls up and down the aisles selling popcorn; but it isn't television and it never will be.

After watching the show for about an hour, I made excuses to Baldy, telling him I had to get back to work. On the way out of the theater I stopped in the restroom for a minute, and there he was, The Listener!

There was a gray-black beard covering most of his face, but his wonderful smile came through in all its glory! He wore a shapeless gray felt hat on his head and, instead of the familiar impeccable tuxedo, he now wore a baggy-kneed blue serge suit. He held his fists together, and a shabby tweed overcoat was covering both wrists. I lifted the overcoat and discovered that his hands were cuffed together. My heart fluttered wildly, and my throat was dry as I wiped my trembling fingers with a paper towel.

"You're The Listener, aren't you?"

He smiled and nodded.

"And you escaped from The Talkers? Right?"

Again he nodded, smiling that beautiful smile.

"Come with me." This simple direct order was my last independent decision, and I've never regretted it. From that moment the course of my life was changed.

We climbed into a taxicab and went directly to my apartment. I hand-fed The Listener and put him to bed in my wife's old room. When he awoke I filed off the handcuffs. For the next three years The Listener lived quietly in my apartment, never stepping outside the door and never uttering a word. He could have walked out any time he felt like it, but he didn't want to leave me. I know he didn't, even though he never said anything.

I followed The Listener's nodding acquiescence in every undertaking, and I soon became rich and famous. When he nodded, I published a book, and it became a bestseller. When he nodded, I purchased the stocks I had listed on the financial pages of the *Wall Street Journal*. When he didn't nod, I didn't buy or I didn't publish. It was that simple.

I was a happy man. Nothing made me happier than waiting upon The Listener hand and foot. He wanted for nothing: he wore the best brocaded robes; he ate the tastiest meals the hotel kitchen across the street could send over; and he drank only the best vintage champagnes. For his relaxation and entertainment, I provided him with a subscription to the current *Reader's Digest* condensed books so he wouldn't have to wade through long-winded verbiage. He had the use of the hi-fi set and a library of rock-and-roll tapes that would play for years. I gave him a private 16mm movie projector and built a pull-down screen for him against the wall of the living room. Although I had to pay through the nose, I purchased complete sets of the old television family series, including real collector's items such as *Lassie, Father Knows Best, December Bride,* and *The Mickey Mouse Club*; and all of them with *unimpaired commercials*! But when I reflected how The Listener had made my fortune for me, I figured that nothing was too good for the great man.

And then the coda to the symphony of my new life. . .

It was almost three years to the day when I entered the apartment after a grueling day at my publishing firm and placed a great pile of MSS. on the coffee table. I had planned to read to him from the MSS. all night long, beginning with three new book-length MSS. of poetry submitted by three southern poets. Ordinarily The Listener eagerly awaited my entrance, smiling and nodding at the blank wall from his comfortable chair beside the fireplace. He wasn't in his chair and I called out to him.

"Yoo hoo! Listener, I'm home!"

I didn't expect a reply because The Listener never talked, but I wanted to let him know I was home. When he didn't come into the living room, I began to search the apartment, and I found him in his bedroom on his bed. His throat was slit, as the saying goes, from ear to ear, and there was a bloody butcher knife on the floor. His eyes were fixed vacantly upon the ceiling, but the broad and tender smile was still on his lips.

I knew he was dead, but I called the apartment house physician, an old retired plastic surgeon, and told him to come to the apartment immediately. The doctor arrived on the next elevator and examined The Listener carefully. He shook his head sadly from side to side.

"Beautiful," the old doctor murmured. "Simply beautiful."

"Is there a chance, Doctor?" I pleaded tearfully. "Any

chance at all?"

"No, he's dead all right. But that's a beautiful job of plastic surgery on his face. At one time this man was badly burned. Do you see that smile? Well, it's a built-in smile; without it he'd have looked terrible. But it must have been a tough decision for the plastic surgeon to make, because a smile like that could be damned uncomfortable. The only way this poor devil could get any relief at all was to nod his head up and down every few minutes. . ."

When the doctor left my apartment, I went all to pieces. I considered the liquidation of my firm, but didn't know whether I should do it or not. I wanted to sell off all my stocks but couldn't decide which stocks to sell first. I didn't know what to do. When the police and hospital people arrived two hours later, I had a decanter of whiskey in my right hand and an empty glass in my left. I was kneeling beside the dead man's bed, asking him if he thought it was a good idea for me to have a drink. . . ֍

# Everybody's Metamorphosis

MORE FREQUENTLY of late, it seems, those of us who are concerned with sociometric and biological uncertainties have been forced to turn back to the late Dr. Franz Kafka for guidance and inspiration. In *The Metamorphosis,* which was once considered to be little more than an entertaining piece of fiction, a closer look at the author's preparation provides the reader with an uneasy glimpse into the future of a life on earth most of us will not be around to share. Now that nuclear testing has begun again (has it ever really stopped?), Dr. Kafka's foreshadowing of the shapes of things to come can no longer be viewed as a routine academic exercise.

Many literary critics have, of course, been dismayed by Dr. Kafka's morbid preoccupation with animal themes. In their exegetical commentaries on Kafka's allegories, scholars have confined their opinions to the pre-1924 social mores of the former's Europe. Kafka died in 1924, and the reluctance of his interpreters to evaluate his social concepts by current standards is not difficult to understand. —Shallow thinking, perhaps, but not unreasonable.

The overlooked key to Dr. Kafka's position and philosophy was stated by the officer in *Aus einer Straf-kolonie:* "Yes, it's no calligraphy for school children. It needs to be studied closely. I'm sure that in the end you would understand it too. Of course the script can't be a simple one; it's not supposed to kill a man right off, but only after an interval."

Idiomatically, Dr. Kafka meant that "the metaphysical handwriting, buddy boy, is crawling on the wall."

In this rarely quoted passage the officer was explaining the complicated diagrams of the harrow to a rather bored explorer, but the patient elucidation is germane to Dr. Kafka's stories featuring animal themes, as well. To be grasped, these stories must be studied closely.

The progress of evolution has been mercifully slow; and now, as Man- and Womankind begin the painful return journey to dusty origins, we can be grateful that the retrogressive physiological mutations will be made manifest sporadically instead of instantaneously. If we are prepared mentally, physically and economically for these inevitable structural changes, one by one, as they make their appearances in widely dispersed primary social groups, the transitory period will not only prove to be a boon for biologists in search of grants, it will provide a stimulating challenge to sociologists and an exciting new area of exploration for philosophers.

Unhappily (especially for those of us who consider phenomenology essential to literary criticism), there are alarmists in every society.

There are vociferous minority groups in every social structure with a sclerotic tendency to resist changes of any kind. And it is these reactionaries in our own American society who must be prepared by education and by unemotional appeals to their reason for the inevitable changes—Now. The incontrovertible truth that radiation produces mutations in genetic material (single- and double-strand breaks, cross-linking, base substitutions, dimerism, etc., in the chromosomal and mitochondrial DNA) has been explicated and reiterated by prudent scientists in responsible journals and periodicals. It has also been discovered that it is too late to change what has already happened. Strontium 90 is present in the air we breathe, the foods we eat, the fluids we drink and, of course, lodged in minute particles within the reproductive germ cells of every male and female animal on earth. At present the amounts are too small to be measured accurately within the animal germ cells, and visible mutations in our offspring will occur so gradually that they will probably appear undetected to an uneducated eye for the next generation or so. However, chance plays its part in the uniting of sperm and egg, and even without radiation-induced mutations, chromosome crossover accidents are reported at a ratio of one to every million births; e.g., the baby who is born with a cute, wagging, practical tail instead of the three or four bone nodules of the coccygeal vertebrae. Do some of these "different" babies arrive un-reported? Yes—I am inclined to think so.

To the bewildered parents of a child born with a tail, excessive hirsuteness, paws-with-claws perhaps instead of hands, or other socially undesirable morphological characteristics, the event is not only disconcerting, it is disturbing emotionally to both parents and to the members of their immediate families. As similar incidents increase, stepped up by radiation mutations of the genes in ever-mounting numbers, we must learn to accept these different children calmly; not as freaks or as something to be ashamed of, but as the result of tampering with the Van Alien belt, nuclear weapons, and the absorbing of fallout particles. Certainly it is much too late to wring our hands and say that "Harry shouldn't have done it."

We are too late to prevent what has happened already, so we must prepare ourselves to love and cherish our mutations as well as we do our normal primate issue. We can do so only by suppressing learned social reactions and immoderate emotions, and by facing our new parental responsibilities with the same exuberance by which we produced such children.

Doting grandparents, I realize fully, will be ill-disposed to shower natural affection upon a furry grandson with a lolling, dripping tongue, but if they will rationally accept the biological principle that the child *must* let his tongue hang out that way for excretion purposes, because he lacks sudoriporous glands, they should be able to overcome their behavioral prejudices without any great hardship.

Actually, we should enumerate our blessings.

Unlike Gregor Samsa, the protagonist of Franz Kafka's novella, *The Metamorphosis,* who awakened one morning to find himself changed overnight to "a gigantic vermin," future primate mutations will occur at birth, not in the mature adult, and for this much we can be sanguine.

The child who is born different from his fellows can be conditioned and educated as he matures, and the realization that he is unlike other children need not be the swift, traumatic shock it was to Gregor Samsa. If families are educated now, well in advance, in precautionary preparation for the unusual children soon to be coming our way, they will be able to cope efficaciously with the social problems involved—avoiding the mistakes made by the shocked, inept Samsa family.

Gregor Samsa had gone to bed as a normal male primate of the class *Mammalia*, and during his sleep had experienced a retrogressive metamorphosis down through several orders and classes to become an off-beat species of phylum *Arthropoda*. Dr. Kafka neglected to point out specifically the exact species, but we know already that arthropods number approximately 750,000 species and, from the clues in the script, the hero can be squeezed taxonomically into the narrow gap between an annelid-like ancestor and the *Onychopora*. For convenience, it will be simpler to rename the hero a *Gregor samsa* on the phylogenetic tree, despite his early demise and unknown reproductive processes.

At this point, I intend to clarify a misunderstanding of grave importance. An ignorant charwoman in the employ of the Samsa family was fond of calling the *Gregor samsa* an "old cockroach." Despite this woman's obvious lack of qualifications for designating the *Gregor samsa* as a cockroach, indifferent literary critics have accepted her hasty classification without examining the text. The misinformation has been passed on to innumerable college students by lazy explicators that Mr. Samsa was turned into a "cockroach" in his bed. This supposition is unsupported. It would be understandable if the charwoman had called the hero, "You old *peripatus*, you!" This mistake would have been natural enough for any untrained observer to make who failed to take the time to examine the arthropod closely, even though the *Gregor samsa* did not resemble a cockroach as much as it did a centipede.

The *Gregor samsa* was segmented into metameres with "numerous little legs," whereas the *Blattidae,* or cockroaches, are characterized by an oval, flattened body, long filiform antennae, and (hexapodic) legs fitted for scampering. Depending upon the species, or in some instances on the sex, the wings of the *Blattidae* are either well-developed or atrophied. But there are wings; always. The *Gregor samsa* was without vestigial wings.

To list, in detail, all of the physical changes Gregor Samsa had to undergo to become a *Gregor samsa* would be impractical. The major changes, however, are important, because it is with the major morphological changes of future mutations with which men and women will be mortally concerned; the observable, obvious differences.

Economically, and certainly this aspect is vital within our capitalist culture, the *Gregor samsa* would have the devil's own time in earning a living in his arthropodic state. It is all very well to say that a retraining program could be designed for new arthropods as they begin to appear among us, but the abrupt transition from a 1,500 gram brain to a simpler supresophageal ganglion would require an altogether fresh set of attitudes and incentives for the species. It is not too early for preliminary studies on the development of training and basic education programs. The *Gregor samsa,* from an economic standpoint, resembles related forms in the order *Orthoptera,* a very destructive order indeed, most of them being pests of domestic grains. And when the enormous size of the *Gregor samsa* is considered (he was unable to squeeze his unwieldy bulk under a sofa), if he were not provided with a feeling of social responsibility, and taught patiently the values of materialism, an inconsiderate, untutored member of such a species would zip through a field of Kansas wheat like an army of hungry Butzes.

Fortuitously, insofar as the brain, or ganglion, of Dr. Kafka's arthropod was concerned, the metamorphosis was incomplete. Or, if it were complete, the abnormally large dimensions of the *Gregor samsa* ganglion enabled it to reason and remember, although it could do neither with any great facility. The emotions were apparently unimpaired during the early stages of the metamorphosis, and any training program designed for the species would have to be based fundamentally on an appeal to the emotions rather than reason. One lesson in the novella was stressed by the author; it was out of the question for the *Gregor samsa* to resume his former occupation as a commercial traveler. To sell products on the road, it is mandatory for a salesman to have a friendly, outgoing personality. And this facet of the *Gregor samsa* evaporated with the altered physiognomy. He was not only sensitive to light, he was embarrassed by his new physical appearance, even in front of his immediate family. To send a member of such a species out on the road with a sample case to face shopkeepers (conceding that a means could be devised for him to carry a heavy sample case) would be cruel and impractical. Occupational therapists and personnel experts will have their work cut out for them in the future, all right; and it will not be a problem they can dismiss so lightly, as they have the current problem of employment for so many of our low-I.Q., welfare-supported citizens.

Communication, verbal or non-verbal, is perhaps the most pressing aspect of any metamorphosis, and Tiresias did not avoid the truth—to his sorrow—when he discussed the matter with Saturnia. Quite early in the story, Dr. Kafka tells us, the *Gregor samsa* "talked," answering anxious queries from various members of his family through the closed and locked door of his bedroom. But did he use human speech? I think not. He made audible sounds, muffled noises acceptable as incomprehensible speech to his family and employer on the other side of the door, but without a mammalian larynx or a set of vocal chords, organs conspicuously absent in arthropods, he was unable to communicate as a normal primate. The sounds he made, in all probability, were the rubbing of his legs together, scraping his legs against the sides of his chitinous armor-plating, or perhaps a disturbingly audible grinding of his mandibles. He thought that he was talking in a natural voice, but this thought must have been a learned, transfer recollection held over nostalgically from his former state as a primate. I believe that it is significant to note that later, when his door was opened, and during the days that followed when his sister and the charwoman made infrequent visits to his room for feeding and cleaning purposes, he never attempted to communicate orally again. We may assume, then, that the metamorphosis, in this respect, was in keeping with the non-vocal nature of arthropods.

However, although the *Gregor samsa* was unable to communicate orally with his family, he could understand every word that they said, indicating the retention of an exceptionally sensitive auditory organ. This auditory faculty was also sensitive enough to appreciate the vibratory sounds of his sister's violin. One wishes that Dr. Kafka had given us more concrete information about his remarkable auditory ability, but as he did not, we can only hope that future mutations will retain this invaluable sense characteristic.

The supposition that the metamorphosis was incomplete in several physiological aspects leads to my reluctant conjecture that the *Gregor samsa* might—just possibly—have been in the terminal stages of a larval form, and that the indifferent feeding of her brother by his sister, Grete, hindered or halted altogether the completion of his holometabolous development. This possibility should not be ignored nor overlooked. The subsequent actions of the *Gregor samsa* following his amazed awakening indicate that he was in a type of quiescent stage interpolated ordinarily between active larvae and the adult (imago) developmental stage. This is a hypothesis indicated, but not confirmed, by textual data. We know positively that the *Gregor samsa* was disgusted by milk, bread, and other fresh foods. He devoured eagerly, at first, rotted stumps of vegetables, smelly cheese, and a leftover white sauce of some kind that his sister brought to him. But to eat at all he was forced to separate these stale food items from the fresh ones. The very odor of fresh foods repelled him, and this is unusual. Ordinary arthropods are not so picky.

The fact that the *Gregor samsa's* eyes became "moist with satisfaction" as he sucked gluttonously at the strong cheese is a further indication that the metamorphosis was, in yet another respect, incomplete. The new arthropod was able to see quite well at first, but after these initial tears of maudlin happiness there was no further lachrymal activity. As the long, lonely days passed, and as the isolated *Gregor samsa* hunkered unloved and unwanted in the window facing the street, his vision dimmed until he was finally unable to discern even the gray outlines of the houses across the way. His faulty diet was undoubtedly responsible for the impairment of the cells constituting the ommatidium, but the unhappiest result of the inadequate, haphazard diet was the early death of the *Gregor samsa* by malnutrition, or dehydration. In spite of an ever-present hunger, he could not bring himself to eat the food with which he was provided. One cannot expect an outsized arthropod to be nourished by mammalian milk; the nutritive materials required to maintain healthy arthropodic mutations will be a serious matter for dieticians to explore thoroughly.

The radical change from endo- to exoskeleton, with the mandatory loss of the all-important notochord, was perhaps the most discomforting change the *Gregor samsa* suffered. The rigidity of the exoskeleton hampered his motor activity and, on one sad occasion, when he was unable to wheel his panoplied body quickly enough to reenter the ostensible safety of his bedroom, his irate father threw an apple at him with enough force to pierce the armor-plating of his rounded back. That he did not bleed to death from the terrible wound can be explained by the rudimentary nature of his unclosed circulatory system, and by the probable existence of a sticky moulting fluid characteristic of pupating arthropoda. In immature insects of many species—granting that the *Gregor samsa* was a new insect—there are gland cells placed either singly or in groups which secrete the fluid facilitating the process of moulting. The hard, inelastic covering of an arthropod must be shed periodically for growth purposes. And although the *Gregor samsa* is always considered by literary critics as an imago—simply because he was an adult primate before his metamorphosis—I am still inclined to believe, by my close attendance to the textual evidence, that the *Gregor samsa* might very well have experienced additional moults if he had been fed the proper foods for such development. The number of moults differs with each species, of course, but the tiny May flies often moult 25 times or more. It is not unreasonable then to advance the hypothesis that the *Gregor samsa—had* he lived—might have gone through several more moults. With the correct diet, and a little love and understanding from his family, it staggers the imagination to reflect upon what his eventual size could have been. At least, it staggers mine. But the *Gregor samsa* received neither love nor understanding from his family. Only his sister Crete, who is presented by the author as a kind of martyr, maintained any pretense of affection for the plight of the family's former breadwinner. That her affection was indeed feigned all along is revealed poignantly toward the end of the story when she beats her hand petulantly on the dining table and says, "We must find some means of getting rid of it." To speak of her brother as "it" cannot be interpreted as an expression of either affection or respect.

Dr. Kafka, if a reminder is needed, stacked his cards against the hero from the opening sentence. In every morphological change, including the pungent odor of the arthropod, which was unpleasant to the members of the family, the author implies that the only way the Samsa family could love its changed Gregor was to work at least three shifts. (If the author had provided the *Gregor samsa* with the alluring glands of a moth or butterfly instead of endowing him with pentamidal stink glands, the story might have been concluded with a note of hope.)

And it is hope that I am concerned with here, not unhealthy, negative pessimism. We cannot afford the dubious solace of feeling sorry for ourselves. The damage has been done, and we must learn how to live with the future as we have learned how to live with our past. As new mutations appear in our society with increasing regularity we must resist, with all of our resources, our natural inclinations to destroy them at birth.

The future of the world rests in mutations. To mention Malthus and Darwin again this late in the century is to repeat common knowledge. No one questions seriously the theory of survival of the fittest. The mutations caused by radioactivity on genetic material are merely Nature's way of ensuring a continuation of species—*some* kind of species—when mankind, as we know it now, is gone. If we will train ourselves to love our offspring, regardless of outer and inner physical changes, and help them to grow into useful, valuable members of society, life of some weird kind or other will not die out altogether on this planet. When a mutation confers an advantage on the individual, *no matter how slight,* natural selection becomes operative. And this slight advantage, given enough time and a little bit of luck, leads to the mutation's eventual replacement of its allelomorph in the population majority. There is no need to elaborate on elementary genetics. Instead, I would prefer to end this short paper hopefully, manfully.

Let us face the truth. Have pity on the meek and humble *Gregor samsas.* Those great big buggers are destined to inherit the earth. ◉

## Sand Dollar

FERNANDO AWOKE suddenly. A man on the dock a hundred yards away had shouted to a girl in a speedboat, "Cut your engine!" Fernando didn't understand the words (they were in English); but as he sat up, feeling the coral-rock retaining wall behind his back, he noticed that the girl was coming into the dock at too great a speed. At the last moment the small boat swerved, and she circled in a wide arc, narrowly missing a cat boat with furled sails, and cut the engine.

The man on the dock laughed. "Perhaps you'd better paddle in."

Fully awake now and feeling hunger pains in the pit of his stomach, Fernando shifted his gaze to a blue heron. The heron, ten yards away, peered intently into the shallow water, ignoring Fernando.

Fernando got stiffly to his feet and climbed over the low wall into Peacock Park. The nacreous light on the gray-green water and the scattered sailboats with their furled sails would have made a challenging scene for a water colorist, but Fernando was too hungry to appreciate the beauty. He was grateful that he had been allowed to sleep through the night on the beach without being bothered. Another Marielito had told him that the beach was a safe place to sleep-not in the Park itself-but to climb over the seawall and stay hidden. The police did not often patrol the narrow beach at night.

Fernando crossed the street and walked up the inclined sidewalk past the Coconut Grove Library to Lum's Restaurant. Lum's wasn't open as yet, but two men were working behind the counter. Fernando went behind the building and looked into the Demsey Dumpster. He ripped open a gray plastic bag, put his arm through the opening, and rummaged something to eat. He pulled out a hard roll with only two bites taken out of it. The roll was stale, but crunchy and good.

He ate it as he crossed the street at the stoplight and checked the doorway of the Kwik-Chek supermarket. There were four plastic crates of milk beside the door. Fernando took a quart of milk from the top crate, hid it under his T-shirt, and ran from the empty parking lot. His tennis shoes, two sizes too large, made a ka-flapping sound on the sidewalk. He didn't run far; he was much too tired, and the sun, now that it had cleared the condos and hotels along the bay, had raised the temperature another ten degrees. He sat down on a bus bench where no bus stopped and slowly drank the quart of milk. His sour T-shirt, which advised people to "Nuke the Whales," was wet beneath the armpits and damp across his back as he leaned against the bench.

The cold milk tasted good as he let it trickle from the carton down his throat, but when he set the empty carton down, his stomach began to rumble. A moment later the milk, together with the half-chewed hard roll and mixed with the wine he had drunk the night before, spewed from his mouth into the street. He gagged and coughed, and then he was emptied completely. His brown, red-rimmed eyes ran with water as he coughed and gasped for breath. It was the wine, he thought, bad wine. He felt weak. His legs trembled, and his arms were heavy as he lifted them to the back of the bench to brace himself. He inhaled deep breaths of humid, sticky air.

"Aie...Miami...Miami...aie." He repeated the rhyme several times, smiling. He closed his eyes, put his head back, and dozed.

A hand grasped his shoulder lightly. "Wake up, man," the voice said. Fernando blinked, suddenly alarmed. A young Anglo leaned over him, smiling. The man had thick blond hair, a red, closely-shaven face, and even white teeth. He was wearing jeans, blue-and-red jogging shoes, and an embroidered blue work shirt.

"Want to make two dollars?" The young man gestured to the parked long-bodied Datsun pick-up. "Get in the truck." Fernando understood "dollars" and the jerking thumb. Fernando nodded and clambered over the tailgate. He sat with his back against the cab as the truck drove away from the curb. A middle-aged black man wearing a tattered shirt sat inside the cab with the Anglo driver.

The truck went down 27th Avenue, headed for Coral Gables. Soon they were traveling down a residential stret. The trees were so tall on both sides of the street that the foliage formed a shaded canopy over the truck. The driver pulled into the driveway of a two-storied, white brick house, and then backed the truck to the low concrete porch. When he beckoned, Fernando went into the house with the driver and the black man.

"My mother's letting me take the piano," the young Anglo explained.

"It looks heavier than two dollars," the black man said.

"Okay, I'll give you four, but only two for the Spic. He isn't going to be much help anyway."

Fernando said nothing. He didn't understand what they were saying. He admired the high-ceilinged room. The furniture was old, but well-preserved and polished. There was a scent of lemon and oil. An oil painting of an enormous bullseye in three primary colors dominated the room from its place above the fireplace. There were many potted green plants, tables at each end of the white couch, and smaller tables holding tall lamps beside three brocaded armchairs. There were small knickknacks, sculptures carved from onyx and marble on the coffee table. The upright Story & Clark piano was flush against the wall in the dining room. The piano was on casters, and it was easy enough for the three men to maneuver into the living room, but it was very difficult to roll on the deep carpet. As they paused for a moment to steer the piano toward the foyer, Fernando picked up a heavy cutglass paperweight from an end table and dropped it into his right front pocket.

The driver had brought two heavy boards in the truck, and the incline from the porch to the truck bed was about a foot and a half. Fernando, as the driver predicted, wasn't much help. He didn't understand the instructions he was given, but pushed and tugged with the others anyway, and they finally got the piano onto the truck. While the black man threw a quilt over the piano and tied it down with rope, the driver went inside and got the piano bench. He checked the door carefully to see if it was locked, and then gestured for Fernando to hop into the back.

On the drive back to Coconut Grove, Fernando sat on the bench. His T-shirt was soaked, and the air felt cool on this wet skin. A block from the Coconut Grove public tennis courts, the driver pulled into a side street and then backed the truck up a driveway to a small cottage that was well-hidden behind a three-bedroom concrete, brick and stucco residence. The fenced backyard was a jungle of scrub palmetto and large-leaved green plants.

Unloading the piano down the steep ramp of boards took considerable effort. One of the casters came off, and there was a long scratch made on one of the legs as it scraped the tailgate. The piano would not slide on the uneven patio of well-separated paving stones, and the men had to half-carry and half-drag the piano to get it into the cottage. When the piano was finally in place against the living room wall, it took a fourth of the small room. Nevertheless, the driver seemed to be pleased. Fernando brought in the piano bench, and the men got back into the truck. The driver drove both men-with Fernando in the back again-to Douglas Road and U.S. 1. Fernando didn't see the driver give any money to the black man, but when Fernando was handed four quarters, he smiled and, "Gracias."

The driver departed, and the black man joined three other black men who were standing around a small fire in the vacant lot. Fernando walked briskly away from the four men before they could take his four quarters away from him.

It was almost two P.M. before Fernando reached Eighth Street and the heart of Little Havana. There was no one he knew in Domino Park, and he walked to the restaurant he frequented when he had a little money. He ordered a cardboard bowl of rice and black beans and a café con leche with extra sugar. He gave the woman three of his quarters and received three cents in change.

With his back to the wall, he sat on a wooden bench and ate his rice and beans. He sipped the cafe con leche noisily, feeling new energy in his shaky legs. He put the plastic spoon in the hip pocket of his jeans and tossed the empty cardboard bowl into the trash can. He entered the men's room and locked the door. After relieving himself, he examined the glass paperweight. Rounded on top and about three inches in diameter, the glass weight was much heavier than it looked. Imbedded inside, and centered perfectly, was a white, well-dried sand dollar. Because of the rounded top, the sand dollar ws magnified slightly and quite beautiful. Tonight, Fernando thought, I shall take a shower and sleep in a bed.

Fernando walked down Calle Ohco for two blocks and entered a religious store. A copper bell attached to the top of the door jingled as he closed it behind him. The shop was dark and religious statues, none of them smiling, stared at him. There were statues of Jesus on the cross and many more of Mary. There was a life-sized statue of Saint Sebastian to the right of the door. Bright red paint dripped from the arrow wounds, and the right hand, palm up, implored. The bearded face was anguished. Fernando dropped three pennies on the floor beside Saint Sebastian, which was already littered with pennies, nickels, and dimes.

A balding man behind the counter fanned himself with a hand-woven straw fan that advertised Purvis Funeral Home in red letters. His black moustache looked like a dirty word that had been crossed out. The man eyed Fernando shrewdly, but said nothing.

"I want to sell this, Señor," Fernando said, placing the paperweight on the counter.

Without touching it, the proprietor stared at the paperweight for almost a full minute. He nodded, pursed his lips, and took a handful of change out of his pocket. He placed three quarters, two dimes, and a nickel on the counter beside the paperweight.

"No, Señor!" Fernando said. "It was my mother's. I brought it from Cuba!"

A .32 caliber pistol appeared in the proprietor's hand. "Take the dollar, or I'll call the police."

Fernando picked up the paperweight. He looked at the

change on the counter. He looked at the proprietor's impassive face, and then shook his head. He wasn't afraid of the pistol; he knew that the man wouldn't shoot him. Fernando turned toward the door, wheeled after two steps, and threw the paperweight with all his might at the balding man. The heavy glass paperweight struck the proprietor's forehead an inch above his right eye. He fell backwards, and as he fell, his finger squeezed the trigger. The round hit Fernando on his left side, just below the rib cage. The bullet felt like a hard blow, but it wasn't forceful enough to knock him down. He kneeled by the doorway and scooped up two handfuls of change from the floor beside the Saint Sebastian statue. He crammed the money into his pockets, opened the door, and ran down the street.

After he covered the first block, the pain in his side hit him hard, and he doubled over. He clutched his side and stumbled on, unable to run. At three-thirty on a hot afternoon, there were very few people on the street. No one, apparently, had heard the shot. Fernando looked over his shoulder. No one was chasing him. He continued down the street, however, afraid to turn into one of the unfamiliar side streets. He wondered how much change he had scooped from the floor. No much, he thought-and he had foolishly left the dollar in change on the counter as well. The man was probably knocked unconscious, but he would wake soon and call the police.

He was at the cemetery now, and once, when the pain doubled him over again, he clutched at the wrought-iron fence. When he reached the gate, he entered. He looked around and saw no one. There were bouquets of flowers-some of them silk, some of them real-in little pots in front of many of the headstones. Fernando took a bouquet of red carnations out of one of the pots and continued down the gravel path toward the back of the cemetery. If the police saw him now, he would look like a man taking flowers to a grave.

He could go no farther. He left the path, walked a dozen yards, and stretched out on the grass with his head in the shade of a narrow Australian pine tree. He could breathe much better this way, lying face down. The sharp pain in his side soon ebbed to a dull, throbbing ache. With each throb he could feel blood pump from the wound. He pressed his body deeper into the dry, hot grass. His T-shirt and pants were wet with blood. By sucking in deep breaths, the throbbing wasn't as noticeable. His arms and legs were weak, and Fernando knew that he could not get to his feet again, even if he had wanted to get up.

A middle-aged woman, visiting her dead husband in the cemetery, paused on the gravel path when she saw Fernando lying there. She saw the red carnations clutched in his right hand and crossed herself.

*Ah, pobrecito*, she thought, *his mother is dead.* ◉

## About the Author

Charles Willeford worked as a professional horse trainer, boxer and radio announcer. He wrote over a dozen novels, including *Miami Blues*, *The Burnt Orange Heresy*, *Cockfighter* and *Kiss Your Ass Goodbye*, numerous short stories, essays, poetry and two autobiographies. He was a tank commander with the Third Army in World War II. For his courage he received the Silver Star, the Bronze Star, the Purple Heart, and the Luxembourg Croix de Guerre. He also taught English and philosophy in Miami. He died in *1988*.

# ACKNOWLEDGEMENTS

"To a Nephew in College" in *Books Abroad: An International Literary Quarterly*, University of Oklahoma Press, Autumn 1957

"Some Lucky License" *Alfred Hitchcock's Mystery Magazine* vol. 10, No. 8, Aug 1965

"Citizen's Arrest" *Alfred Hitchcock's Mystery Magazine* vol. 11, No. 8, Aug 1966

"How Warren and Lee College Came to Florida..." *Tropic*, vol. 1, No. 6, Nov 19, 1967

"The Old Man at the Bridge" (as "Burning One's Bridges to the Past") *Sports Illustrated*, vol. 38, No. 18, May 7, 1973

"An Actor Prepares" *Savannah*, Vol. 9, No. 5, Nov 1977

"A Matter of Taste" *Savannah*, Vol. 10, No. 4, Nov-Dec 1978

"The Man Who Loved Ann Landers" *Zantia*, Vol. 2, No. 2, Spring 1979

"The Gardener and the Princess" *Tropic*, Apr 19, 1981

"The Tupperware Party" (as "The Party") *Tropic*, Jul 11, 1982

"The Condemned" *Something About a Soldier*, Random House, 1986

"Checking Out" *Florida*, Jun 7, 1987

"Give the Man a Cigar" *Florida*, Aug 16, 1987

"Saturday Night Special" (as "Strange"), "The Deserted Village" and "Everybody's Metamorphosis" *Everybody's Metamorphosis*, Dennis McMillan Publications, 1988

"The First Five in Line..." *Orange Pulp*, University Press of Florida, 2000

"The Pop-Off Caper", "One Hero to a War", "Behind Him Goes His Dream", The Emancipation of Henry Allen", "The Laughing Machine", "The Listener", "Sand Dollar" previously unpublished.

*available in trade paperback*
*Fall 2003*

**"A fast, tough tale..."**—*John Updike*

---

## Douglas Fairbairn's
# SHOOT

---

"This is what happened. Myself and four friends were hunting along the Sturrup River one weekend in the deer season . . . When we got there we noticed that there was another party of hunters standing over on the opposite bank . . . Then, all of a sudden, without any warning, and I swear to God without the slightest provocation from us, one of them raised his rifle and fired at us, hitting Pete Rinaldi in the head."

Ranked by Stephen King along with Robert Louis Stevenson's *Dr. Jekyll & Mr. Hyde*, Stephen Crane's *The Red Badge of Courage*, Henry James' *The Turn of the Screw* and James M. Cain's *The Postman Always Rings Twice* as a "masterpiece of concision," this shocking tale of violence escalates from this spare beginning into a full scale war. . .

**"Unusual, gripping, menacing."**
—*The New York Times*

"Action and adventure up there with the best . . . painfully realistic . . . A novel easy to read, but difficult to forget."
—*Los Angeles Times*

A WITSEND BOOK—WWW.SENDWIT.COM

CPSIA information can be obtained at www.ICGtesting.com
Printed in the USA
LVOW12s1952081214

417811LV00001B/198/P